The Mysteries of Tomorrow
Volume 1:
The Fiancés of the Year 2000

BY THE SAME AUTHORS

Paul Féval, fils. *Felifax, The Tiger-Man*

The Mysteries of Tomorrow
Volume 1:
The Fiancés of the Year 2000

by
Paul Féval, *fils* & H.-J. Magog

Translated by
Brian Stableford

A Black Coat Press Book

Visit our website at www.blackcoatpress.com

ISBN 978-1-61227-945-9. First Printing. March 2020. Published by Black Coat Press, an imprint of Hollywood Comics.com, LLC, P.O. Box 17270, Encino, CA 91416. All rights reserved. Except for review purposes, no part of this book may be reproduced or transmitted in any form or by any means, electronic or mechanical, including photocopying, recording, or by any information storage and retrieval system, without permission in writing from the publisher. The stories and characters depicted in this novel are entirely fictional. Printed in the United States of America.

Introduction

Les Mystères de Demain (here translated as *The Mysteries of Tomorrow*), subtitled *Roman d'aventures scientifiques*, was originally published by Ferenczi in five volume, as follows:

* *Les Fiancés de l'an 2000* [The Fiancés of the Year 2000] in 1922;
* *Le Monde des damnés* [The World of the Damned] in 1923;
* *Le Réveil d'Atlantide* [Atlantis Awakens] in 1923;
* *L'Humanité enchaînée* [Mankind in Chains] in 1923; and finally
* *Le Faiseur de folles* [The Maker of Madwomen] in 1924.[1]

Paul Féval *fils* (i.e.: Paul Féval Jr.) was born Paul Augustin Jean Nicolas Féval on January 25, 1860. He was the third of eight children and the eldest son of Paul Henri Corentin Féval, who was then 42 years-old and at the height of his literary success. The elder Féval had published his most successful work, the historical swashbuckler *Le Bossu* [*The Hunchback*], in 1857, and became a *Chevalier de la Légion d'Honneur* in 1865; that same year, he was elected president of the *Société des Gens de Lettres*.

However, five years later, in 1873, the elder Féval's streak of good fortune began to wave. He was a candidate for the Académie Française, but the Academy was not yet ready to recognize the respectability of literature practiced as a trade rather than a vocation, and his candidature drew a hostile response. He diplomatically withdrew in favor of the popular

---

[1] Despite the mention on French Wikipedia that a sixth volume entitled *Le Poison du monde*, written by Magog alone, was part of the series, this is incorrect.

playwright, Alexandre Dumas *fils*. Much worse was to follow. In late 1875 and early 1876, the elder Féval lost his fortune gambling on the stock exchange and plunged the family into bankruptcy.

The elder Féval reacted to this disaster by recommitting himself to the ideals of the Catholic faith, loudly repenting all the sins for which God might have been punishing him. We can only speculate as to what effect all this had on his teenage son, but it must have been profound, and it certainly blighted what had previously been his exceedingly bright prospects of a handsome inheritance. The elder Féval still had his literary capital to draw on, and almost managed to recover his solvency, but he suffered a second financial disaster in 1882 when the official in charge of his funds absconded with them—a blow compounded by a paralyzing stroke, which prevented him from writing anything further.

Paul Féval *fils*, who had come of age by then, had no alternative but to earn his own living—which he set out to do just as his father had done. He eventually became a writer of such thoroughgoing tradesmanship that he became a conspicuous example of the literary hack: a casual mass-producer of what would eventually become known as "pulp fiction."

He was first published in book form in 1890, when a collection of his *Nouvelles* appeared alongside two novels, *La trombe de fer* [*The Rain of Iron*] and *Le Dernier Laird* [*The Last Laird*]. In *Le livre jaune* [*The Yellow Book*] (1891), he attempted to combine melodrama with thematic elements borrowed from the Decadent Movement. *Maria-Lauria*, published the same year, also attempted to respond to contemporary fashions, but with equally modest success. He never stopped trying to do distinctive and original work, but he had little success in establishing a literary career that extended much further than the blurred edges of his father's shadow.

Féval *fils*' commercial breakthrough came with an epic account of the adventures of *Le fils de Lagardère* [*The Son of Lagardère*], written in collaboration with Albert d'Orsay and published in 1893. Lagardère is the hero of *Le Bossu*, and

Féval *fils* went on to add several more novels to the expanding series on which he was now collaborating with his late parent. *Les jumeaux de Nevers* [*The Nevers Twins*], also written with d'Orsay, followed in 1895 and both *Les chevauchées de Largardère* [*Lagardère's Rides*] and *Cocardasse et Passepoil* in 1909, while *Mariquita* (1923), *Mademoiselle de Largardère* (1929) and *La petite-fille du Bossu* [*The Hunchback's Grand-daughter*] (1931) were added towards the end of his career and *La jeunesse du Bossu* [*The Hunchback's Childhood*] (1934) was added posthumously.

Like his father, Féval *fils* also dabbled in eccentric supernatural fiction in *Histoire d'outre-tombe* [*Story of the Afterlife*] (1903-04). His *Les bandits de Londres* [*The Bandits of London*] (1905) was clearly modeled on, although it was not an explicit sequel to, his father's *Les mystères de Londres*. Although he wrote several *romans de cape et d'épée* of his own–most notably *Mam'zelle Flamberge* (1911)–his derivative works sold far better.

It must have seemed a natural expansion of this activity to begin plundering other *feuilletonistes*, and the younger Féval was by no means the first writer to produce a sequel to Alexandre Dumas' most famous work, *Les trois mousquetaires* (1844; tr. as *The Three Musketeers*). He published *Le fils de d'Artagnan* in 1914, some years before bringing Dumas' hero together with Cyrano de Bergerac–whose personality had been extravagantly celebrated in Edmond Rostand's play of 1897. Féval *fils* also wrote a further sequel to Dumas' novel in *La vieillesse d'Athos* [*Athos' Old Age*] (1930). The actual d'Artagnan was presumably acquainted with the actual Cyrano de Bergerac, as both men had fought at the siege of Arras in 1640, but the younger Féval's literary versions of the two heroes, and his fanciful account of their changing relationship, owed far more to the exemplars provided by Dumas and Rostand than to history. His posthumous works included a further two volumes detailing *Les exploits de Cyrano* [*Cyrano's Exploits*]. The younger Féval thus became his father's literary heir in more ways than one, similarly becoming a prodigiously prolific writer whose work was mostly doomed to be forgotten.

Féval *fils* never gave up trying to apply his skills to work of a more immediately fashionable nature, and his pursuit of new fictional trends led him to produce a five-volume sequence of short novels hybridizing occult fiction with science fiction, *Les mystères de demain* [*The Mysteries of Tomorrow*] in collaboration with H.-J. Magog in 1922-24. *Félifax* (1929),[2] written near the end of his career, when he was in his late 60s, was a further exercise in much the same vein, attempting a similar hybridization of related but not-entirely-compatible genres, with a science-fictional element.

Paul Féval fils passed away on (d 15 january 1933) having written around 80 novels, two volumes of poetry, one collection of short fiction, several plays and a volume of dramatic monologues, leaving several more volumes behind for posthumous publication; he also wrote unpublished scripts for the fledgling movie industry.

Henri Georges Léon Charles Jeanne was born on May 29, 1877 in Laon, the son of Georges Léon Jeanne (1841-1883) and Marie Caroline Hortense (1851-1894, born Teissonnier d'Areste). His father was captain at the 45th Regiment of Ligne. He does not seem to have had any brothers and sisters.

In 1902, Henri Jeanne married Marie Pauline Chauvin (1881-?) in Entrevaux. At that time, he was working as a recording officer for the local tax office, a job he kept until 1907, when he became a full-fledged writer.

Inspired by his childhood reading and the adventures of a certain "Magog," the hero of a medieval Hungarian folk tale that claims that the Huns, as well as the Magyars, are descended from twin brothers named Hunor and Magor[3] who settled

---

[2] Black Coat Press, ISBN 978-1-932983-88-3.

[3] The version of this legend in the 14th century *Chronicon Pictum* equates this *Magor* with Magog, son of Japheth.

by the sea of Azov after the Great Flood, and took wives from the Alans, Henri Jeanne took the nom-de-plume of "H.-J. Magog."

At first, he published articles and humorous essays in the *Provençal* Weekly Bulletin, which were later collected into two volumes entitled *Scenes et Silhouettes* and *Mieux vaut en rire* [Better to Laugh]. By penning those faithful but amusing descriptions of the provincial people, their officials and other bourgeois types, Magog gained famed as an accomplished writer of comedies of manners.

He published his first novel, *L'Attentat de la Rue Royale* [The Attack of the Rue Royale] in 1910. Drafted in 1915, he nevertheless continued to write and published three novels during the war years. He occasionally used his real name, as well as a number of other pseudonyms, either for new works or reprints, which make his bibliography exceedingly difficult to compile. Most of these were inspired by his hometown or family names: Henri Jeanne, Jean de la Tardoire, Jacques Noal, Jean de Brévalles, Jean de Laon (or Delaon), Yves Chorsin, Henri d'Areste (from his mother's maiden name), etc.

Magog was the author of a great number popular adventure novels, many of which displayed a wild and unique imaginative streak, but, from a literary standpoint, they were often marred by their pulpish nature. In *Extraordinaires Aventures de Deux Fiancés à travers le Monde* [*Extraordinary Adventures of Two Fiancés Across the World*] (1922), which took place in the year 2050, a Japanese mad scientist used the heat from the Earth's core to cause the oceans to dry up, but the ensuing volcanic eruptions ended up destroying Japan.

In *L'Île Tombée du Ciel* [*The Island Which Fell from the Sky*] (1923), a chunk of a wandering planet fell near Australia; its human explorers discovered that it was inhabited by invisible aliens who turned out to be benevolent.

His best-remembered novel is *Trois Ombres sur* Paris [*Three Shadows Over Paris*] (1928) which also took place in the 21st century and featured the artificial creation of a race of supermen, and their conflict with the political powers of the times. Its conclusion was remarkably similar to the 1935 Olaf Stapledon novel, *Odd John*, in which the supermen were exiled to an island where they eventually destroyed themselves.

As a man of letters, Jeanne was vice-president of the *Société des Gens de Lettres* and founded the *Syndicat des romanciers français*. He was made *Chevalier de la Légion d'Honneur* in August 1929, under the patronage of Pierre Benoît, and seven years later, was promoted to the rank of Officer, under the patronage of Jean Vignaud, He died on January 13, 1947, at the age of 70.

Jean-Marc Lofficier & Brian Stableford

Chapter One
THE MENACING APPARITION

In the luminous spiral of the glass staircase, descending from the terrace, a gracious silhouette was blurred and dissolved, becomes increasingly vague; after a few minutes it ceased to be distinct when the thickness of the crystal paving slabs of several successive landings were interposed between it and the admiring eyes that were following it.

Then, Jean Chapuis raised his head, moved away a few paces and came to lean on the edge of the terrace of the magical Villa, the abode of the celebrated scientist Oronius, the father of the exquisite Cyprienne, who had just left him, and of whom he was the fortunate fiancé.

At his feet—which is to say, below the heights of Belleville, on which the troubling crystal Villa was built, where the laboratory of the greatest and most mysterious of scientists was located—the Paris of the twenty-first century extended.

The twenty-second hour had just chimed. In outdated epochs, people would have said that it was night. But did night still exist for the capital of the United States of Europe, equipped, thanks to the science of Oronius, with all the miracles consequent on the adaptations of his marvelous discoveries? From the top of the 1500-meter tower that had replaced the legendary Eiffel Tower, a timid trial of a metallurgical science in its infancy, an artificial sun projected torrents of light as dazzling as daylight over the entire valley of the Seine.

The most powerful arc lamps of old—the luminous intensity of which would have seemed very pale compared with that extraordinary source of light and heat—had rejoined in the past gas, oil and all the outmoded luminaries with which humans had experimented over the centuries. Now, a certain quantity of solarium, the last-born of the "luminous radioactives" isolated by Oronius, was sufficient to illuminate a whole world.

That was, moreover, only a step toward less costly and more fantastic realizations, Oronius having promised to appropriate directly the fiery arrows of the star, by means of profound vats of mobile mercury, and to distribute them at his whim.

Thus, night no longer existed, nor cold. In truth, humankind would have been able to do without the good old sun, the utility of which only remained certain in a few remote corners of the globe. One could judge now the fragility of the predictions of Camille Flammarion regarding the end of the world by cold. Oronius had already vanquished cold permanently. Perhaps the Earth owed him its present life.

It goes without saying that that uninterrupted daylight—sometimes natural, sometimes artificial, but succeeding one another without interruption—had profoundly changed the manner of human life, most particularly that of Parisians. Activity never ceased there; it did not diminish at any moment of the division of twenty-four hours, which remained the unit of time. Whatever the hour launched by the Tower, aerial Paris, like terrestrial Paris, continued to swarm with people going about her affairs or their pleasures. And if some revenant of olden times had been able to contemplate, as Jean Chapuis was doing, the spectacle from the height of the terrace of the magical Villa, he would certainly have asked the question: "But when do they sleep?"

Sleep! How amused they would be by that obsolete expression, that antique word devoid of any significance. Yes, how they would have laughed, those moderns of the twenty-first century: Jean Chapuis, preferred pupil of Master Oronius, or his gracious fiancée Cyprienne, who had just gone downstairs to take her daily repose.

That repose did not consist of going to lie down on what was once called a bed and stupidly closing her eyes in order to abandon herself to the semi-death of sleep. Bed? Bedroom? Words erased from the new vocabulary. In order to dissipate fatigue and restore the body to a condition to furnish further effort, one now went to the relaxation room. There, under the action of judiciously selected and combined radioactive currents traversing the body and the brain with their effluvia, all the cells of the organism were rid of the toxins accumulated by physical or cerebral effort, cleansed, reconstituted, revivified and rejuvenated.

The body and the mind were renewed, as all garments woven from asbestos fibers were renewed and purified by flames; for there were no longer any dyers, bleachers or laundries, but only *ustorians*, or burners, attached to electric furnaces of cremation.

Thus, the human machine, on emerging from the relaxation room, found itself ready for a new course of action.

Clad in one of the harmonious garments of repose, which had been readopted for interior usage, borrowed from the fashions of antiquity, notably Greece, Jean Chapuis allowed his gaze to wander distractedly toward the upper regions of the atmosphere, traversed by the purr of aerial autobuses and ferries continually landing on the mooring ports or rising from the ground toward the Palaces of the stratosphere.

In fact, it was now up above, in the serene regions surrounded by the first layers of the terrestrial atmosphere, that the fortunate went on vacation. Why remain in the midst of the tumultuous and noisy fever of Paris when, high above, bold architects had suspended in space, in an artificial atmosphere created by means of oxygen currents launched from the ground, and immobilized by an ingenious combination of gliders and electromagnetic forces, crystal "buildings", the luxury and comfort of which ceded nothing to the most reputed of terrestrial palaces. The billionaires of that fortunate epoch lodged at an altitude of ten or twelve thousand meters in aerial palaces, bathed in light and surrounded by space; at their whim they could stare into infinity or contemplate the singularly shrunken panoramas of the poor earth beneath them. They lived above the clouds in the perpetual warmth of an atmosphere warmed and unified by Oronius' solarium.

Nearer to humans—with regard to whom he professed the same love as his venerated master—the young engineer

Jean Chapuis did not envy those semi-astral dwellings, in spite of the charm of their magical gardens enclosed by crystal cupolas. To the privileged few who benefited from them he preferred those whose laborious occupations maintained them close to the ground: ants whom progress had nevertheless rendered winged, buy giving them the marvelous little flying machines that were named, because of their gracious appearance, dragonflies, which permitted everyone to transport himself at will from one place to another by the aerial route. At any moment they were seen flying in thousands, giant insects soaring along the radiant highways of the sky.

Flying over the magical Villa—so well-known to everyone and so popular, by virtue of the innumerable discoveries that Oronius had made to the benefit of transformed humankind—they sent greetings as they passed, via the wireless or speaking sparks. But that spectacle was too familiar to Jean Chapuis for him to be able to take any real interest in it. Did he not have other subjects of reverie, especially the most agreeable of all: his imminent marriage to the charming Cyprienne, whose beauty was only equaled by her marvelous intelligence, by which she was affirmed as her illustrious father's daughter?

Moved and dazzled by the evocation of that promised near future, Jean Chapuis never wearied of admiring the predilection that Destiny marked for him by reserving for him, after the father's lessons, the favor and love of the daughter.

Cyprienne loves me! Oronius consents to give her to me! I shall be the husband of that young woman in every unique point! he thought, ecstatically. *What mortal has ever known such happiness?*

As he thought rather than pronounced those words, a violent shudder shook his entire body, interrupting his dream. His features decomposed; panting with alarm, his eyes staring, he watched—without bring able to wrench himself away from that contemplation, in spite of the horror that it inspired in him—a luminous patch that trembled and grew moving nearby over the glass slabs that formed the floor of the terrace.

It resembled exactly the patch of light formed by a beam of light emerging from a projector and seeking a screen in order to constitute an image thereon.

"Where has that fallen from?"

Making a superhuman effort, Jean Chapuis succeeded in raising his head; instinctively, his gaze searched the sky.

Stupor! There was nothing above him but empty air, an absolute void—or, the put it better, the immense vault, the limpid ceiling filled with the sunlight of the Tower.

What projector could have pierced that fiery sky? No sufficiently powerful luminous source was in view. Jean Chapuis could not see anything...

And yet, he felt something. He felt unknown waves coming from the enigmatic space traversing his body and colliding with the obstacle of the glass on which they displayed that luminous halo.

Suddenly it became a mist, appeared to suspend itself above the floor of the terrace, and became more precise, acquiring shape and substance.

Then, quivering with emotion, Jean saw before him a woman's face, a face endowed with the accursed beauty of the Angel of Evil, which was looking at him with glittering eyes.

Impossible to doubt it: that image, of a reality so gripping that it seemed to be alive in spite of its immateriality, held him under the fixity of its eyes. It seemed to want to search his consciousness, to steal his intimate thoughts.

Horror! It succeeded. He was laid bare—him, Jean Chapuis.

To crown everything, suddenly, a voice resounded in his ear, as strange and inexplicable as the image, which said: *"So you're marrying? You're marrying the daughter of Oronius? Beware, Jean Chapuis... beware!"*

Horrified by having been able to allow the secret of his soul to be discovered by a powerful enemy—oh yes, powerful, and disposing of an unknown force, since she had been able, in spite of his resistance, to exteriorize and lay bare his thought—the young scientist felt a cold sweat running over his entire body.

Losing all initiative, he became as pale and inert as a corpse.

Chapter Two
THE IMMORTAL ORONIUS

The contemporaries of Oronius—insofar as he had contemporaries, as we shall see—said of that extraordinary scientist of genius, that he was the greatest marvel of the era. They could have pronounced that statement in the previous century, and there was every chance that they would continue to say it in the following century, still applying it to the same Oronius.

To what century did he belong? Or, to ask that question in a less abstract and simpler form, how old was he?

No one could have responded with any precision; the oldest of living scientists—the nonagenarians and even a few centenarians who were still alive—recalled having heard mention of the illustrious Oronius even at the most tender age, and as far back as their memories could go. In their estimation, therefore, he must have surpassed a hundred and fifty years; perhaps he was even older.

Knowing that, the few privileged individuals admitted for the first time to have the honor of contemplating the features of the Master expected to find themselves in the presence of a venerable scholar with a long white beard and parchmented skin; they imagined him speaking in a faint and quavering voice and rubbing together hands stripped of flesh that ought to produce a sound like castanets.

Thus, how amazed they were as soon as the father of Cyprienne, that beautiful young woman twenty years of age, showed himself in his real form. The announcement of their respective ages would have enabled the supposition that the pretty Cyprienne—born, moreover, of a twelfth or fifteenth bed—ought to be less the daughter than the great granddaughter of the ancient Oronius.

Well, she was nothing of the sort, and if, in the presence of both of them, spectators experienced some surprise, not to say incredulity, it was, on the contrary, by reason of the extraordinarily youthful appearance of the phenomenal scientist. One might have mistaken him for his daughter's brother rather than her author. He had the same admirable purity of features, bright gaze, and even the solar hair. Those two individuals were equally beautiful, equally youthful in body and mind, and equally vigorous. But that youth, which, in Oronius, defied the claws of time, was a veritable enigma. How did he escape the implacable human law that gradually inclines mortals toward the tomb and steals a little life from them every day? Had he found the secret of immortality, then? Did he make use of an elixir of youth discovered by him, and with which he did not judge it appropriate to give other people the benefit? Many people believed so!

Strange legends ran around on that subject. According to some, Oronius was simply the latest reincarnation of the famous Comte de Saint-Germain, whose multiple existences—especially the last, several centuries before, had excited lovers of the marvelous.[4] But others—occultists—sustained a different thesis; according to them, the remarkable longevity of Oronius and the eternity of his youth was explained by the fact that it was necessary to see in him one of those mysterious spirits maintained among humans at the expiration of the period of their reincarnations in order to sustain and inform humankind. In other terms—those of which initiates make use—Oronius was a delegate of the Great White Lodge.

When his close acquaintances were sufficiently emboldened to make allusion to these different assertions and to question him on the mystery of his existence, the scientist, without denying or confirming anything, limited himself to smiling in an enigmatic manner. Such an attitude was bound to reinforce the legend. It was therefore admitted, in a general fashion, that the singular being in question, in spite of his human appearance, did not belong to our humankind, or at least that he was not submissive to its laws, notably that of ineluctable death.

---

[4] Author's note: "The story can be found in *Mam'zelle Flamberge* by Paul Féval *fils*."

Even Jean Chapuis was subject to the influence of those legends and the sincere admiring affection that the Master inspired in him was mingled with a sort of respectful dread.

For him, as for everyone, the laboratory of the enigmatic scientist, from which so many sublime discoveries emerged—remained a sanctuary into which one only penetrated tremulously, and only after having be duly authorized by the god himself.

That was, let us admit, elementary prudence, for a barrier of sword-blades is child's play compared with the redoubtable surprises that would have greeted and immobilized any undesirable visitor.

In addition, it was absolutely necessary to be admitted into that laboratory in order to be able to glimpse that high priest of official science in the midst of his retorts, his crucibles and all the apparatus of modern alchemy, extracting from Nature secrets of much greater importance and more marvelous than that of the transmutation of metals.

Did Oronius not live in a house of glass, though? His work and his meditations could be witnessed—but no one could penetrate the enigma unless he deigned to explain it.

For several days already, he had been cloistered, in a way, in his work-room and a prohibition had been issued to everyone to importune him on any pretext whatsoever. He only came out, at widely-spaced intervals, to submit himself for a few moments to the action of the regenerative currents and absorb the concentrated chemicals that had replaced meals some years before, and possessed the advantage, at least, of suppressing the laborious work of digestion. Evidently, he was pursuing the solution of a problem of capital importance. A new and sensational discovery was surely about to emerge from his retreat.

That was the opinion of all the inhabitants of the magical Villa, that of Jean Chapuis and Cyprienne, of the mechanic Laridon and the scientist's domestics.

Let us introduce the latter. The first was named Julep: an exuberant black man, he had the singularity of being a "dappled negro"; in fact, his skin, of an appearance as comical as it was bizarre, bore the traces of experiments to which Oronius has subjected him.

The second was the disquieting Wiwar. Welcomed by virtue of charity, and showing servile obsequiousness, because of his shifty appearance, he was antipathetic to everyone, save for the scientist, who was too absorbed to lower himself to observations qualified by him as secondary.

Given that Wiwar fulfilled the functions of laboratory assistant, Jean Chapuis and Cyprienne thought privately that the Master showed a confidence in him that was very imprudent in the circumstances. It is necessary to recognize, however, that thus far no harm had resulted from it—which justified in a certain measure Oronius' lack of suspicion.

Nevertheless, could one fail to remark that curiosity was Wiwar's venial sin? Excluded from the laboratory, like everyone else, during the period of the Master's research, he furnished a new proof of it by prowling obstinately around the corridors with translucent walls, from which he could perceive the Master agitating around his electric furnaces and delivering himself to an entire cuisine that would have seemed quasi-diabolical in other times.

Thus, Wiwar observed him, or, to use a more exact term, he spied on him with a very suspicious perseverance. That discretion would have been dangerous for his own person if the scientist had reserved the smallest fraction of his faculties for maintaining surveillance of the external world. He did not, unfortunately. Wiwar saw his master, absorbed in the contemplation of a mysterious mixture, suddenly straighten up, sponging his brow and casting a triumphant glance around him.

At the same moment, in spite of the rigorous order, the door of the laboratory opened and Jean Chapuis hurtled into the room. That was an unusual event, a sort of sacrilege without precedent, which would have consternated all the inhabitants of the dwelling and struck them with terror. To dare to trouble the meditation of the laborious seeker, to push audacity so far as to infringe his prohibition, was enough to attract the thunderbolts of Oronian wrath!

Wiwar remembered once having heard its explosions, comparable to those of thunder. He sniggered with joy at the thought of the formidable remonstration that the intruder was about to attract. Alas, contrary to that venomous hope, legitimated by his own experience. Oronius did not even frown.

Better than that, the Master's face lit up and he held out his hands to his favorite pupil.

"You've arrived at the right time!" he said. "*I've succeeded!*"

"You've succeeded in capturing...?"

With his open right hand, rapidly extended, the scientist gagged his future son-in-law. "Shh!" he whispered. "That, you know, must remain secret until the day when I'll be able to experiment practically. It's necessary to wait for the opportunity. Between now and then, you and Cyprienne must remain my only confidants. Apart from the two of you, no one must suspect the goal that I've been pursuing, and hope that I've now attained.

Suddenly, however, in spite of the fire of his enthusiasm, he stopped and considered his pupil attentively. The latter's features were covered by a livid pallor.

"What's the matter with you?" he exclaimed. "I forgot to ask you the cause of your coming here before I sounded my summons. Something serious has just happened? It's sufficient for me to look at you to sense it."

"Something terrifying!" stammered Jean Chapuis, passing his hand over his brow. "To make me forget the deference that I'm proud of testifying to you, it required nothing less, in fact, than an incomprehensible event that has bowled me over."

"What is it?"

"You're about to know, Master."

Mechanically, the young man searched with his eyes for a seat, which Oronius, seeing him totter, hastened to advance for him.

"Speak!" he said. "But first, recover your calm and remember that there's no harm so grave that I can't boast of being able to remedy it."

"I'm in great need of the comfort of that conviction, Master. If I didn't know that you were with me, ready to support me, nothing would prevent me from ceding to my fear. If I only listened to my present emotion, I'd renounce the hand of my beloved Cyprienne immediately."

"What foolishness are you saying?" said the scientist, astounded. "And what reason would you give for inflicting such despair on yourself, and on my daughter at the same time?"

"I can't cause Cyprienne's misfortune!" groaned Jean Chapuis.

"Marry her, then!"

"We're not understanding one another. It's by marrying her that I'm afraid of attracting to her what threatens her."

"Stop talking in riddles, my friend. I have too much esteem for your intelligence and the solidity if your brain to yield to the suspicion of a dementia, so your trouble must originate from a real and sensate cause. Explain yourself."

The young scientist passed his hand over his forehead in the manner of a magnetizer waking his subject.

"Master," he commenced, striving, as Oronius had advised him to do, to recover his sang-froid, "you know what a sincere and profound love I have for Cyprienne. If I had not believed myself to be sure of being able to consecrate all my aspirations and all my strength to her happiness, I would never have had the audacity to accept that she might render me the most fortunate of mortals"

"I know that! Go on!" replied Oronius, shrugging his shoulders.

"Well, Master, since a quarter on an hour ago, an atrocious doubt has been torturing me. A remorse is clawing me. I an reproaching myself, at the moment when you have deigned to accord me Cyprienne and promised her to me as my wife, for having hidden from you an incident that I judged insignificant, but which it is impossible now for me to keep to myself any longer, because it clarifies the adventure that has just discouraged me. It's a consultation that I've come to ask of you, because, in truth, I no longer know what to think, nor what to do. Where does my duty lie? Ought I to continue, or to renounce Cyprienne? I believed that I was free to consecrate my life to her, but perhaps I'm not. The shadow of misfortune extends over my head."

"Some pretend to see a shadow in me," laughed the scientist. "You'll permit me, therefore, not to be moved and give you this assurance: I shall be able, if necessary, to struggle victoriously against a shadow."

"I will confess, then, and you shall judge. But in order to understand me fully, and before arriving at what has just terrified me, I first need to take you back into the past."

"Speak."

Chapter Three
THE EYES OF THE INVISIBLE

Before commencing, Jean Chapuis collected himself for a few moments. He was prey to an indescribable emotion, which had thrown his ideas into disorder. He found himself obliged to reassemble them before proceeding.

He passed his hand over his brow for a second time, and finally began.

"Master, because you have pushed back the boundaries of the possible and admit miracles as normal events, it has become very difficult to be moved in your presence by a manifestation of the forces around us and talk about them as if an explanation can be furnished for them. Personally, for two or three years, I have on several occasions, sometimes in a continuous fashion, had the impression of being enveloped by a mysterious influence. I didn't want to believe it—wouldn't that have been admitting that that your power might be equaled?"

"Why didn't you speak to me about that doubt? Why have you concealed the events that gave birth to it from me?" asked Oronius tranquilly, without referring otherwise to the final allusion, nor attempting to respond to it."

"I was afraid of seeming ridiculous to you. It resembled so closely the beginning of a hallucination. Only its persistence, as well as the continuity of its action, obliged me to think that it was a matter of a reality. Master, can you admit that, through walls and even in the dark, someone—I don't know where, but assuredly a long way away, and perhaps in another world—can see us constantly, hear us think, watch us act and keep us under surveillance to the point that none of our gestures escapes him?"

Oronius closed his eyes in order to concentrate his mind better.

"Why not?" he replied, simply. "I'm only occupied in perfecting optical instruments by applying the forces of radioactive currents to them. Only the immediate utility directs my discoveries. However, if some circumstance had spurred my research on that path, I imagine that I could have arrived at the result revealed by your question."

"In your estimation, is it possible to project one's own image across space and reveal it to another person, separated from you by a considerable distance?"

"Realizable."

"To be heard by him? To speak to him?"

"I can admit that."

At each of the scientist's affirmations Jean Chapuis' voice deteriorated further, while the pallor spread over the young man's face became livid.

"But to realize such prodigies," he stammered, "Wouldn't it require a science… that only one man has boasted of possessing thus far? And that man is you, Master!"

"Can one ever boast of being the only one of one's species?" riposted Oronius, placidly.

Again, Jean Chapuis passed one of his hands over his brow, which was streaming with sweat. It seemed that he was having a bad dream.

"That's frightful," he murmured.

"Will you tell me your dream?"

"It wasn't a dream!"

The master's eyebrows furrowed imperceptibly. On his part, the gesture could as easily express impatience as irritation or anxiety; but he remained silent and contented himself with looking at his disciple with a sustained attention.

Evidently, what Cyprienne's fiancé had said had awakened thoughts in his mind that were worrying him.

"No, it wasn't a dream," Jean Chapuis went on. "In the beginning, however, I agree, I couldn't believe that it was anything other than a series of hallucinations, at which I smiled to begin with; and then they irritated me. I would have blushed to confess that weakness of my nervous system, so I didn't mention it to anyone. I struggled alone, subjecting my mind to a severe discipline destined to prevent it from going astray in a similar fashion. Nothing worked... the troubling symptoms persisted."

"And of what did they consist?"

"First of all it was only a simple malaise, the sensation of embarrassment and sometimes of irritation that one feels when one senses the obstinacy of a strange gaze upon one. You turn your back and suddenly sense someone looking at you; you make an abrupt, almost involuntary half-turn and you find someone staring at you...except that when I turned round, more than twenty times a day, I didn't see anyone—no one at all—until the day when I saw..."

He interrupted himself and hesitated, genuinely embarrassed at having to recount the fantastic story.

"You saw what?" asked Oronius, impassively.

"A woman's face... nothing but a face in a halo of fog."

"A woman's face," Oronius repeated, slowly. He seemed disappointed. Had he expected something else, and had Jean Chapuis' specification surprised him? "Known or unknown?" he asked, laconically.

"Completely unknown, Master. I was seeing that image for the first time in my life, and I will add that I have never contemplated the original... if it exists."

"If it exists," Oronius approved, with a visible satisfaction. Without a doubt, that restriction corresponded to the explanation that his secret thought had suggested.

"The face was, moreover, unforgettable," said the young engineer. "Beautiful but terrible... the face of an angel transformed into a demon."

"Go on—that detail is devoid of interest."

"Since then, it hasn't ceased to obsess me... but on the condition that I'm alone. It only appeared to me in solitude. That is why I could believe that it was a hallucination, of which I sought in vain to cure myself. It soon got worse, in the sense that one night, I heard the voice murmur in my ear: *'Someone is following you with her eyes, constantly... con-*

stantly. *I am present everywhere you go. I am the gaze of the invisible, which you cannot escape. My thought envelops you, like my will. Already, you belong to me. Try, then, to chase my image away. It's inside you! Your eyes will not be able to forget it!*'"

The young man clutched his temples with an enervated hand, and all the despair accumulated within him by the long persecution supported in silence suddenly burst forth.

"Those words, how many times must I have heard them?" he exclaimed. "They become odious to me, and yet I only attributed them to an aggravation of my enervating phantasmagoria: auditory disturbances accompanying visual disturbances. I conserved that illusion. In time, the discourse changed; I heard the voice say to me, imperiously: '*Now you have seen me and you know my power. You will come to join me; I wish it. You will soon receive a proposition to depart. Accept it.*' Three days later, Master, a stranger came to offer me an advantageous situation; it was a matter of accompanying him in a voyage of study. Imagine my exacerbation: the voice seemed to have foreseen that offer. How could I believe it to be a simple hallucination?"

"It was, at least, a curious coincidence," said Oronius, pensively.

"It was worse than that. Naturally, I rejected the proposition. Brilliant as it was, the conditions offered to me could not persuade me to leave you. That would also have been to distance myself from my dear Cyprienne. On the other hand, the strange circumstances that attached the offer to my apparitions could only inspire the keenest reluctance. I therefore responded with a categorical refusal, on which there was no possibility of my going back."

"What happened then?"

"Taking account of my resolution, the stranger did not insist. Some time afterwards, however, in the course of a solitary excursion I was making on foot, like our ancestors who were fond of walking, an airplane landed a few paces away from me with the rapidity of a bird of prey. Three men came out and threw themselves upon me. It was definitely an attempted abduction."

"You got out of it, it appears."

"Yes, fortunately, and thanks to you. In fact, in view of that dangerous excursion, especially nowadays, when few pedestrians risk themselves on the roads, I had dressed in the protective suit of which you are the inventor, which a electric current, unleashed at will, renders fatal to attackers. As soon as they had laid hands upon me, my fellows executed the most beautiful series of pirouettes that any clown or acrobat had ever contrived and fell to the ground, gasping. They remained inanimate there and I drew away peacefully. The same evening, I saw the face again, but irritated and menacing, and I heard the voice growl: '*You've escaped me: beware!*'"

"It was necessary to inform me of that," said Oronius frowning again.

"I dared not. In any case, reassured as to my mental equilibrium, since I was certain of the reality of the persecution, and proud of having shown myself to be invulnerable, I thought that I had nothing much to fear from my unknown woman. It ought to have been sufficient for me to remain on guard; she had invited me and I had refused. Events appeared to justify my confidence. The face ceased to appear to me... until this evening."

"You've just seen it again?" Oronius had not started, or made any gesture of surprise. He was a man of admirable *sang-froid*.

"Yes, Master. Only a moment go I saw it again, and heard the voice again. It was on the terrace; she pronounced threatening words... regarding my marriage. Can I take that lightly? I'm not the only one in danger...Cyprienne! Is someone not taking aim at her? Strange presentiments are overwhelming me; frightful doubts are tearing me apart. Have I not been wrong to take all that so inconsiderately? What can the mysterious being do who, from a place nearby or far away—I don't know which—can follow my thoughts and my steps, can impose on me he illusion of seeing her and hearing her? Mas-

28

ter, I need to be enlightened and reassured. Forgive the blasphemy that I'm about to pronounce, but the circumstance is too grave for me to hesitate to let you see the extent of my fears, even if you qualify them as chimerical or they offend you. Do you not think that the frightful prodigies of which I have been simultaneously the witness and the object announce a considerable science, a power approaching yours?"

"Approaching: the word is just," said Oronius calmly.

"You have a rival, then?"

"Approaching doesn't mean equaling, even less does it signify surpassing," riposted the Master, with an ironic assurance.

Undoubtedly!" agreed Jean Chapuis, slightly confused. "However, it's terrible none the less to think that you might have to measure yourself against a similar science, which might perhaps, in certain respects, hold yours in check, or cause such misfortunes that you'll only retain the possibility of avenging yourself."

"No childishness!" snapped Oronius, disdainfully. "I have no rival in the world. I nearly had one—only nearly—once, a long time ago; I can't tell you how many years… you'd believe in your dreams again. At that time, a man stood up against me; he intended to snatch my scepter, eclipse me and crush me. The presumptuous individual had, you will have guessed, the demon of pride. He did not belong to the genre of those who toil for the benefit of humankind. In those conditions, I could not hesitate; I accepted the contest, I defeated him and humiliated him… he disappeared…"

A sudden anguish—an inexplicable anguish, as if it had been suggested to him by a superior force—took possession of Jean Chapuis.

"That man—what became of him?" he exclaimed, almost involuntarily.

Oronius smiled, shrugging his shoulders.

"What a state you're in! What does my man matter? In your case, it's a matter of a woman… the face of a woman. In any case, the man was…."

His voice was drowned out by a sudden din, which made the walls of the magical Villa vibrate...

Chapter Four
SCIENCE AGAINST SCIENCE

In the state of agitation that Jean Chapuis was in, the slightest incident was bound to have an unfortunate repercussion on his nerves and throw him into further trouble.

On hearing that racket, which was truly terrible, he immediately attached the cause to the object of his present preoccupations, and imagined a catastrophe.

"What's happening?" he exclaimed, precipitating himself toward the door, trembling with emotion and anxiety.

More simply, Oronius had placed himself before a "speaking screen," which ought to bear his question into every covert of the Villa.

"What's the cause of that noise?" he asked, in a perfectly calm tone.

An obsequious voice, that of Wiwar, the excessively curious laboratory assistant, immediately responded: "It's a slight accident, Monsieur. Monsieur de Sainte-Barbe's aerocab has just crashed on the terrace."

"Has he broken anything?"

"Personally, he's unharmed, but his apparatus is badly damaged."

"But how the devil did the maladroit idiot come a cropper? Did he think he was in his chair at the Institut?"

Wiwar's voice marked a hesitation. "Monsieur de Sainte-Barbe claims to have collided with a cloud."

"A collision with a cloud!" scoffed Ormnius, almost amused by the enunciation of that fantastic accident "In truth, if the honorable academician weren't the most tedious of serious men, I'd suspect him of wanting to play a practical joke on us. He had descended from the Moon, I imagine, and the cloud that caused him to crash was composed of the fog by which his own brain is beset."

"Monsieur de Sainte-Barbe is asking to see you," said the speaking screen, again.

"I'm flattered by the honor. Have him come down, Wiwar, since I can't disturb myself."

Quitting the communication post, Oronius turned to Jean Chapuis, who had stopped, reassured by the first words.

"You were wrong to tremble," the master said. "It was only an old bore falling out of the sky. The loss wouldn't have been disastrous if his teeth had severed his tongue."

He struck a gracious pose. Monsieur de Sainte-Barbe came in, very upset. Doubtless the emotion consequent on his fall, Oronius judged. Amiably, he offered a comfortable arm-chair—which, in truth, might have alarmed the member of the Institut slightly, for it was an electrocuting armchair generally reserved for certain experiments.

Monsieur de Sainte-Barbe paid no heed to that, and let himself drop into it. "Oh, my dear friend, if you knew!" he exclaimed, with a tremolo in his voice.

"Pull yourself together," Oronius advised. "You've got away with a scare. That's lucky."

"You're talking about my fall? Oh, as extraordinary things go, it's extraordinary. Think of it: crashing into a cloud."

"The presence of a cloud in our pure and carefully swept sky would be very surprising in itself," Oronius put in, skeptically.

"Well, it's a fact," riposted Monsieur de Sainte Barbe, piqued by the irony. "Master, I'm announcing something unexpected to you… a meteorological phenomenon that we haven't contemplated for at least a quarter of a century: battalions of clouds are rushing toward Paris. There's going to be a storm!"

A storm? Jean Chapuis thought. *My father has never been able to see one. Shall I see one?*

"Is that true?" Oronius exclaimed, at the same time; his expressive physiognomy appeared to betray a joy that was as sudden as it was incomprehensible.

A storm! A storm over Paris!

As the academician had just said, and the engineer had thought, the Parisians had lost the habitude of that disturbing phenomenon since artificial currents had been carefully sweeping their sky, now filled with a carefully-measured atmosphere that excluded all elements of trouble. A storm!

That improbable event did not seem to displease the illustrious Onorius in the slightest.

"Your science had doubtless not foreseen its advent?" said the vindictively ironic Monsieur de Sainte-Barbe in his turn. "It wants to prove to you that water vapors still exist in the free state. They can't all be constrained to imprison themselves in your machines. Those Bohemians of the skies wouldn't accept without revolt the slavery of boilers; they don't recognize any authority—even yours. So a storm is in preparation, and it's inexplicable... perhaps less so for me than for you..."

The academician produced the last words in a singular manner; after which he interrupted himself, as if he were waiting for them to be queried.

"Well, let the storm come," said Oronius, phlegmatically. "It's welcome. I've had the greatest desire to observe one." And he exchanged a rapid glance with Jean Chapuis, the meaning of which remained impenetrable for Monsieur de Sante-Barbe.

"You'll be satisfied," the latter declared, with increasing aggression. "Damn it! The most menacing horizon seems to be appearing. To see one as black as that I have to go back to the time of my distant youth. One might think that all the clouds in the world were galloping toward Paris!"

"Let them come," Oronius repeated, without flinching. And he added, maliciously: "It's doubtless one of those that you... bumped into. That's a fine exploit! To pass through a cloud, fine—but to bump into it... that's a record. You're exaggerating, my dear master."

"I never exaggerate," the member of the Institut riposted, dryly. "And my word ought to be sufficient for you, for I'm an observer with a critical mind nourished on scientific methods. If I pronounce a fact that appears inadmissible to you, ripe for your sarcasms—a collision with a cloud, matter ordinarily inconsistent and impalpable—it's because the collision occurred. I can add that it was passably rude."

"The cloud enveloped a rock, then?"

Monsieur de Sainte-Barbe replied seriously: "It might have! Yes, my word, it might have! For I remember that, after having entered the apparently inoffensive cloud, which the wind seemed to be pushing toward me, and which I thought I could traverse without any inconvenience, I suddenly had the impression of finding myself confronted by a wall. A collision occurred. That impact in thick fog caused my apparatus to capsize and precipitated me on to your terrace, fortunately at close range. All that was so rapid that it would be an impertinence on my part to say '*I saw it...*' One fact subsists: I collided with a massive and hard surface, wrapped in a cloud."

"Get away! I recognize that the impact must have been hard, since you're still troubled by it," Onorius pronounced, with an indulgence that was rather mortifying for Monsieur Sainte-Barbe, "but why the devil were you traveling through clouds, at a speed such that you couldn't avoid them? Such feats are unworthy of your character."

"Master, you're trying to vex me, but you won't succeed. If I was traveling at speed it was because I was flying to you... yes, literally!" cried Monsieur de Sainte-Barbe, bounding to his feet and showing once again the same emotion as when he entered the laboratory. "I was in haste to see you... to tell you... for you doubtless don't know what has happened... the vain rumors of the world come to die against your walls of glass without crossing them..."

"I don't intend to allow myself to be distracted from my work, my dear colleague."

"For the ordinary circumstances that are the background of our preoccupations, so be it... but today... today! It's you who are involved; it's because of you that Paris is frightened..."

"Frightened? Why is that?" asked the master, negligently.

Monsieur de Sainte-Barbe struck a tragic pose.

"Because of this challenge," he proclaimed. "Because of the challenge by which we're threatened with total destruction in twenty-four hours, in order to prove to the world that you, the illustrious Oronius, are only a simple hack incapable of defending us. Yes, that's what the voice of the Tower announced, transmitting a message received by it from an unknown point in space."

"And this is aimed at me? What does this madness signify?"

"It's a matter of a challenge that is being thrown down to you," riposted Sainte-Barbe forcefully. "These are the terms of the challenge; I noted them down for your benefit."

Taking out a minuscule parlograph, he set it in motion. A voice, which made Oronius tremble at the first words, resounded in the room.

"Oronius, Hantzen is not defeated. He has put the years to profit. Today, certain of his strength, he proclaims himself your master and issues you this challenge: Science against science, Oronius! Defend the world, which I shall destroy because it shelters you and has believed in you. Today I will deliver the first blow. Parry it, if it is in your power. Tomorrow, Paris will be no more than a heap of ruins, not even a pile of ashes, for I shall scatter its dust to the four corners of space. Hantzen challenges you to prevent that, savant Oronius!"

For the first time since Jean Chapuis had known him, the Master permitted his face to reveal a slight emotion.

He had let his head slump on to his breast and he murmured in a strange voice, not loud enough to be understood by those who were listening: "Otto Hantzen! Have I not defeated you already? You're back... You're challenging me again... it's the two of us against each other!"

Chapter Five
A SCIENTIST'S HATRED

Forgetting his listeners, seemingly sunk in a meditation that must be made of memories, Oronius had started marching back and forth across the laboratory. His grim expression and his concentrated gaze, as when he was pursuing the solution to an arduous problem, were not calculated to diminish the anxiety that had taken possession of Jean Chapuis, and which Monsieur de Sainte-Barbe certainly shared.

They both contemplated the Master from whom they expected salvation; at the same time their gazes implored the explanation that his attitude required; for it seemed only too certain the Oronius' adversary was of similar stature and that the scientist deemed him worthy of attention.

What was it necessary to fear? That was the question that Jean Chapuis and Monsieur de Sainte-Barbe were asking themselves. The latter, in spite of the ironies that he had permitted himself with regard to his illustrious colleague—too far above his modest person for him not to be jealous—had evidently come with the goal of hearing words of appeasement and to acquire the conviction that the menace of the mysterious Hantzen was only an inconsequential boast.

Now, things were not turning out as he had expected. Oronius had greeted the news with a seriousness that was a bad omen; and what was more serious, he seemed not to be unaware of Hantzen. Who, then, was the person that was causing the Master to reflect?

In order to learn that, and simultaneously to glimpse the gravity of the peril, Jean Chapuis and Monsieur Sainte-Barbe waited anxiously for the words that were about to fall from the scientist's lips.

Finally stopping his pacing, the latter turned to face his pupil, and his mouth sketched a bizarre smile.

"This is one of those coincidences that makes one believe in the ironic tendency of chance," he pronounced. "The man about whom I was talking when the honorable Monsieur de Sainte-Barbe interrupted our conversation with the noise of his fall was the man on the subject of whom you interrogated me as to what had become of him; it's him of whom there is question—it's Otto Hantzen."

"What!" stammered Jean Chapuis, going very pale. "The man who opposed you as a rival, and whom you defeated..."

Oronius nodded his head affirmatively. "It's him," he repeated. "I had obliged him to observe that he couldn't hold a candle to me, and he went to hide his shame who knows where. In short, he disappeared, and I would have found it difficult to respond to you just now. I'm scarcely better informed now, but he's finally showing signs of life again; he's rediscovered his pride... and his arrogance. He's challenging me again!"

Straightening up, Oronius launched sarcastic laughter across the laboratory, affirming: "So we're going to amuse ourselves!"

"Do you think that it's anything to laugh at?" asked Monsieur de Sainte-Barbe, timidly. "This Hantzen has made precise threats; he's announced the destruction of Paris in twenty-four hours. Might he not carry out his threat?"

"He might..."

"Oh! Are you joking?"

"If I weren't here to counteract his work," Oronius concluded, proudly.

"But can you counter it effectively," Monsieur Sainte-Barbe hazarded, "without knowing his plans or the means at his disposal?"

"Whatever his means are, I'll annihilate them," snapped the Master. "Yes, I'm strong enough to riposte, tit for tat. I repeat to you that Otto Hantzen, in spite of his intelligence—which is, I recognize, remarkable—has never been and never will be anything but a child in comparison to me."

"Let's accept the augury," said the academician, slightly calmer. "Will you authorize me to go and take that reassurance to the Parisians?"

"Go tell them this: Oronius is at his post; he is awaiting the enemy, in order to reduce him to dust."

The member of the Institut took a few steps toward the door, and turned round in order to bow to the man of whom he was taking his leave.

"It will be a terrible contest!" he could not help murmuring. "Properly speaking, two great scientists have just declared war on one another. May humanity not have to pick up the pieces! I imagine that the world is going to see frightful things."

"Let the world be reassured," sniggered Oronius. "What Hantzen breaks, I shall repair. In this little game, he won't have the last word."

"Undoubtedly, undoubtedly," said Monsieur Sainte-Barbe, in a conciliatory tone. "At any rate, personally, I'd prefer not to be broken... in order not to have to be repaired."

He disappeared after that irreverent remark, which caused the Master to frown.

Oronius remained alone with his pupil. "Are you no more reassured than that old bird?" he thundered, point-blank.

Cyprienne's fiancé sighed. "Alas, Master, I must admit, frankly, that this succession of events has upset me and inspired the keenest apprehensions. How can I help being struck by the coincidence of these two threats: the one I've received and the one addressed personally to you? Can we not fear that they come from the same source?"

Oronius shook his head. "I don't see how that could be," he replied. "Your mysterious adventure seems to be entirely personal. It is only addressed to you; you alone are involved. It's a matter of a woman. You have been signaled out, you have not responded to advances that are flattering, but too strange; you rejected them. Offense has been taken and there is an intention to make you repent. That rancor is very feminine, and has nothing to do with me, for the challenge that

Otto Hantzen is launching at me intends to liquidate an old quarrel dating from an epoch in which you were not yet born. You can see that there can't be any link between the two events. Your mysterious woman has nothing in common with my evil demon."

"May you be telling the truth—I'm frightened by the mere idea of an alliance between these two hatreds... and also, it's necessary to say, since my unknown woman has proved her power, and you recognize that this Hantzen has a certain genius, between these two forces!"

"United or separate, I'm capable of standing up to them and annihilating them," proclaimed Oronius, disdainfully, "but the greater probability is that there is no correlation between the two manifestations, that simple coincidence has made them manifest almost simultaneously. Thus far, in any case, your unknown woman has not been able to do anything except frighten you, which is very little. Hantzen's threat is not of the same caliber; I was wrong to treat it as childish; it's that one, therefore, with which I ought to occupy myself immediately. Leave me alone; I need to meditate in the most complete calm."

He pushed his pupil gently toward the door. The latter was manifestly still anxious and apprehensive.

As Oronius opened the door, a tumult burst forth in the corridors of the glass villa.

"Ah! I've caught you again, spy of the devil, impudent sneak!" an indignant voice proclaimed. "Do I have to turn your vile olive skin inside out and crush the nucleus to take away the desire to eavesdrop at doors?"

Furrowing his Olympian eyebrows, the scientist shouted angrily: "And do I have to cut out your tongue in order no longer to be importuned by the noise of your disputes? What is it now?"

While he was speaking, Oronius and his pupil had advanced a few paces outside the laboratory; they discovered then the most singular of spectacles.

One might have thought that a mob—an angry mob—was beating an individual with an olive mask, who cut a truly piteous figure in the middle of the hostile group/

The mob consisted of a negro, an ape, two dogs and a young man. They were all agitating, screeching, barking, threatening and manifesting the most eloquent indignation, each in accordance with the physical means provided by nature, against the man in the olive mask, which proved to be Wiwar, the laboratory assistant.

The assault was manifestly being led by the aforementioned young man; he alone could be the leader of the band. Supple, lithe, muscular and mocking, he had a tongue as prompt as his fists; he was a Parisian, who answered to the name of Laridon, and whose employment at the Villa was in the capacity of mechanic, maintaining and, if necessary, piloting the flying machines, particularly the Halcyon-Car, the most advanced of them all.

The negro affected a singularly new aspect, of which no treatise of anthropology had yet identified the marvelous species. In fact, he was mottled from head to toe with all the colors of the rainbow. He owed that singular costume of natural skin to the whim of Oronius, who studied from time to time the effect on that dark backcloth of the coloring and decoloring effects of luminous currents, and was striving to reconstitute by that means the secret of the pigmentation of the various human races.

The multicolored individual was supposed to answer to the name of Julep, but most of the time, he preferred to play deaf, idly.

Another inmate consecrated to serum experiments, the ape, an orangutan of tall stature and exquisite humor, came running without reluctance when the name of Bambo was pronounced. Like Julep, and as much as him, he adored the mechanic Laridon, and obeyed his finger and his gaze.

Pipigg and Kukuss, the two little papillon lap-dogs, favorites of Cyprienne, habitually frolicked throughout the dwelling. There was thus nothing astonishing in the fact that, seeing the troupe launched by Laridon against Wiwar, considered by him as a spy, they had seized the opportunity to amuse themselves by nipping the laboratory assistant's calves.

Beaten, shaken, pinched, scratched and simultaneously insulted, Wiwar really was not having a good time. On perceiving Oronius he started uttering loud screams.

"Help, my good Master," he wailed. "They're killing me! Murder!"

"Let him go, Laridon," ordered Oronius, authoritatively.

Intimidated by the Master's gaze, the mechanic obeyed, but not without protest.

"He's nothing but a dirty spy!" he fulminated. "I've been keeping an eye on him for some time. I've even warned M'sieur Jean. If I were you, Boss, I'd throw this vermin out. I've just spotted his villainous muzzle stuck to your door. In order that you wouldn't notice him, he was lying belly-down and he approached like that, crawling."

Needless to say, young Laridon had no affection for Wiwar. On the other hand, by the hateful and sly manner in which the latter looked at him, there could be no doubt that he nurtured sentiments that were no more cordial in the mechanic's regard.

In response to Laridon's words there was a concert of approval.

"Him bad!" growled Julep.

The orangutan grunted and the papillons yapped.

Oronius had to block his ears.

"Are you trying to deafen me?" he shouted. "Laridon, I hold you responsible for this racket. Take your gang away, and if you take it into your head to come and break my head again with your stupid speech, I'll deprive myself of your services. I have spoken."

His dominating gesture compelled a retreat, which was executed in disorder under the guidance of the disappointed Laridon.

"Good!" he muttered. "That's all it needs! Me getting sacked because of that bird of ill omen! Damn it! Take the side of the villains! Devotion is pointless here. He doesn't see what's going on, M'sieur Oronius. No need of spectacles, though! It leaps to the peepers that Wiwar's always prowling around the lab. On whose account? That's to find out. But me, it's a waste of time keeping an eye open and sticking my oar in. I've been rebuked unjustly; they won't catch my plating watchman again. The green ape can snaffle all M'sieur Oronius' bottles and play tricks with his scientific grub. I won't tell! Enough! I've had it! Only I'll keep a dog for my bitch. No, Pipigg? No, Kukuss? Let him laugh now… one day or other, I'll show him how I make plum jam!"

Muttering thus, he emerged on to the terrace flowed by his flock: the negro, the ape and the lap-dogs.

Prudently, Wiwar had disappeared into the depths of the basement.

A lively brunette with a sparkle in her eyes greeted the appearance of the discomfited group with a loud burst of laughter. That was Turlurette, Cyprienne's chambermaid.

"Oh-ho!" she remarked, mockingly, "Marlborough's off to war! Now you're the commander-in-chief, Monsieur Laridon. What's the matter then? We could hear you shouting from Mademoiselle's apartment!"

"Nothing!" replied the ill-humored mechanic. "It's not at Monsieur de Wiwar that one can shout, is it? He's a fellow who's entirely correct and lovable. If I said that his mug didn't suit me they'd criticize me for my bad taste. So, what can one do but give him a pat on the back? But frankly speaking, I'd rather look at your pretty face than his ugly mug, Mam'zelle Turlurette."

So saying, he slid an insidious arm around the chambermaid's waist. She pulled away with an elegant and skillful pirouette.

"A thousand regrets, Monsieur Laridon—Mademoiselle is waiting for me."

She fled, laughing, calling to the two minuscule dogs, which launched themselves in her pursuit.

With a chagrined gesture, the mechanic dismissed Julep and Bambo.

"Go away, you two! Me, I'm going into town! I need to cheer myself up. It eats you away to be misunderstood!"

And the worthy fellow moved off in the direction of the hangars.

Chapter Six
A CLOUD ON THE HORIZON

Oronius having shut himself in his laboratory, Jean Chapuis had gone back up to the terrace, and he was leaning on the balustrade again.

In spite of the Master's confidence, he was assailed by somber preoccupations—presentiments, a less stern mind might have said.

He allowed himself to be absorbed to such an extent that he neglected to observe the remarkable spectacle that was presented by one entire side of the horizon.

Had Monsieur de Sainte-Barbe been correct in prognosticating an imminent storm, announced by a veritable offensive of clouds? Perhaps...

To the east, a managing black band was beginning to bite into the silvery cap of the luminous sky, and restore the nocturnal color that it ought to have had at that hour. But Jean Chapuis paid no attention to that, any more than he remarked, almost directly overhead but very high in the sky the singular fixity of one cloud—just one—the roseate whiteness of which could, in any case, easily be confounded with the surrounding colorations.

The young engineer might, however, have remembered the bizarre accident to which the member of the Institut had nearly been a victim. Had it not been caused by that cloud— the cloud that remained obstinately motionless, as if anchored in space, above Oronius' villa?

No; the apprehensions of Jean Chapuis were interior and devoid of precise form, with the consequence that the idea did not occur to him of applying them to that reality, visible if not tangible.

In any case, if he had applied them to it, he would not have had time to dwell on the solution of the problem for long. A hand was placed on his shoulder and a soft and tender voice suddenly caressed his ear; he abandoned his preoccupation for more amiable realities.

Cyprienne, infused with new strength in the relaxation chamber, had just come up to rejoin her fiancé.

Mademoiselle Cyprienne Oronius, aged nineteen, possessed a rare beauty, although it had not yet blossomed completely. Tall, slim, svelte, with serpentine curves that the light fabric of her fashionable tunic allowed to be divined, she presented in combination all the elegances of a virgin and all the seductions of a mature woman. Above a high forehead, as befit a person given to study, was a rich florescence of golden threads, which steamed over the whiteness of her neck and her blonde shoulders. She had breeding, and her ultramarine blue eyes, which were able to smile or command, would have troubled the hearts of all those on whom they fixed.

"What are you thinking about?" she asked the engineer, gratifying him with her sweetest smile.

Jean Chapuis shuddered. Could he confide his dreads to that delectable child? Could he talk to her about his troubling vision? That would awaken two sources of alarm in her, of which the crueler might be the one that disturbed her affection.

Resolved to hide the recent incidents from his fiancée, the young man replied: "What could I be thinking about, except you, my dear Cyprienne?"

"You had a very serious expression for such a subject of reverie," riposted the young woman maliciously. "Does the future of happiness for which we are hoping justify such a melancholy meditation? It's bright, it's joyful... nothing can darken it or threaten it..."

"Nothing," Jean acquiesced, sighing.

The stabilized cloud enlarged its underside above their heads, but neither of them saw it; they were looking at one another.

And looking into the eyes of his fiancée, the engineer forgot his anguish and rediscovered a new confidence.

"Dear Cyprienne!" he murmured, with a tender fervor. "Near to you, how could I doubt the future? To you, above all, it cannot refuse its smiles."

Perhaps we have forgotten to mention that Jean Chapuis was twenty-eight years old? And Cyprienne was approaching her nineteenth spring. At those respective ages, a man and a woman are well-matched for marriage; the future of such a couple is woven of beautiful hopes.

At the moment when the young man finished pronouncing his last words, the multicolored silhouette of the polychromatic negro appeared at the top of the staircase.

"Visit, M'sieur... Visit, Mamzelle," he announced with an expression of compunction.

"Visit for whom?" asked Cyprienne, turning round and mechanically matching Julep's manner of speaking.

"For both of you."

Jean Chapuis intervened. "A visit supposes a visitor... male or female. Tell us the name. That's how you should have commenced, my worthy Julep."

That criticism did not diminish the mosaic negro's natural joviality. Showing all his teeth, he announced: "Visitor is M'sieur Jarrousse."

There was a silence; the faces of Jean Chapuis and Cyprienne both froze. In the young woman, it was a sort of annoyance and embarrassment, whereas in Oronius' pupil, anxiety was dominant.

"What does that revenant want?" he murmured, addressing Cyprienne.

She responded with a moue, and said: "We can refuse to see him." Her tender eyes, anxiously fixed on her fiancé's, declared her ardent desire to be spared any difficulty and to sacrifice the entire world for him—for Cyprienne was in love, as amorous as a fiancée ought to be.

Reassured by that gaze, Jean Chapuis smiled at the young woman and replied: "No, it's better to learn from him the reason for his visit. We have no reason to send him away;

let's see him together." Addressing a sign to Julep, he added: "Have Monsieur Jarrousse come up."

As soon as the negro had disappeared, he said, slowly, in a low voice: "Forgive me, my dear Cyprienne, for the movement of stupid jealousy that you just saw. Can I forget that this Jarrousse, before disappearing mysteriously, had dreamed of marrying you? And then, I can't get over the coincidence of his reappearing on the eve of our marriage."

"Jean," the young woman replied, gently, "I rejected Monsieur Jarrousse's request, as you're not unaware, and you also know that he has never inspired the slightest sympathy in me. On the contrary, I've always experienced a sort of repulsion for him. It was instinctive. Nothing in the world could vanquish that sentiment."

"I congratulate myself for it!" said the fiancé ardently, seizing Cyprienne's hand.

They exchanged a confident gaze; but they straightened up abruptly and their hands separated. Conducted by Julep, Thomas Jarrousse had just appeared in the doorway.

He was a tall, thin, ugly man, but with a savant ugliness, if that expression is permissible, for his brow, broadly uncovered, denoted a high intelligence.

In fact, the engineer Thomas Jarrousse, a Norman from Cherbourg, not yet forty, had already attracted the attention of the scientific world. Had he not been, before Chapuis—and this was what had occasioned the latter's fit of jealousy— Oronius' pupil? Like Jean, he had lived in the intimacy of the Master, and like him, he had been subject to Cyprienne's charms. He had been the first to be ambitious to marry the young woman.

Oronius appreciated his intelligence; Cyprienne had been less sensible to it.

It is necessary to recognize that Jarrousse had nothing seductive about him. In terms of character, he was a taciturn man who said very little, confining neither his despairs nor his hopes—a hard worker, to be sure, but even more mysterious.

For a time, his research had not been discouraged by Oronius, and he had hoped to obtain the hand of the Master's heiress; but, having consulted the latter, a very clear and definitive word had discouraged his fine ardor and annihilated his hopes.

On the evening after that refusal, Thomas Jarrousse had abandoned the magical Villa of Belleville after brief goodbyes, and since then, nothing had been heard of him.

What had become of him? Why had he come back?

Jean Chapuis, as much as Cyprienne, had a perfect right to ask those questions.

One thing was certain: he was arriving after a long journey; his costume furnished the proof of that. A kind of combination smock enveloped him and he was wearing an aviation helmet fixed by a chin-strap.

He was not embellished. Oh no! Little eyes sunk beneath bushy eyebrows, a nose like an eagle's beak, brutally angular cheekbones and a thick blond beard falling over a bony chest.

Unfastening his helmet, he sketched a rather awkward bow, and in the glances that he darted, first at Cyprienne and then at Chapuis, very different sentiments were legible; an invincible passion for the former, the most ferocious of hatreds for the latter.

Cyprienne shivered; Jean Chapuis' ideas darkened.

In a detached tone that attempted to affect ease, Jarrousse began the conversation in this fashion: "Excuse me, Mademoiselle, for the suddenness of this visit, which you were probably not expecting. I've scarcely been prodigal with my news. Observe, however, that I have retained the best memory of you, since I'm taking advantage of passing through Paris to come and inquire about your health and bring you my felicitations. I learned from afar about your engagement with Monsieur Chapuis."

Again he darted a glance at the couple, sinister this time.

"You're too kind," stammered Cyprienne, without the slightest conviction.

As for the engineer, in spite of his customary urbanity, he could not succeed in taking it upon himself to pronounce the slightest polite remark. His instinct warned him that he was in the presence of an enemy.

How many apparitions of evil augury are succeeding one another today, he thought, his brow furrowed. *The mysterious woman... Jarrousse... that coincidence would strike a mind more impressionable than mine. Certainly, the man is less to be fared than the woman... but no matter... in any case, he displeases me!*

"May I ask for your news?" Jarrousse continued, contemplating Cyprienne with a pleasure so marked that it irritated the young woman as much as her fiancé. "In truth, Mademoiselle, they must be excellent, for you're even more beautiful, which seemed impossible."

"It's rather of you that it's necessary to ask for news of your existence," snapped the young woman. "Your disappearance gave birth to many hypotheses."

An imperceptible twitch of Jarrousse's chin communicated a kind of little wave to the flamboyant cascade of this beard. His eyes flashed, and a singular smile creased his lips.

"It would have been wrong to worry about me," he riposted. "I believe that I have spent my time passably well working in view of the future... a future that is now very imminent."

The tone in which he emphasized the final words caused the fiancés to shiver. But, perhaps taking account of that impression and probably desirous of effacing it, the visitor hastened to go on, in a jovial fashion: "How is the Master? Will I be able to salute him? Having heard—entirely by chance—about the terrible challenge of which he is the object, it's for him that I've come. Yes, above all for him. On the eve of frightful events that can't fail to materialize, as these competitions, supported by scientific weapons, menace his security... and yours... I wanted to come to bring him the assurance of my profound sympathy."

Jean Chapuis started at him insistently. His gaze said a great deal about his secret thoughts. "You're exaggerating somewhat the importance of Otto Hantzen's words," he could not help riposting. "The Master welcomed them with laughter."

"Perhaps he was wrong," Jarrousse insisted, in an enigmatic tone. "With an inventor of that caliber, does one ever know whether it's necessary to laugh or tremble?"

"Oronius knows!" declared Jean Chapuis, dryly.

Jarrousse shrugged his shoulders, and said, flippantly: "Really? I admire so much confidence, and incline before it. My task would certainly be superhuman if I undertook to oppose him; I shall refrain carefully from doing so... in any case, the future is here."

Again, his malevolently pinched lips formed an ambiguous smile, which appeared to imply a vague threat.

Again, too, Cyprienne and Jean could not suppress a shudder.

"May I present my homage to the Master?" Jarrousse repeated, visibly satisfied by the effect he had produced.

Cyprienne hesitated, and consulted her fiancé with her gaze.

The latter decided: "I don't think so. No, in truth, it seems to me to be quite impracticable. The Master is shut in his laboratory, working."

An involuntary flash of curiosity traversed Jarrousse's eyes.

"A new discovery?"

"I don't know."

"He's never short... it's very probable."

"Perhaps."

The visitor's face became impassive again. "In that case, I won't insist," he declared. "I'm reluctant to snatch from science the slightest parcel of such precious time... and so well-employed. Alas, time is measured for us all... even for Oronius."

More forcefully than ever, Jean Chapuis had the impression that the ironic and sibylline remark dissimulated a threat.

You, my lad, are on Hantzen's side, and I wouldn't be surprised if you were in cahoots with him, he thought. *That would also explain your disappearance and the mysterious existence that you seem to be leading. If my suspicions are well-founded, you've come here to play the role of Judas. I'd be acting sagely in sending you away.*

Jarrousse, however, without appearing to be unduly troubled by his check, seemed resigned and ready to take his leave.

"Please present my regrets to the Master," he said, bowing to Cyprienne. "And for yourself, Mademoiselle, accept the good wishes of a sincere friend for your happiness. May the grave events that are in preparation... or, at least, that have been announced and are dreaded... spare you, and permit me to find you again, beautiful and radiant, in my path."

"Mademoiselle Cyprienne is certainly very sensible to the thought that dictates those good wishes to you," Jean Chapuis put in, in a taut voice. "Reassure your sensibility, however; it is wrong to be alarmed. The daughter of Oronius is shielded from all danger, presumed or real."

"Who knows?" said Jarrousse, again, staring at his successor with a sort of bravado. And as that insolence drew a gesture of anger from Jean Chapuis, he pretended not to notice it, and withdrew.

"Adieu, Monsieur... Au revoir, Mademoiselle."

He had disappeared into one of the cages of the double elevator, always en route for the ascent and the descent, with an automatic or facultative pause at every landing.

Tenderly, Cyprienne retained her fiancé, who had almost bounded after the impudent individual.

"Jean!" she implored. "What do the incoherent words of a jealous man matter to you? Only chagrin and rage inspire them... but that chagrin and rage are impotent."

"You're right, my delectable Cyprienne. We ought to be scornful of that hatred. It can't attain us, the Master is here!"

He drew the young woman to his bosom.

Above the lovely couple, lost in their ecstasy, a cloud passed slowly… a white cloud, which they did not see

Chapter Seven
THE FLYING DRAGNET

While he was retiring rapidly, Thomas Jarrousse crossed the path of the silent Wiwar on the ground floor.

Without stopping or looking at one another, the two men exchanged rapid words.

"The mechanic?"

"Gone," replied the laboratory assistant.

"Where he usually goes?"

"Yes."

"Good. Expect me in an hour."

And Jarrousse quit the Villa in order to climb back into his airplane, while Wiwar drew away in another direction, a louche and silent shadow.

Still on the terrace, the fiancés had had no suspicion of that dialogue, which confirmed Laridon's suspicions so eloquently. They only saw the airplane transporting Oronius' former pupil fly away and descend over Paris.

"*Bon voyage!*" murmured Jean Chapuis.

Those words, with which he saluted the departure of the dismissed and rancorous suitor, certainly could not be taken literally. Although he strove carefully to hide that impression, in order not to sadden Cyprienne, Thomas Jarrousse's visit had left him in a dark mood, his mind haunted by further presentiments. No matter how hard he tried to defend himself, it appeared to him to augur ill.

It was necessary, however, to leave Cyprienne and go back down to his personal laboratory in order to continue his own work, collaborating with the work of the Master. Leaving his fiancée on the terrace, therefore, where the chambermaid Turlurette immediately came to join her with the two little dogs, Pipigg and Kukuss, he went down the vaporous steps of the glass staircase.

The principal laboratory was in full action. There, Oronius, his hair in the wind, resembled a black demon agitating in his inferno, pursuing in the midst of the dazzling reflections of electric furnaces the experiment to which he had made mysterious allusions.

Returned to his own laboratory, the young engineer went to lean on a window sill. From there he could see, on the edge of the terrace, the silhouette of his fiancée outlined against the sky.

Next to her, indifferent to the chatter of Turlurette, the minuscule lap-dogs were pointing their little muzzles toward the sky. They appeared anxious, and seemed to be observing the extraordinary invasion of clouds, the cohort of which was incessantly reinforced, ever thicker and ever darker.

On the silky and snowy coats of the vigilant Lilliputians, two black dots stood out: their ears. Those ears were pricked up; one might have thought that they could hear something.

However, no sound was perceptible in the calm sky.

It was not the same down below. A dull, confused rumor was rising from Paris, which increased, diminished and returned, like the voice of the ocean battering the foot of cliffs.

Under the mysterious threat of Otto Hantzen, the lungs of the immense city no longer seemed to be respiring normally. The pulse of Paris was feverish and its breath gasping.

Leaning over the parapet, the two young women listened to the immense breath of that oppressed respiration.

Suddenly, Jean Chapuis shivered. In the dark sky he had seemed to see squadrons of sooty clouds open and close, as if they had been traversed by one of their peers that was denser and more compact, almost solid.

Jean rubbed his eyes. Was he dreaming?

No; on the terrace, the little dogs, having become invisible, were barking in unison, and madly. It is true that the two beasts might as well have been insulting with their furious yapping the importunate noise rising from Oronius' laboratory.

Having run to fetch binoculars, the young man returned to the window, but before he had had time to apply them to his eyes, he felt a suffocation and went frightfully pale. Above him, approaching the terrace with the fulgurant rapidity of an eagle swooping on its prey, the disquieting cloud was arriving.

Pipigg and Kukuss, vigilant guard-dogs of the lovely Cyprienne, were barking furiously. Brave to the point of intrepidity, those pocket-sized sentinels, infimal mites of the canine species, in imitation of the chevalier d'Assas,[5] were giving the alarm.

For his part, Jean tried to cry out. No sound was able to emerge from his contracted throat.

How could he not be amazed by what he suddenly discovered: the cloud was towing an immense aluminum net!

The bulging eyes of the young man gazed fearfully as that strange aerial trawl descended from the sky and advanced toward the terrace. What inhuman harvest were the invisible fishers meditating, who were racing across the sky, embarked on a cloud, dredging the earth?

Guided by a mysterious power, the trawl advanced, opening the mute pike's maw of a hawk. It swept the terrace, breaking the shrubs, knocking over the tubs and carrying away everything it encountered in its path.

Everything was engulfed therein... everything! Like a devouring monster, it sucked in beings and things.

An apocalyptic spectacle!

---

[5] Nicolas-Louis d'Assas (1733-1760), also known as Chevalier d'Assas, was a captain of the French Régiment d'Auvergne, whose celebrity depends on a single act of defiance. Having entered a wood to reconnoiter it the night before the battle of Kloster Kampen in 1760, he was suddenly surrounded by the enemy English soldiers, and defied with bayonets at his breast to utter a cry of alarm; "To me, Auvergne! Here is the enemy!" he exclaimed, and fell dead on the instant, pierced with bayonets, to the saving of his countrymen.

The scene that followed only lasted for a second, but it seemed as long as a century of torture to Jean Chapuis.

The menacing net was still advancing.

A table placed in front of Cyprienne was overturned. Panicking, Pipigg and Kukuss tugged the tunic of their young mistress in order to call her attention to the imminent peril.

His body covered in an agonized sweat, the fiancé made new efforts to cry out, but his strangled throat still remained mute.

Then, a supreme effort having launched him outside the laboratory, he climbed the stairs four at a time, and emerged on to the terrace...

Too late!

The brutal impact of a rope whipped in a semicircle like the edge of a sail inflated by the wind knocked him down flat on his back at the moment when he set foot on the platform.

Panting and bruised, incapable of movement, he was able to see the inferior frame of the trawl scythe down the two your women at ankle-height and tumble them into its shiny mesh.

The unhappy engineer, maddened, his ears filled by an afflux if blood, thought he perceived something frightful: their double scream of horror.

It was finished. The pretty target coveted by the infernal fisher was captured,

Jean lay gasping on the flagstones, unconscious.

The net rose into the sky and returned into the cloud, carrying Cyprienne, Turlurette and the two papillons into the unknown, rolled up on the aluminum mesh of the diabolical flying dragnet.

Chapter Eight
A TWENTY-FIRST CENTURY BAR

In order to descend into Paris from the heights of Belle-ville—which is, in truth, only a simple jump—Laridon had no need of an apparatus of great range. He had therefore content-ed himself with slipping on a dragonfly, and as soon as he took off he headed straight for the Place de la Concorde in order to cast an eye over the evening news.

It was the hour when numerous Parisians were imitating that curiosity, so he was not astonished, on touching down in the vicinity of the obelisk, to find the square and the Champs-Élysées swarming with a crowd, in which all eyes were staring westwards, gazing in the direction of the Arc de l'Inconnu—the former Arc de Triomphe.

Like Laridon, that crowd had come to "read the newspa-per."

It is necessary not to understand that expression in the old sense that had once been given to it. Many years ago, the employment of printed sheets, so reduced in format and so difficult to edit and compose, had been renounced. Documents of every kind—books and newspapers—were now published by less obsolete methods; the invention of Gutenberg, im-proved by Marinoni, had had its day. Henceforth, thought was conserved and expressed in two forms, one addressed to sight and the other to hearing. Libraries were composed entirely of phonograms and cinegrams. People no longer read; they lis-tened to the voice of an author declaiming his work, or fol-lowed on a screen the succession of images that spoke to the eye and translated ideas.

In particular, in the newspaper those two modes of ex-pression were employed simultaneously to inform the crowd assembled in one of the consecrated centers, the most consid-erable being the cinephonojournal of the Arc, whose extraor-dinarily powerful "howlers" could   launch forth news perceived and understood by thousands of passers-by. At the same time, its apparatus projected filmed events in the sky, in such dimensions that five thousand spectators could perceive the details simultaneously.

Having folded up and fixed on his back the wings of his flying machine, Laridon mingled with the multitude of viewer-listeners. But scarcely had he lent an ear to the news clamored by the howlers and let his gaze wander over the projection by which the sky was illustrated than his physiognomy took on an expression of absolute shock.

"What? What?" he said, in his loud, authentically Parisian drawl. "What are those idiots singing? There's a hothead who wants to make a match with M'sieur Oronius for the Championship of Science? Good! What's got into the individual? Hey you, M'sieur! Perfectly, my dear Madame! Pantruche [6] can sleep easy on his lugs; the boss will take charge of settling his account with M'sieur Hantzen. That's my opinion! I beg you to infiltrate that I know what I'm talking about, because I'm M'sieur Oronius' own mechanic, in person. Not necessary for you to get into a funk. Do as I do, don't get excited; he'll arrive soon enough... to prove it I'm offering myself a round at the Bar of Dreams, to the health of the daddy and the little lady!"

Without worrying any more about the cinephonojournal stupid enough to broadcast such news and to appear to take it seriously, the joyful Laridon went up toward the Madeleine, in the vicinity of which as the establishment that he had just named.

Do not allow the denomination of "bar" to alarm any member of the temperance society. In the twenty-first century, people no longer drank, any more than they ate. It was far from the time of eateries and drinking-dens, and no poet, for fear of not being understood, would have taken it into his head to put the pleasures of the table or Bacchic joys into the hexagonal or polyhedral verse, which were the last word in poetic

---

[6] A nickname of Pantin, a popular neighborhood of Paris.

form, in the taste of the epoch. Oh, the worthy Ponchon [7] would scarcely be cheered up in that epoch. The temporary dryness of America was only base flattery by comparison with the integral abstention of today.

The custom of meals—a custom said to go back to the remotest antiquity—had no more reason to exist. The contemporaries of Oronius would have been profoundly shocked if some impolite person had delivered himself in their presence to the repulsive exercise of mastication. They would surely have considered him to be a savage. In any case, it would have been difficult for that retrograde individual to satisfy such primitive tastes, since aliments were no longer presented in any other form than liquid drops or solutions injected directly into the organism by means of *ad hoc* syringes.

Even domestic animals were subjected to that regime.

Deprived of that pleasure, which was also a repose, humanity, doubtless yielding to the imperious demand of ancestral instincts, had been obliged to invent a replacement that would also be an equivalent. Notably, in regard to the habit of drinking, erased from the program of twenty-first century life, it had been agreed that people had not only drank in order to absorb tisanes but also—and very often—in order to extract from the various, mostly alcoholic, beverages they consumed a cerebral stimulation destined to abstract the mind for a while from insipid and irritating realities.

Now, to escape life—the consciousness of life—constitutes, it is necessary to recognize, a profound human need. And it is in that need that it is necessary to seek the reason for an incontestable fact: the excessive development in that ultra-civilized society, intellectually far superior to its predecessors, of the appetite for artificial paradises.

---

[7] Raoul Ponchon (1848-1937) was a French poet and noted alcoholic. A friend of Arthur Rimbaud, he was a contributor to the satirical weekly *Le Courrier français*.

Not that in the Paris of Oronius people used ether or morphine, nor that they took cocaine, smoked kif or opium, or chewed hashish.

They had a better means.

That was the Bar of Dreams, the door of which Laridon was opening at that moment.

Like all the cities in the world, Paris had a certain number of those establishments. Their interior aspect and their furnishing did not resemble in any way the ancient cafés: no little tables of wood or marble, around which arrogant waiters circulated, parading above humbly curbed heads trays laden with glasses and bottles.

The Bar of Dreams, in the interior of which a soft and mysterious half-light reigned, blue shadows and inky reflections fell from veiled lamps on to a mass of divans, cushions and carpets, offering to the gaze the silence and meditation of a temple.

One did not go there to argue or gesticulate, but simply to dream—which is to say, to be transported into an unreality fashioned to the taste of the dreamer's subconscious.

Indifferent to everything that surrounded them, the clients of that singular bar were lying around the room, torpid in the bliss of their dreams. All of them wore on their faces the "inhaler masks" that procured them those dreams, freely chosen.

As he passed through the door, Laridon had received one of those masks from the "barman," which he immediately applied; then, taking care not to bump into any of the bodies lying on the thick carpet, noses in the air, he undertook an excursion around the room. While walking he consulted the little labels discreetly fixed to the walls above the orifices of the reservoirs.

Let us say right away that it was not curiosity, but with the goal of making his selection of a "consummation" appropriate to his taste, made by attaching the tube of his inhaler to the valve of one of the reservoirs.

The labels gave the names of the new alcohols or alcoholic gases. There were the laughing gases and the melancholic vapors, the effluvia of poetry, the radiations of heroism and the passions... all mirages, all aspirations, all states of mind could traverse a brain, on condition of submitting to the action of the appropriate current, radiation or gas. Scrupulous study had determined the action that each could have on the cerebral cells, and had catalogued the sensations. It was thus that the Bar of Dreams could provide its clients with the entire gamut of joys and pains, artificially obtained: melancholy, lyricism, enthusiasm, exaltation...

One could even—still artificially, with no prejudice to the body—give oneself the illusion of savoring the ancient joys of humans, so vulgar and so material. Yes, one even had the faculty of offering oneself the sensations—or the malaises—that they experienced when they emerged from the table after an excessively copious meal, or when they delivered themselves to exaggerated libations... one could stuff oneself or get drunk!

But that genre of bliss had few connoisseurs—only the curiosity of an experiment that they rarely recommenced caused the seekers of sensations to stop before the *ad hoc* reservoir.

Laridon did not belong to the backward category of the last degenerate and rare representatives of a species that had once made the celebrity of Montmartre. Healthy and cheerful in temperament, he generally requested the stimulants of the bar to transport him on the wings of rosy dreams toward the joyful vagabondage of the imagination through marvelous décors.

He stopped, therefore, in front of a label bearing the enticing words: *Dreams of fortune and glory*, fixed the tube of his inhaler to the valve and, uttering a sigh of contentment, lay down on a heap of soft cushions.

Minutes went by. Laridon had gradually lost the notion of time.

However—were the contents of the reservoir tricking him?—the sensations were not at all what he had expected.

Undoubtedly, it had commenced perfectly, but abruptly, in the middle of an enchanting dream that transformed him into a conquistador of the stars, he had fallen back to earth and, since that moment, disagreeable impressions had not ceased to succeed one another. Did he not feel prey to a strange vertigo? It seemed to him that his brain was filled with noxious vapors; his ideas were troubled; around him everything was grimacing, colliding, and spinning, and he allowed himself to be overtaken by the worst ill-humor.

Truly furious and disappointed, if he had had the strength he would have castigated the landlord of the bar for permitting himself to put into service faulty products of such execrable quality.

Alas, wanting to do something and being able to do it are two different things. The means of proceeding with that merited execution were lacking; his tongue felt thick and almost as paralyzed as his ideas.

Where the devil was it coming from?

Suddenly, his foggy gaze, in parading sullenly over all the surrounding objects, attained and fixed upon the place in the wall to which his inhaler was fitted. And, mechanically, he deciphered the label.

Stupor! Who, then, had played the nasty joke on him of displacing the tube?

Instead of the words selected by him as promises of enchantments, *Dreams of glory and fortune*, now he read on the reservoir of the toxic vapors of which he was inhaling: *Fumes of alcohol; intoxication.*

The innocent Laridon was in the process of getting drunk, unwittingly.

With a heroic effort, he tore off his mask, uttered an oath, and tried to get to his feet.

Presumptuous mechanic: his legs were like lace, soft, vague and floating, and refusing obstinately to sustain him; he collapsed.

Then a burst of mocking laughter resounded nearby.

Laridon could still move his eyes; he turned them immediately toward the place from which that laughter had come and saw...oh! nothing extraordinary. He saw on the cushions nearby the body of another consumer. He had probably arrived during his voyage to the land of dreams, for he did not remember having seen him when he arrived.

That neighbor, a red-haired man of very unsympathetic appearance, by virtue of the mocking fashion in which he was presently staring at poor Laridon, would certainly have attracted the mechanic's invective if the latter had been in full possession of his means. But the young man tried in vain to get up and to mutter insults.

The impolite stranger leaned over him, picked up the mask, and, acting with a great liberty and an astounding casualness, replaced it on the poor fellow's face.

"What's this, then?" he sniggered. "One wants to play the rebel? Fortunately, one can't. I've provided for that. Complain, then! I'm offering you one of the memorable blow-outs of which only our ancestors had the secret. You'll believe yourself rejuvenated by twenty lustrums, and it's to me that you'll owe it. Let's go! Another little glass of schnick... and then another... and yet another. Drink, then, friend Laridon! These days, no one knows how to drink any longer! Drink! It's my round. While you sleep off your drunkenness, I'm going to occupy myself with your master Oronius. As for poor Jean Chapuis, I think that at present he must have registered and qualified, as he should, your stupid absence. Rest in peace, *mio caro*. It's much better for your repose if you aren't mixed up in the events that are about to unfold out there."

With those enigmatic words, being assured of the perfect innocuousness of the involuntary drunkard, the unknown man, hearing snoring, got to his feet briskly and drew away discreetly, thinking: *Like the robe of Nessus of the so-called Hercules, his mask will stick to his skin. The imbecile won't trouble us.*

63

His confidence was ill-founded, however, for scarcely had he disappeared than the heroic Laridon raised himself on to his knees and, with a supreme effort, snatched the tube of his inhaler away from the reservoir of alcohol vapors

Having succeeded in that, the brave lad collapsed on his back and remained still for a few moments, gasping and groaning.

The stranger's words had resounded terribly in his ear, and provoked such an emotion in him that his intoxication was partially dissipated; so he had been able to extract from the hypertension of his reanimated will the strength to play the comedy that would rid him of the presence of the infernal individual.

Having profited from the other's disappearance to abstract himself from the deadly effect of the poison, Laridon concentrated again, in order to struggle against the fog of drunkenness. After a moment of cerebral effort against the weakening substance, when he thought he had accumulated sufficient strength, he got up, stiffened himself, and attempted, vacillating as he was, to make another tour of the room decorated with indicative inscriptions. He was approaching the end of his circuit and commencing to despair of his luck when, in front of the last label—the last!—he leaned over and uttered a grunt of satisfaction.

Ammonia, he had just read.

Then he started inhaling again, with delight, while congratulating himself for having learned by a chance reading, the usage that as once made of ammoniacal vapors to clear the fog from the brain of drinkers.

There's a God for drunkards! He might have cried, if he had not been ignorant of that obsolete turn of phrase.

A few moments later, still staggering, but with a sufficiently lucid mind and more docile legs, he was able to quit the Bar of Dreams, swearing that he would not return there soon. Outside, he deployed the wings of his dragonfly, started the motor and took to the air.

Well, his flight was certainly a trifle zigzag, of a nature to worry anyone who crossed his path, but he succeeded nevertheless in attaining the magical Villa without encumbrance.

Suspecting that the Villa was to be the theater of unusual events, and that he could not intervene usefully if his return were not secret, the worthy fellow descended prudently behind the hangars.

As he landed, he had to make a violent effort to stifle an exclamation.

A few meters away from him, in the garden, at the end of the perspective of an avenue bordered by giant rose-bushes, two silent silhouettes were sliding toward the low door of an entrance that was generally unused. Laridon smiled. The indiscreet individuals were about to bump their heads. But no; with a familiar gesture, one of them opened that door and drew his companion inside.

In the intruder introduced in that clandestine and mysterious fashion into the abode of the savant Oronius, Laridon, with a start of anger, had just recognized the individual from the Bar of Dreams—the same one who had poisoned him insidiously. As for the introducer, he was none other than Wiwar.

"Wait, bandit, wait!" growled Laridon, running forward.

Unfortunately, he had spoken too loudly. Wiwar heard him, and turned round.

"How the devil is that one still on his feet?" he murmured, fearfully. "In truth, so much the worse for Jarrousse; he's going to come unstuck, and I don't like that!"

And lifting his legs, he fled.

At that precise moment, a rightful bolt of lightning zigzagging in the clouds, appeared to descend on the Villa. Above Paris, black clouds were circulating in battalions.

The storm foreseen by Monsieur Sainte-Barbe burst in all its violence; but, amazingly, the lightning was not followed by any roll of thunder.

Laridon had other fish to fry; he neglected to be astonished, and even to perceive the phenomenon. Surprised by

Wiwar's flight, he hesitated. Should he pursue him, or occupy himself with the other, who had just disappeared into the interior of the glass villa?

He was doubtless about to decide on the latter solution when the voice of Jean Chapuis resounded above his head; it was calling for help. Then Laridon forgot everything else, in order to respond to his master's appeal.

Chapter Nine
THE ARTIFICIAL STORM

Jean Chapuis' faint, caused by his fall, had only lasted a few seconds. An unconscious, as if latent, will, acting upon the brain at the instigation of a powerful psychic reaction, recalled him almost instantaneously to the sentiment of the incredible situation and the dangers menacing his fiancée.

That was the first thought that imposed itself on his mind when he opened his eyes of the terrace of Oronius' villa.

"Cyprienne!" he groaned, trying to get up.

Above his head, in the sky, the kidnapper cloud now only formed a white dot among all those that were now circling Paris, all the more reason why the flying dragnet, having climbed back into that fog with its captives, was no longer visible.

The young man could have believed that he had had a bad dream. Alas, he was only too certain of the horrible reality. He had seen with his own eyes the pitiless net descend from the sky, sweep the terrace, knock over and carry away, caught in its mesh, his beloved Cyprienne and the devoted Turlurette.

A cast of an aerial trawl!

What a fantastic vision!

Jean imagined that he could still hear the furious barking of the two little dogs, Pipigg and Kukuss. Where were they, those courageous pygmies? Doubtless, they had shared the fate of their young mistress.

Could he, in those conditions, conserve any other preoccupation? Everything was effaced before that obsessive thought: to fly to the aid of Cyprienne!

He did not see the strange storm unleashed above the capital, nor the long, silent streaks of lightning that appeared to envelop Oronius' villa. What did that phenomenon matter to him henceforth?

The spectacle ought, however, to have reminded him of Otto Hantzen's threat. Was it not being executed? Never in human memory had such monstrous preliminaries been seen to accumulate. What could the unleashing of that atmospheric perturbation signify? What singular discipline was animating those clouds, marching as if to attack? One might have thought that a conscious will—a human will—was directing the vapors.

Was it necessary, then, to see it as the realization of the announced intention to destroy Paris? Would the first proof furnished by Otto Hantzen of the power of his science be the frightful phenomenon of the first artificial storm?

But that terrible vision, which Jean Chapuis was to remember later, was eclipsed for the moment by the abduction of Cyprienne. That alone counted in his eyes. For all the rest he was afflicted by an amnesia that was both explained and excused by amour.

Tottering, he dragged himself to the edge of the terrace as, gathering his strength, he appealed in a loud voice: "Laridon! Julep! Help! The Halcyon-Car! Immediately, right away!"

Leaning over the balustrade, he watched for the effect of his appeals. From down below, a voice rose up. "What's the matter, boss?"

"A terrible thing!" replied the young engineer, feverishly. "Obey without delay. The Halcyon-Car... quickly, quickly! It's a matter of life and death."

Thus stimulated, the mechanic hailed Julep.

"Ha! At the gallop, my friend!"

"Will they be ready in time?" lamented Jean Chapuis, raising his anguished eyes toward the kidnapper cloud, fleeing amid the bursting of the storm.

Carried away by his impetuosity and his despair, he did not ask what enemy he would find in the heart of the artificial cloud, nor whether he would have the strength to attack it. He had seen, emerging from that cloud, the aluminum net sweeping up its prey. Thus, there was an enemy within it... a diabolical machine, which the grappling-hook of the Halcyon-Car could grip.

"Pee-wit!" someone cried down below.

At the same time, a loud purr, departing from the ground and rising toward the terrace, calmed the engineer. Manned by Laridon and Julep, the Halcyon-Car was taking off. It climbed toward the sky almost vertically, brushing the walls with a temerity to cause a shiver.

Two seconds later, the marvelous apparatus was hovering above the terrace. Jean Chapuis seized the cords of the flexible ladder that Laridon had just thrown down with both hands; he scaled it nimbly and took his place in the cabin next to his faithful companions.

"En route! En route!" he ordered. He was in haste to launch forth into the unknown. Was that foolish temerity?

In any case, the Halcyon-Car represented a famous trump card. It was truly the marvel of that epoch, which boasted of having completed the conquest, attempted by its predecessors, of the infinity of the heavens.

There was no longer any limit to adventurous journeys; isothermic walls and atmospheric generators permitted the attainment of the most vertiginous altitudes; the employment of radiogenic apparatus gave birth to the combined forces of magnetic, electric and radioactive current, capable, by application to a point on a given surface, of counterbalancing any exterior action, even that of weight or aerial currents, assuring the apparatus of free movement along a trajectory fixed in advance, or of absolute immobility at any point in space.

To those advantages, the Halcyon-Car added a few others, which permitted it to maneuver in all milieux and to transform itself, in accordance with the needs of its occupants, into a terrestrial charger or a fish of the surface or the depths, after having been the most rapid and most intrepid of birds.

It was the Protean Aircraft, by turns an airplane, an auto, a boat or a submarine.

One can understand that, knowing the scientific marvel that the apparatus was, none of those whom it was about to carry into the adventure hesitated to launch forth.

"All right!" Laridon replied. "One could ask for nothing better, M'sieur Jean... I would have thought, however, that there was more to do at the house than in the air. Never mind! You see more clearly than I... because, for reasons I'll tell you when there's time, I have vertigo in my compass-housing! But the fist is still solid... just tell me what heading to take."

The engineer's hand was extended.

"That cloud!" he growled. "The white cloud that's drawing away from us while all the others are coming toward us. That's what we're dealing with; it's necessary to catch up with it."

"We'll catch it," Laridon assured him. "No matter how fast it goes, we'll have it. Damn! You're right: what trick is that thing playing? It's curious to see it trotting like that instead of staying with its comrades. They all seem to have it in for Paris! Can that be a cloud-automobile?"

"You don't know how true you are," Jean Chapuis affirmed, somberly. "That nimbus isn't ordinary vapor; it certainly constitutes a diabolical invention put n the service of the hatred of an enemy... whom we're going to fight."

"Fight?" Laridon repeated.

Having scarcely recovered from the disturbance in which his adventure in the Bar of Dreams had left him, but still thinking about the unknown man's threats, Jean's words only surprised him slightly. He expected it.

"Yes, fight... or at least confront," Jean Chapuis repeated, more gravely still. "You'll understand the importance I attach to catching that cloud when I've explained the terrifying spectacle that threw me into the state in which you found me. Oh, my impotent rage in seeing... witnessing...a lmost touching that crime, without being able to intervene! My presentiments have been cruelly realized, and my good master was wrong not to take my confidences more seriously."

"What presentiment are you talking about, M'sieur Jean, and what crime?" the worthy mechanic queried, moved by that visible pain. Had he not seen the engineer extend his clenched fists in the direction of the fleeing cloud? What was the cloud carrying away, then? What had happened on the terrace before Jean Chapuis shouted for help?

He was about to find out, and Julep also. The good multicolored negro, frightened by what he had heard, was rolling white eyes—and, something less common, he reddened, paled or took on a darker hue, emotion modifying the various colors that dappled his skin simultaneously.

In a voice strained by dolor, Jean Chapuis told them the story of the rapid drama that had unfolded above the magical Villa. He depicted the frightful anguish that had taken possession of him when he had seen the aluminum trawl descend to envelop and carry aloft his dear Cyprienne.

Laridon uttered a cry. He understood the meaning of what his antagonist at the bar had said.

"Mademoiselle Cyprienne has been kidnapped?"

"Before my eyes! And I couldn't oppose it! I couldn't defend her!" said Jean Chapuis, tearfully. "With the speed of lightning or a swooping eagle, the net carried away it prey. The faithful Turlurette, a victim of the odious abduction, and the two little dogs, shared a fate of my fiancée."

A roar emerged from the mechanic's threat.

"Turlurette too! Then she's inside it? That diabolical wisp is carrying her away?"

"Alas. I saw it with my own eyes."

Assuredly, the pretty Turlurette inspired a keen interest in the young scientist's companion, for his anger burst forth tempestuously.

"Oh, but it isn't going to end like this! Kidnapping Turlurette! That surpasses the frontiers of the imagination! Apologies, M'sieur Jean; I can't say that I wouldn't bat an eyelid if only Mamzelle Cyprienne had been attacked... You know my heart; that's frank! For you and M'sieur Oronius, his family included, I'd have myself broken in two... but I can

admit to you that Turlurette, that touches me in the quick...
There! Yes, my word. that's a nasty blow. I need to find out
who's stolen that kid! And I want to get my hands on whoever
pulled the dirty trick. Faith of Laridon, they'll learn a new
dance for the gibbet! Again, many apologies! What I'm saying
won't prevent me from doing my duty and thinking first about
Mamzelle Cyprienne. You can count on me... and doubly!"

"I know, my brave Laridon, and I understand," said Jean
Chapuis, emotionally.

Already, the mechanic had got over the shock that he had
just experienced. He was a positive and energetic fellow. He
thought before anything else about action. His face had taken
on a resolute expression. Giving the Halcyon-Car all the impe-
tus of which the marvelous bird was susceptible, he headed
straight for the cloud, to which they were visibly drawing
nearer.

"Don't let go of the broomstick! We'll sweep them up,"
he murmured. "Yes, we'll have them. First and foremost, I'm
going to get under the skin of that dummy."

"Don't get carried away, my friend. Think about those
we want to liberate. It would be a poor solution to provoke a
catastrophe that would cost them their lives as well as those of
their abductors... not to mention ours."

"Damn it! You're right. We'll maneuver quietly. Necessary first to know what we're dealing with. You have an idea
about that, M'sieur Jean? What's that cake made of?"

"I don't know... but I suspect a diabolical invention... a
ruse of this Hantzen."

"The fellow who wants to challenge M'sieur Oronius,
and who claims to be cleverer?"

"Yes. He utilizes his scientific knowledge to make
weapons and perpetrate his crimes more surely. That cloud is
certainly artificial; it encloses a flying machine in its bosom."

"Possible. For me, the read-head's at the bottom of this,"
Laridon declared. In fact, while listening to the engineer, he
had been unable to help pursuing his own train of thought,
incessantly chewing over his adventure at the bar.

"What red-head? What do you mean?" asked Jean Chapuis, shuddering. The mechanic's allusion suddenly reminded him of the suspect visit of Jarrousse—who, by virtue of the color of his hair, merited Laridon's disrespectful epithet. In Jarrousse, Jean Chapuis could not help seeing a discomfited, rejected, but not resigned, rival who might be nourishing the most perfidious designs.

From there to imagining that Jarrousse could not be a stranger to Cyprienne's abduction it was only a short step; Jean Chapuis made it.

Who knows? he thought. *Perhaps I was wrong to hypnotize myself with my vision and immediately accuse the strange woman. That was to spur myself on a false track. This Jarrousse represents an enemy much more real.*

"Yes, the red-head," Laridon replied. "I found one of them in my path just now, M'sieur Jean. And truly, I haven't had to congratulate myself! He caught me out, the fellow."

He gave his young master a brief account of his adventure, including the reappearance of the suspect silhouette clandestinely introduced by Wiwar into the glass Villa.

"It's shady!" he concluded. "I can't get the conviction out of my noggin that all of this is connected; the individual only nobbled me at the Bar of Dreams to immobilize me during his accomplice's attempt. Have I been stupid!"

"Perhaps you're right," reflected Jean Chapuis. "In any case, there must have been a double attack. Jarrousse can't be in the cloud, since you saw him going into the Villa after the passage of the meteoric aircraft."

That thought soothed him. In his mind, if the individual in question had not participated in the abduction, the danger run by his dear Cyprienne was reduced.

"You call him Jarrousse?" said Laridon. "Well, he certainly suits his name.[8] He's a dirty rat. And if M'sieur Oronius wasn't the solid fellow we know, it would torment me to have left him to deal with that individual!"

---

[8] *Roux, rousse*: a person with red-hair.

"Oh," said Jean Chapuis, smiling. "In that regard I don't have any dread. My master can defend himself; he'll take care of anyone who risks attacking him. Let's just think about the prisoners. The decisive moment is approaching."

In fact the Halcyon-Car had reached the immediate vicinity of the fugitive cloud. A final maneuver of the bold Laridon launched it into the fumigenic layer—"into the cotton wool," as the mechanic put it himself.

Then they saw...

"Cyprienne!" cried Jean, extending his arms.

"Turlurette!" cried Laridon by his side

What a singular apparatus was finally revealed to their bewildered eyes.

It was very close, the nucleus of the meteor, so close that it seemed to them that they only had to extend a hand to touch it—but perhaps that as an optical illusion due to the vaporous armor.

The flying machine in question differed entirely from all known models, including the Halcyon. It was only a metallic sphere, probably hollow, but externally smooth, without any apparent opening and without any asperities except for singular propulsors similar to the fins of a shark, which girdled it completely. Under their disconcerting action the sphere advanced in space, rotating upon its axis, like a miniature Earth describing its orbit around the Sun.

On its upper half it had a glazed cap; that must be a cabin. In that cabin, their hearts beating faster, Jean Chapuis and Laridon had just recognized the women they loved. They were so close that they could hear the furious barking of Pipigg and Kukuss, imprisoned with their mistress.

Forgetting all prudence, putting the upper part of his torso out of the compartment that he occupied next to Laridon, Jean Chapuis shouted madly: "Cyprienne! Cyprienne, can you hear me?"

Faint, but sufficiently distinct, a tremulous voice reached him. "Yes, Jean, I can hear you!"

"Can the people who kidnapped you hear me too?"

"I don't know. We're alone!"

"We haven't seen anyone," confirmed the chambermaid Turlurette, paler and seemingly even more frightened than her young mistress.

Alone! They were alone, imprisoned in that infernal instrument of nightmare!

Stupefied, Laridon, who was listening intently while supervising his controls, nearly let go of the handgrips. "What!" he cried. "You haven't seen the people who snatched you from the terrace?"

The two young women shook their heads in unison. They were visibly terrified.

"Oh, Jean!" moaned Cyprienne. "What's happening to us? It's so strange, so supernatural, that we're dying of fright! From the moment when we were drawn inside the sphere through an open trap-door, which closed automatically, we've been gripped by an impression of anguish. We're only surrounded by machines. I've already told you, Jean, that there's no one aboard this flying machine that is carrying us away."

At that repeated affirmation, the young engineer shivered involuntarily, turning his eyes away, forbidding himself to allow her to divine his anguish.

"Are you sure?" he exclaimed.

Certainly, he was familiar with the marvels of pilot-less aircraft, directed at a distance by Hertzian waves, but the phenomenon took on disquieting proportions here. What magical power had been required for the aerial abduction to be carried out without a human presence! Who, then, had been able to command and to guide from afar, not merely the evolution of the flying machine but also the maneuver of the metallic trawl?

In truth, that guidance without a conductor surpassed the bounds of comprehension. Very well-informed of modern mechanics, Jean Chapuis racked his brains without being able to resolve the problem of that intelligent gravitation of a machine left to its own devices. In his view, to permit the machine to progress, it required a brain and an arm acting at a distance—which was, after all, not impossible—but it also required eyes in order to monitor the incidents of its operation and, in certain cases, to determine action at the desired moment.

That was satanism! For one could not decently qualify as a miracle the disconcerting discovery of a demon.

"Such a power!" he stammered, confounded. "Who could have it? Who?"

Suddenly, as if in response to his thought, he thought he perceived the image of the woman with nocturnal eyes in the bosom of the fog. A smile of triumph was on the lips of that phantasmal obsession.

"Her! It's her who has abducted Cyprienne from me!" Jean Chapuis stammered, chilled by fear.

At the same moment, as if by a phenomenon of telepathy, divining that her fiancé was experiencing a need for stimulation, Cyprienne resumed crying out.

"Help, Jean! Save me! I'm too afraid of his silence, this solitude—the rigid regularity of this sphere that is carrying Turlurette and me away into the troubling unknown!"

Electrified, the young man stiffened himself. "Yes, I'll save you, dear Cyprienne!" he replied, in a vibrant tone. "Make contact, Laridon. Even if I have to break my fingers, I'll pierce the metal of that sphere!"

That recognition, and the conversation at a distance that had followed, had not, of course, been operated with the tranquil facility one experiences in reading it, each aerial apparatus having continued its course in the meantime, following their route in concert amid the din of motors.

In response to Jean Chapuis' last threat, a strident burst of laughter resounded.

The vision was effaced… at the same time, alas, as the sphere appeared to plunge abruptly into the bosom of the thick fog. By the same token, the almost inconsistent mist that surrounded the Halcyon-Car suddenly became completely opaque; the airplane and its passengers found themselves in complete darkness.

"Damn!" swore Laridon. "Have I gone blind? I can no longer light up."

"Go straight ahead!" roared Jean. "It's a maneuver of the enemy to escape us. Get out of the fog, quickly."

He combined his efforts with the mechanic's, but it was in vain, at the risk of a collision analogous to the one that had nearly annihilated Monsieur de Sainte-Barbe, that they increased the aircraft's speed. The fog did not release its prey; it stuck to the fabric of the Halcyon-Car and continued to surround them in a prison of darkness, the wall of which they could not pierce.

That blind course lasted for half an hour. Then the vapors dissipated and vanished in the air. Chapuis and Laridon found themselves in an open luminous sky—but alone... frightfully alone!

Carrying its prisoners away through the mysterious space, the sphere had disappeared.

Chapter X
THE ABDUCTOR OF LIGHTNING

The singular storm, of which the young engineer and his mechanic had only contemplated the preliminaries, had scarcely begun when Wiwar took flight in order to escape the inconveniences of a private conversation with Laridon.

But Wiwar did not take the road to Paris. Without quitting the heights of Belleville, being in haste to put a reasonable distance between himself and the victim of the bar, he ran in a zigzag through the florid paths serving a handful of cottages and the rarer buildings that were in the vicinity of the magical Villa.

After having made sure that he was not being followed, he slipped into the last of those buildings and threw himself precipitately into an elevator, which took him up to a terrace.

"I only just have time," he muttered darting an anxious gaze toward the darkened shy. "Yes, just the time I need to flee that condemned Babylon. It's up to Jarrousse to strive to conquer Oronius' secrets, if Hantzen's impatience leaves him the time. That, I can hardly believe. The rain of fire will certainly begin within the hour, and everything will be destroyed."

Feverishly, he brought a flying apparatus out of its shelter, in which he took his place, and launched himself into the sky, following a direction opposite to the one that the Halcyon-Car was to take a moment later.

As he flew over Paris, he could hear the clamors of fear of the crowd emerging from the houses. The firmament was already black with dragonflies, airbuses and aerial ferries, loaded to capacity; they were carrying the tremulous far from the menace of the storm.

"And there are people who don't appear to have great confidence in the science of Oronius," sniggered Wiwar. "They judge it more prudent to take to their heels. Damn! Can any refuge exist against the destructive rage of Hantzen? Everything will pass... the city, the brave and the cowards... everyone and everything."

The odious spy affirmed that with conviction, while using wings to take him personally to shelter. At a certain distance from Paris he slowed his speed and turned around, thinking: *I'm out of the danger zone, I can take a look. It'll be worth the trouble. I'm my youth I was told a Biblical legend in which the Eternal caused the fire of his Heavens fall on five culpable cities, Sodom, Gomorrah, Seboim, Adamah and another... Segor, I think, although the name doesn't matter... it was so long ago! It ought to be an agreeable spectacle to contemplate...*

Opening the case containing his binoculars, he continued: *Paris is worth as much as the five cities, I imagine, and Otto Hantzen can stand in for the Eternal. Let's see, the upheaval must have begun... no? Why haven't I heard any thunderclaps? Will Hantzen's storm be a damp squib?*

Having borne the binoculars to his eyes, he immediately uttered an exclamation, and stammered in a troubled voice: "Ah! What's happening? Is Oronius going to prevail? But what is Jarrousse doing?"

For a quarter of an hour, the spectacle of the cataclysm that was threatening Paris had been terrifying, and all those who had not been able to flee thought that their last hour had come.

Bearing the destructive lightning in their bosom, all the clouds in the world were hurrying to the rendezvous that the science of Otto Hantzen has assigned to them.

Yes, that was how it was necessary to translate Wiwar's words and explain the threats of Oronius' rival. There was nothing in all directions, but distant rumbles that increased and drew nearer; incessant lightning, a rain of fire, commenced. Could the capital of the United States of Europe, menaced with conflagration, escape disaster? No one thought so, and the Parisians awaited death, lamenting; the most beautiful city in the world seemed doomed to suffer the fate of the Pentapolis of Palestine.

A dazzling flash of lightning suddenly sprang forth from the sky, now filled with somber clouds; a veritable wave of fire raising crests fringed with blue flame rose up and appeared to be making ready to fall back on Paris, to envelop it and annihilate it. Cries of terror resounded. Overwhelmed by horror and respiring with difficulty the fiery air filled with the odor of sulfur, the condemned believed that their last hour had come... that they were all about to die... unless there was a miracle.

But could they hope for one? For Science had abolished the species a long time ago.

Well, science or magic, it was manifest, amazing and incomprehensible!

In fact, the gigantic flash of lightning was suddenly extinguished, as if pumped way by a colossal invisible aspirator.

Another lit up; it suffered the same fate.

From that moment on, throughout the sky, there was a stupefying conflict between the lightning, previously victorious everywhere, and an unknown element, perhaps less powerful, but surely superior in energy, since it attracted it and captured it silently in mid-air in the course of its fulgurant trajectory, without leaving it the time to strike.

One by one, as they were born in the bosom of the clouds, the zigzag tongues of fire were stretched, thinned and extinguished, always in the same direction.

And it was toward the magical Villa that they all seemed to be irresistibly drawn.

Oronius, the Master, riposting to his rival's scientific attack, had just entered the stage.

He was capturing the lightning.

From the corridors of the Villa, into which he had slipped, thanks to the complicity of Wiwar, Jarrousse, the felonious disciple, the disdained lover of the beautiful Cyprienne, had witnessed the attack of the atmospheric elements regimented by Otto Hantzen, and then the unexpected riposte, before which the storm had been resorbed.

That spectacle filled him with both amazement and rage.

"What new physical combination has the inexhaustible Oronius found, then?" he muttered. "I'm beginning to fear that Hantzen doesn't have the strength. Let's go! I've decided to get mixed up in it; ought I not to earn my reward?"

A diabolical sigh accompanied those words, and Jarrousse's physiognomy took on a sinister expression. With the ease of someone familiar with the places that he had often visited in the days when he was the Master's pupil, he headed for the forbidden laboratory, and soon, through the transparent walls of that eccentric dwelling, he was able to perceive the meditative silhouette of the great scientist.

Then, as if against his will, he remained nailed to the crystal floor, so to speak, by an invincible sentiment of admiration.

"That man is almost a god," he murmured, with terror. "He truly is *the Master*."

Who would not have formulated the admiring judgment that Jarrousse had just made it on perceiving the calm figure of the scientist standing in the middle of his laboratory, strangely illuminated by the fulgurant reflections of the celestial fire? In fact, sliding along one of the glass walls in a silent cascade that descended from the terrace, the atmospheric electricity, still incandescent but definitively vanquished, even domesticated, went meekly to disappear into the bosom of a reservoir of singular form.

Before the wonderstruck and frightened eyes of Jarrousse, Oronius stored the lighting unleashed by his enemy—the lightning hurled at him by the stormy cloud. Before the spectacle of such a formidable power, Jarrousse remained inert; he was invaded by a sentiment of terror and discouragement, which dominated him for several seconds.

One can't do anything against such genius, he thought. *It would be pure dementia to dare to confront it.*

But his jealous nature and his deeply vindictive mind did not take long to extract him from that abnormal dejection, so, pulling himself together quickly, his villainous features contracting, he murmured: "To the Devil with fear! I'll see whether he's only a man, or whether he's the immortal that people claim!"

With an audacious decision, he opened the door of the laboratory, without his unexpected intrusion seeming to extract the Master from his reverie.

Only the ape Bambo, the scientist's placid and silent companion, in his corner, where he allowed himself to be forgotten, perhaps dreaming about the impenetrable forests of the heart of Africa, greeted the new arrival with an unfriendly gaze. The flair of animals is sometimes far superior to human reason; in Jarrousse, Bambo had scented an enemy.

"Bonjour, Master!" pronounced the traitor, in a honeyed tone. "Don't you recognize me?"

Distractedly—perhaps disdainfully—Cyprienne's father turned his head and leveled his bright eyes at the indiscreet intruder.

"Why, it's Jarrousse," he observed. "Where have you come from, deserter?"

"A harsh word, Master. I only wanted to stay with you, as you know very well. You're not unaware, either, that it would have been pleasant to attach myself to your glory by even tighter bonds. You preferred a newcomer to me."

"Rather say that he was able to make himself preferred," Oronius put in. "Sympathy isn't commanded, Jarrousse."

"I know that, Master, so you can't be astonished that I went to take mine elsewhere."

"That was your right, my boy."

Gradually, Jarrousse, humble and submissive at first, straightened up and stared mockingly at the man whom the Parisians, not without reason, had made their idol.

"It was very difficult," he said, with a bantering intention, "to find an equivalent of the illustrious Oronius."

"Say that it was impossible."

"I'd like to leave you that illusion, Master, but beware of the truth."

"Leave the truth alone; it has never counted you among its fervent adherents."

"No matter," Jarrousse persisted, piqued. "It's proven nevertheless that I've encountered another genius, who can, with just title, claim to be your rival."

"Ah!" Oronius smiled maliciously. "You've become Otto Hantzen's pupil? Poor fellow, I didn't think you had such bad taste."

"His pupil and his friend," affirmed Jarousse, in an ill-tempered tone.

"I don't congratulate you."

"Perhaps you'll have reason not to congratulate yourself," insinuated the renegade, malevolently.

"Because?" Oronius queried, raising his head and staring at Jarrousse.

The later evaded the question. "The science of Otto Hantzen, isn't so negligible..."

The Master smiled. "What can it do?"

"You've just had a rather splendid example."

"Bah! Where is it?"

"The storm that threatens Paris..."

"Threatened, you mean," the scientist corrected, pitilessly.

Jarrousse reddened with anger. "It's nevertheless an appreciable proof of what Hantzen can do. For it is, as you've certainly divined, artificial in origin. Hantzen can unleash lightning at will."

"It isn't prime quality, his lightning. Your new employer is a leper; scientifically, he's stingy. Like bad gunpowder, however, bad thunder can have its dangers—can one ever tell? So I collected Hantzen's toy and rendered it inoffensive... while waiting to use it myself, after having improved it. Look, here's your scarecrow!"

While speaking, superbly casual, Oronius indicated with his hand the reservoir in which, silently and continuously, the sheet of fire was still being stored.

Jarrousse went pale, only then realizing where the intolerable heat came from that had made him sweat copiously since his irruption into the laboratory.

"So you've found a means of capturing the electric spark?" he exclaimed, paralyzed by envious admiration.

"Capturing it, conserving it and making it my weapon of choice, in the fashion of Olympian Jupiter," the scientist specified.

"It's an admirable discovery," murmured Hantzen's ally, taking a step forward.

"Among a hundred others. In that regard, there's no lack of choice here." And with a broad gesture, showing the treasures that his laboratory contained, Oronius added: "All the forces of the universe, all its secrets, deciphered by me, are in my hands. You can repeat that to Otto Hantzen when you give him an account of your mission."

"Of my mission?" Jarousse stammered, paling further.

"You imagine, then, my poor boy, that I haven't penetrated the ridiculous goal of your visit?" said Oronius, with a scornful irony. "You intended to witness the spectacle of my defeat and my despair; you thought you would be able to regale your master with the story that you would have concocted for him. Admit it—you came as a spy, Thomas Jarrousse."

He marched toward his former pupil in order to throw his scorn in his face.

Jarrousse did not recoil; the two men came breast to breast.

"I haven't come with that sole intention," roared the intruder, at the peak of his rage. "Why, by insulting me, are you obliging me to throw away the mask? You're foolishly imprudent, Oronius. In spite of all the legends running around on your account, you're only a man, after all... and I'll add that you're only a play-actor, since you don't deny them. Well, humans and play-actors are mortal. Be careful. I've come, as you've awkwardly divined, with a very definite mission: that of extracting your secrets from you... in other words, to disarm you. It's necessary to deliver them to me, you hear? Alive or dead, you're going to let me take these treasures, to which you've just made allusion. To me, the science, Oronius!"

He leapt upon the Master, enclosing him in his powerful arms. He possessed the muscles of a wild beast, as they say in the bush, and he was endowed with a Herculean strength. In spite of his robust constitution, Oronius did not seem to have the strength to be able to resist him.

In such an unequal struggle the Master seemed vanquished in advance, all the more fatally because the unscrupulous Jarrousse would not hesitate to employ the most disloyal weapons. It was not a battle he was meditating, but an assassination.

Already, slyly, one of his hands had released his adversary in order to plunge into a pocket in search of a dagger.

But the criminal gesture was not completed. Unexpected reinforcements arrived for Oronius at the moment when he had the least right to expect any.

Uttering a war cry, the ape Bambo, intoxicated by anger, pounced on his master's aggressor and grabbed him by the hair.

The pain made Jarrousse let go; abandoning Oronius, he concentrated all his strength in getting rid of the ape-man of the woods, a redoubtable adversary.

In fact, rolling on the glass floor and overturning everything with which they collided, the furious adversaries caused irreparable damage in the laboratory.

That was not what preoccupied the scientist, however; fearfully, he saw them roll in the direction of a flask three-quarters full of a colorless liquid. He tried to launch himself forward to stop them.

"Look out!" he cried. "Look out, wretches—the nitrocolle..."

He could not finish. Overturned by the combatants, the flask shattered.

The air was shaken by an explosion so formidable that Paris entire undulated, as if moved by a seismic shock...

Chapter XI
A VOLCANO AT BELLEVILLE

Desperate and dejected, Jean Chapuis and Laridon were returning toward Paris. They had not abandoned the pursuit of the mysterious sphere; they had not renounced liberating the captives of the woman with the enigmatic visage. No! But the sudden check, and the proof that the persecutrix of the young scientist had furnished of the immensity of her power, overwhelmed them and left them with an impression of complete impotence.

Which way should they turn? What corner of the sky should they explore? Were they even sure that their enemy inhabited the Earth?

Beyond the stratosphere explored by humans as far as the confines of the ether, there was all the enigma of space, through which no one had yet dared to take flight. But at that moment, Jean Chapuis felt less convinced that no one had risked it.

The illustrious Oronius and he would have to struggle, he now knew, against two enemies: Otto Hantzen and the unknown woman from space.

Which of the two was the more powerful?

Already, the young engineer no longer hesitated to respond, and if the choice had been left to him, he would immediately have asked to be rid of his persecutrix, taking personal responsibility for defending himself against Otto Hantzen.

Was he seeing clearly? Was he mistaken?

In any case, for the moment, his mind was only occupied by the unknown woman and her prisoners. For him, she alone counted. The storm and its consequences, and Hantzen's threats? Negligible quantities—Jean Chapuis had forgotten them. So had Laridon; he did not even remember any longer hang seen the traitor Jarrousse slipping surreptitiously into the transparent Villa overlooking Paris, even though the behavior of the fellow and the trap he had contrived for the mechanic announced and proved evil designs.

The abduction of the two young women, however, and the vain attempt at pursuit, however, absorbed Laridon's thoughts to such an extent that everything else was eclipsed. So, negligent of the danger that Oronius might be running personally, the young mechanic instinctively invoked his God of Science.

"Only M'sieur Oronius can get us out of this," he decreed, in his distress.

That was also the opinion of Jean Chapuis. He too believed in the power of Cyprienne's father; he needed to believe in it at the present moment more than ever.

He'll advise me and I'll act, he said to himself. *Why did I launch myself into the sky like an insensate? First, I should have brought my Master up to date with what was happening, and consulted him. He would have found a means of thwarting the ruses of that infernal woman. He would have vanquished the cloud! Unfortunate that I am, my great confidence in myself has only delayed and compromised Cyprienne's liberation. I wanted to act alone, and I've failed. I've certainly been punished!*

He conserved the hope, however, that Oronius would be able to repair that fault and indicate the tactics to employ in order to find the sphere again or follow its course.

Was not science omnipotent?

That is why, instead of exhausting himself in vague courses through the air, he had sagely preferred to turn the Halcyon-Car around and return to Paris.

That return appeared likely to be accomplished without incident. In the distance, the storm, vanquished and tamed— by what? they could not tell—had calmed down. The sky had become serene again, and was beginning to fill with flying machines, whose passengers were joyfully acclaiming the name of Oronius, their savior.

Already, the passengers of the Halcyon-Car could see Belleville and the magical Villa.

Instinctively, Laridon increased he sped of the Halcyon; he too experienced the need to strengthen himself again in the presence of the Master and to place Turlurette under the protection of his science.

"Fortunately, he's there," he murmured. "We're coming back empty-handed, and no prouder for it."

Jean Chapuis gave his melancholy approval; but the proximity of Cyprienne's father acted upon him as a consolation; on seeing the Villa again and the laboratory in which so many marvelous discoveries had been born, he told himself that with the support of the inexhaustible genius of Oronius victory as finally certain.

He would rediscover and liberate his fiancée!

Suddenly, a frightful explosion shook the air... and precisely above the heights of Belleville. It seemed to the two aviators that the entire landscape, shaken like a fruit-tree, blurred and was ripped apart.

The Villa toward which they were flying disappeared from sight as if by magic and without it being possible to tell whether it had been volatilized or swallowed up by the ground. In the place that it had occupied a second before a column of flame rose vertically into the sky, tapering, spreading out and surrounding itself with a plume of vapor. And from the flanks of the mountain of Belleville, dislocated, disemboweled and transformed into a crater, torrents of fire surged forth.

Jean Chapuis and Laridon uttered cries of horror.

Instead of the pleasant landscape they had been contemplating a moment before, there was no longer anything but a volcano in full activity, launching its streams of fire and ash into the air, which fell back upon Paris in red clouds.

"Oronius! My poor master!" moaned Jean Chapuis, his heat atrociously crushed by a new dolor. And that too related to Cyprienne. Was not Oronius his principal support, almost his unique hope?

That catastrophe, implausible on ground that was reputedly not volcanic, attained Jean and Cyprienne simultaneously.

"Gone!" lamented the mechanic, for his part. "We're done for now!"

More picturesquely expressed, it was the same thought and the same despair.

Neither of them was able to divine as yet what had happened. They could not imagine the drama of the laboratory and the accident provoked by the treacherous Jarrousse, who had probably been its first victim. But before knowing, before understanding, they *saw*. And the spectacle was sufficiently terrible to break their hearts. They looked at one another, equally pale.

"Did you hear?" stammered Jean Chapuis.

"And saw," Laridon affirmed. "Everything's fried. Everything's burned. "Necessary to go there, M'sieur Jean. If there's a chance of saving M'sieur Oronius..."

"A chance!" moaned the young engineer, bitterly, profoundly discouraged by the spectacle that he had before his eyes. "How can we hope that he has survived that catastrophe? Look at those sprays of fire.. .those whirlwinds of flame and smoke... it's a volcano..."

"A volcano in Belleville!" exclaimed the mechanic. "If anyone had predicted that in my youth, I'd have had the medium carted away."

"The Villa no longer exists," sighed Cyprienne's fiancé. "Everything that it contained must have been destroyed; everyone inside it must be dead."

Rendered mute by terror, Julep was huddled in a corner of the cabin, his eyes fearfully closed, in order not to see anything, but at those final words he began to utter howls of despair.

He was thinking of Bambo, his friend, and the petty treasures he possessed in the house that was now volatilized, and finally, above all—let us recognize it in praise of the worthy man—of his teacher Oronius, for whom he professed a blind devotion, perhaps in recognition of the value he attributed to his sumptuously multicolored skin.

"Ah!" cried Laridon, with a sudden fury. "It's that evil individual, I'll wager, who's done this! Why didn't I smash his face in before departing?"

Belated regret, futile regret! Jean Chapuis did not even pick up the allusion.

"No matter!" he said. "However little hope there is of finding the Master alive, we ought to try. Let's get closer, as you proposed."

They set about flying over the furnace, describing great circles around the crater, but they only perceived a crimson lake, and blue and yellow roaring flames, twisting like snakes. From the gulf opened by the explosion, into the depth of which Belleville had disappeared, new jets of fire were emerging incessantly.

It was as if the violence of the deflagration had split the globe all the way to its center, and that the igneous mass attained and liberated was rising to the light from the depths of the fissure.

"I only know of one explosive capable of producing such formidable effects," murmured Jean Chapuis, thoughtfully. "That's nitrocolle, one of the Master's recent discoveries. But he was too well aware of the danger it represented; how could he have committed the imprudence whose result we're witnessing?"

"It was committed for him," riposted Laridon, with conviction. "Probable that the guilty party won't do it again. What a misfortune! The poor fellow was so good!"

They had landed some distance away. Quitting their apparatus, they strove to get closer on foot to the frightful furnace.

A consternated crowd, hastened from all parts of Paris, surrounded the volcano. Rescue parties were organized—but what could they do? They quickly had to take account of the fact that nothing could be done to attenuate the effects of the cataclysm. Everything had been consumed.

91

They could not risk themselves in the immediate vicinity of the crater; it was throwing out flaming matter and giving off a unbearable heat. How, in those conditions, could anyone envisage for a single instant the hypothesis that the gulf might still contain living beings? At this hour, everything that had been swallowed up by it at the moment of the explosion must be carbonized. However, Jean Chapuis and the two servants of the uncontested Master of all the sciences could not decide to abandon hope. They continued to wander lugubriously around the furnace, obstinately calling out to the savant defender of Paris.

"He was the cleverest of the clever," said the mechanic. "Not possible that he let himself slide. Could he have clung on to something?"

Alas, it was necessary to render to the evidence a few hours later when they discovered a skeleton amid the debris ejected from the volcano. Doubt was no longer possible; it was all that remained of the illustrious Oronius. The mortal had shed his terrestrial form, conserved for such a long time that it seemed to be associated with his immortality. Otto Hantzen had prevailed—for in the eyes of them all—Laridon and Jean Chapuis did not hesitate to share that opinion—the catastrophe in which the greatest scientist of all time had just found death could only have been provoked by his enemy.

"We'll avenge him!" swore Cyprienne's fiancé, his eyes glittering.

He extended his right hand in the direction of the crater, above which the spirit of Oronius might perhaps still be wandering. "May your thought pass into me and be my guide, Master!" he pronounced, fervently. "You can't abandon your daughter. Help me. I swear to associate in my hated the person who has kidnapped Cyprienne and the man who has caused your death. Without respite, even if I have to go to the ends of the universe, I'll pursue them, and I won't rest until I've attained my double goal, and fulfilled my doubt task... to deliver Cyprienne and avenge your death!"

As he finished that oath, a tremor that his two companions were able to observe shook him from head to toe. It seemed to him that an electric current had passed through him.

"The thought of the Master," he murmured, going very pale. "I sensed him. He heard me. He'll help me!"

The next day, while Paris, in mourning, gave the skeleton that was presumed to be that of Oronius an imposing funeral, the Halcyon-Car resumed its fight, carrying Jean Chapuis, Laridon and Julep, all three equally resolved to triumph over all obstacles in order to accomplish the oath made to great Death.

Chapter XII
THE MOTIONLESS VOYAGE

Grief and anger, succeeding the dejection into which the death of Oronius had initially plunged Jean Chapuis, had the effect on the organism of the energetic young man of a whiplash. As soon as he was resolved to action and fixed in his double duty, he recovered his mental lucidity—lucidity such that the thought of aid from beyond traversed his brain.

He did not stop there.

Between the living and the dead, alas, in spite of the affirmations of psychics, it seems that the link has been broken forever. The living and the dead do not speak the same language; how can they understand one another. Cyprienne's fiancé admitted, nevertheless, that the piety of the memory he conserved of the dead Master might perhaps be an inspiring comfort to him. Intimately penetrated by the thought of the man who had been his initiator and had awakened him to the scientific life, he admitted as possible, even probable, a prolongation of he action of that marvelous genius beyond the tomb. That is why he had said: "He'll help me!"

His heritage remains to me, he thought. Had he not elevated me to the rank of confidant? How much information and how many precious indications he threw into my memory. It registered everything without classifying it, almost without taking account of it. Today, now that he is no more, it's necessary to reconstitute that part of him. I want that!

He pronounced those words forcefully.

As if obedient to that order, his thought was suddenly revivified, so to speak; a feverish activity took possession of it, and projected light that made all the science of Oronius appear in a griping summary.

Was that not really the automatism of memory entering into play? Jean Chapuis neglect to marvel at what he was able to consider as a mental phenomenon. He simply abandoned himself to the current of cerebral energy that seemed to be impelling him more than he was provoking it, and did not ask himself whether that new force emanated from himself or a foreign source.

He embraced the situation with a glance.

The Halcyon-Car was flying through the open sky. Laridon and Julep were awaiting his orders.

"What are we going to do, M'sieur Jean?" asked the mechanic, encountering the young man's gaze, in which he read a sort of awakening.

Cyprienne's fiancé searched the immensity of space with his eyes.

"Searching there for the sphere would be a foolish enterprise," he declared. "And yet, to get to the end, it might be necessary for us to visit all of the sky, travel all the earth and perhaps take our investigation even further."

"Further than the base and further than the ceiling? We're not at the starting-post, then," riposted Laridon, shaking his head dubiously. "There's no lack of room for playing hide-and-seek. It's not only once around the Great Everything that it's necessary for us to go. That'll take time, rapidly as our Halcyon flies!"

"The Earth travels even more rapidly," Jean Chapuis put in, with an inspired expression. "Don't worry. We can easily go as quickly as that."

"How?" asked the mechanic, opening his eyes wide.

"By remaining motionless," Cyprienne's fiancé replied, smiling.

The mechanic looked at him anxiously. Had chagrin troubled the young boss's brain, perhaps, to the point of "de-railing" it? Laridon was not reassured.

Without paying any heed to that anxiety, the engineer quit the direction cabin and went to a cell suspended in the exact center of gravity of the apparatus. There he shut himself in and immediately activated a complicated mechanism, opening certain taps and closing others, pulling levers and turning wheels...

Sonorous vibrations, which gradually fused into a harmonious accord, filled the cell.

Then, rotating the needles of six dials, placed respectively on the six walls whose adjustment formed the cell, Jean Chapuis set them all to the figure zero.

Having done that, he rejoined his companions.

"Look," he said, simply, to Laridon, showing him the ground, which was traveling at high speed beneath them.

Given the low altitude at which, by virtue of a savant maneuver, he was maintaining the Halcyon, the surface of the earth remained clearly visible. Amazed, Laridon observed that mountains, forests and rivers, like all the other accidents of the terrain, the railways, the canals, the towns and villages, and constructions of every species, appeared to be racing beneath them with a veritably vertiginous rapidity. By virtue of that crazy course, everything melted into a series of horizontal stripes that did not permit any details to be distinguished.

"Oh la la!" he exclaimed, darting an anxious glance at the speed indicators. "What's got into the Halcyon? My opinion is that it's bolting like out ancestors' horses when they'd been fed too much hay!"

But immediately, he rubbed his eyes, and changed his tone and expression. "M'sieur Jean! Help! What's happening? We're no longer moving... and it's the Earth that's trotting! One might even think that it's dragging us along."

"Haven't I told you that?" replied the engineer tranquilly. "Yes, it's running... or rather, it's rotating underneath us... before us... at its ordinary speed of thirty kilometers a minute... eighteen hundred an hour."[9]

"A nice canter. Down with the champions!" exclaimed Laridon, enthused by the fantastic figures.

"Say that we're beating all the records... for that speed is becoming ours," Jean Chapuis went on. "Of two bodies isolated from one another in the bosom of space, one of which is

---

[9] At the latitude of France, the speed is actually closer to 1000 km/hr.

moving relative to the other, the immobility of one is no more than an appearance. Seen from the Earth, it's us who are flying through the void approximately at the speed that I've just revealed to you."

"Approximately?"

"Yes, as you remarked for yourself, our immobility is entirely relative, because, as much by virtue of its attraction as its rapid rotation, the Earth is dragging in its orbit everything near to it..."

"It's going to catch us then? Swallow us?"

"No. Our determined, calculated recoil almost compensates for the attractive force of our planet."

"I'm content... I'm running very fast... very fast!" exclaimed Julep, who was listening, making conscientious efforts to understand. In his jubilation, laughing broadly, he uncovered his gleaming teeth.

"Idiot!" riposted the mechanic, with an air of scornful superiority. "You don't get it! You're not running, since you're staying in the same place, as M'sieur Jean has just inculcated us. That's it, isn't it, M'sieur Jean? The Earth is making tracks and we're in the stands."

"Exactly. Thanks to the ingenious mechanism invented by my poor Master Oronius, a mechanism that's keeping us suspended in space and assuring us of a stability very close to absolute immobility in relation to the Earth. To realize that prodigy, it was sufficient for him to neutralize the action of gravity and currents, automatically developing in the walls of the fixation cell a force sensibly equal and opposite to each of those whose influence we want to cancel. It's that series of electromagnetic currents that I've just developed."

"So we'll be spectators?

"Undoubtedly A screen is displayed before us on which the landscapes will unfurl at a crazy speed. Seas and continents will file before our eyes. It's only a matter of opening them."

"It's also a matter of putting an accelerator on the peep-ers. It's passing too quickly," Laridon complained, disappoint-ed and squinting.

And the worthy Julep repeated, like an echo: "Julep no see! Screen blurred!"

Wait a little, impatient that you are," responded Jean Chapuis. I'll pass you spectacles."

He went down into the Halcyon's storage lockers, where the provisions and all the equipment were lodged. An instant later, he reappeared holding three minuscule items of appa-ratus, which consisted of an assembly of lenses and prisms covered in a radioactive coating destined to augment their power prodigiously.

"Glory to Oronius!" he proclaimed in a voice penetrated with admiration and gratitude. "Yes, glory to that benefactor of humanity, whose indefatigable labor has left us treasures! He had foreseen all the obstacles resulting from the imperfec-tions of our senses, and he was able to remedy them. This is his Cyclopean Eye, which permits seeing a prodigious dis-tances, and even through opaque bodes; this marvelous adapt-er of vision adjust to the relativity of time and space. It slows down or multiples at the whim of the observer the velocity of the observed object. Thus, it arrives at maintaining it in the field of human observation. In other terms, it permits focusing in four dimensions. Turn this little wheel and you can adjust speed and distance—which is to say, time and space—to the measure of your visual faculties."

Having each received one of the marvelous optical in-struments, Laridon and Julep, imitating Jane Chapuis, applied them to their eyes. Both immediately uttered cries of admira-tion.

"I can see!" cried the negro, enthusiastically. "I'm very near a little village. I can see hens laying and hear cocks crow-ing."

"Don't exaggerate," protested Jean Chapuis, smiling. "That second prodigy would only be possible if I had confided another of Oronius' inventions to you, the Ear of Stentor. That magical ear will serve us when the occasion arises."

"What a dab hand he was," murmured Laridon. "He could have remade our poor carcass from top to bottom. That's what's called ameliorating the race. It's a pity that in our epoch, we don't eat any more, as in the time of my great grandmother. I'd have asked you, M'sieur Jean, if you had at my disposal a Mouth of Gargantua and a stomach of corresponding caliber."

But Cyprienne's fiancé was no longer listening. Gripped again by his preoccupations he was searching avidly with his gaze—or, more precisely, with the Cyclopean Eye—the portions of the terrestrial surface that the course of the Earth revealed to him.

Did he hope he find the lair of Otto Hantzen there, or the retreat of the unknown woman?

Perhaps he was committing a gross error in supposing that the mysterious enemy will that was directing the course of the sphere and its prisoners resided on the Earth, and that it was necessary to search for it there.

Jean Chapuis reasoned like a man; he said to himself: *That mysterious sphere can't pursue its course through the sky eternally; it has to land sooner or later; perhaps it has already landed.*

So, that was what he was searching for, or at least some indication of its presence. No matter how he concentrated, and no matter how the Earth rotated, he did not discover anything at all.

His companions were no more fortunate.

Suddenly, an intuition traversed his brain, like an order: *Look up.*

Mechanically, he tried to obey. He could not.

A force of which he was conscious now held him curbed, obliging him to continue his futile exploration of the ground.

For several seconds he had the impression that two forces—two contradictory wills—were competing within him and that he had become a battlefield. But whose? Where did that come from? What were those material powers whose irresistible influences were disputing his brain, installing themselves as masters in his will and wanting to take over its direction?

For having experienced something analogous already while the apparitions had tormented him, it was easy for him to respond partially to that question and imagine that the mysterious unknown woman was no stranger to his malaise.

It was very probable that the entity of that problematic woman was one of those seeking to dominate Jean Chapuis and direct his actions. But what was the other? A friend? An enemy?

Supposing that the latter were favorable to him, only intervening to counterbalance the baleful influence of Jean Chapuis' persecutrix, how could he identify it? How could he recognize the ascendancy to which it was necessary to yield, the advice it as necessary to follow?

Terror and anguish tortured Jean during that combat of mysterious dominations that were trying to subjugate his own. Whichever prevailed, he would not know whether to rejoice or deplore it. By what certain sign could he recognize that he ought to abandon himself to the savior will?

Abruptly, the combat within him ceased; his doubts and his anguish eased; he no longer felt the weight that was curbing his head while another, less powerful effort was attempting to raise it.

Free, he was finally able to look at the sky.

Then he uttered a loud cry, which made Julep and Laridon jump.

"Out there! The cloud! The sphere!"

Chapter Thirteen
THE ENIGMATIC SPHERE

The sphere was there! It was perceptible through the cloud that still enveloped it, but seemed to have been diluted into less opaque vapors.

It was allowing itself to be seen.

It was not a mirage. The vision persisted after Jean Chapuis had rubbed his eyes and Julep and Laridon had confirmed it in turn.

"It's really there, boss,"

"That round machine, that magic cage."

It might, however, be a trap, for it was certainly very astonishing, and also very suspect, that the sphere had come back and had done what was necessary to reveal its form, instead of continuing to flee toward its unknown goal.

Jean Chapuis did not hesitate, nor even reflect upon that singularity. He turned round in the fixation cell and put a stop to the immobility of the Halcyon-Car. Then he turned back to his crew and addressed the mechanic.

"Straight up, at top speed!" he cried, feverishly.

"Good!" said Laridon, philosophically. "Let's go... although I don't trust it. Since it escaped us before, there's no reason for it to come back now to plant itself in our path. Anyway, we'll see. But if it lets itself get caught, it might strike hard."

"What do the risks matter? I want to free Cyprienne... and she is in that flying prison."

Manifestly obstinate, the fiancé refused to modify his tactics. The mechanic understood that it would do no good to preach. He felt an equal impatience himself, and was ready to take any risk to get close to Turlurette

However, he uttered the axiom: "Every return to a point of departure has a reason. Do we know whether they're still in that ball?"

Jean Chapuis shivered. The same idea had occurred to him. His occult enemy might well have employed the stratagem of emptying the sphere of its prisoners and adapting it to fulfill the function of a trap.

"We'll see!" he replied, his expression darkening. "Steer straight up, I tell you."

"In fact, it's the only means of finding out," the mechanic approved. "To touch, it's necessary to approach and take a peep. Too bad if one receives a slap—we'll come out quits by returning it."

And after consulting his azimuth and giving the motors their full thrust, the brave fellow headed straight toward the point of the horizon where the sphere appeared.

Anxiously, Jean Chapuis aimed his binoculars at it.

At first, he had feared seeing the cloud thicken and escape the gaze, as soon as the invisible observer who must be following the course of the machine perceived the approach of the Halcyon-Car. He expected to lose visual contact with the sphere at any moment; logically, he ought to expect that it would not fail to slip away for a second time.

That did not happen.

The distance separating the Halcyon from the flying prison of Cyprienne and Turlurette diminished progressively, and the sphere remained visible. Soon, it became indubitable that it was waiting for the Halcyon-Car and its passengers.

For a second, it even seemed to our friends that a hand drew on its flank, in fiery characters, the seven letter of its name: *SPHERUS*.

"That's suspicious! Look out!" young Victor—for Victor was Laridon's forename—never ceased muttering. "Necessary to keep our peepers open, boss."

"That's what I'm doing, damn it! Don't I have to take a look, to find out whether my fiancée and her maid are still in that singular apparatus?"

The mechanic shrugged his shoulders. *When a valorous man gets knocked for a loop*, he thought, *he loses all wisdom and prudence. If enemies are lying in wait for us, we're going to get a punch in the nose.*

But as he belonged to a breakneck species himself, he continued nevertheless to bring the Halcyon closer to the Spherus, taking care to describe wide circles around it that gradually diminished, and he permitted the machine to be observed without making contact.

Having gained altitude in order that their apparatus was slightly above the enigmatic ball, he and Jean Chapuis could dart glances through the glass cap that surmounted it.

The silhouettes of the two prisoners were still there. The klaxon sound of shrill barking reached the ears of the young men.

"I can see them, Victor!" said Jean, transfigured. And with all his might he started shouting: "Cyprienne! Turlurette! Here we are!"

Amazingly, no matter how he multiplied his signs and appeals, Oronius' daughter and her maidservant remained passive, not manifesting any joy, contenting themselves with turning melancholy faces in the direction of the circling Halcyon-Car.

At the same time, Laridon and Julep said: "That's not encouraging," and "The Mamzelles don't see much happy."

"Perhaps they think that we can't do anything for them," riposted the engineer with the determination of the amorous, ever ready to discover new reasons for hope. "Doubtless they think that, like the first time, the cloud is about to be interposed between them and us. They're afraid of a false joy—that's why they're not abandoning themselves to transports. Anyway, aren't they right? Before crying victory, it's necessary to figure out what it's possible to do to reach them and free them. Tighten the tangent, Victor. Let's quit the horizontal to take the perpendicular and form a concentric spiral passing above and below; it's time to call upon the talents of aerial acrobatics. I need to examine that machine from every angle."

"One can do that for you, M'sieur Jean," the mechanic replied, "but at times like these, no joking, I'd rather have another job. I'm not confident."

"Master, Julep isn't either," grunted the negro lugubriously, who often echoed his friend's reflections.

The young engineer was not listening; he was intoxicated by the proximity of his fiancée. She was there, a few meters away from him, only separated by a glass partition, apparently thin and fragile.

After having feared finding the sphere empty, and trembling with anxiety on the subject of Cyprienne, Jean Chapuis suddenly passed from extreme discouragement to exaggerated optimism. It was as if he were mad with joy and excitement. The most insensate enterprises seemed facile to him; he was almost indignant at the doubts that Laridon's attitude expressed.

"We'll liberate them! I'm convinced of it," he affirmed, joyfully. "In fact, what are we risking by trying? They're alone inside that machine, which a favorable hazard has placed in our path, and we're free..."

"Exactly," remarked the mechanic. "It's too tempting. It reeks of a trap. We're being set up."

"Leave off! You would prefer not to have your picture taken in the high atmosphere? I'm not so proud... especially when it's a matter of saving someone dear to me."

"Agreed. All the same, I'd be more confident if we'd had to play games in order to get close to that treacherous orange, and if we'd been greeted by bullets or some other projectile. At least, that would be frank; we'd know what was what. Instead, of which, it's waiting for us very politely, having the appearance of wanting to be taken. So I say, beware of the catch!"

"You know full well, my brave Victor, that there's no one aboard that sphere except for the prisoners. Our enemy is directing it at a distance. I can therefore suppose some sort of breakdown, an obstacle interposing itself between that spherical aerocab and the conductive waves. It's a very admissible hypothesis; it would explain the good fortune that makes you anxious, and from which I want to profit."

"Listen, M'sieur Jean," said the mechanic, despairing of the cause. "Keep aiming your goggles at that thing while I commence my capers. We'll see about opening the door... if it has one."

With an equally admirable audacity and mastery, he started executing the most fantastic evolutions around the sphere, sometimes passing above it and sometimes below, after having let the Halcyon fall along its flanks by cutting across the machine's route at a vertiginous speed.

It was in the course of one of those perilous tumbles that Jean Chapuis suddenly remarked, in the inferior part of the sphere, a circular opening of small diameter, but sufficient to allow a man to pass through it. Had it existed before, or had it just opened, by a coincidence that as at least singular, which Laridon would have been entitled to think suspect? That was what the young captain could not have affirmed, so he abstained from opening that delicate controversy.

He simply announced: "There's a door. I can see it. We won't even have to break it down, since it's open."

"Hmm!" said the mechanic, decidedly suspicious— which was explicable by the necessity of reacting against the manifest recklessness of Jean Chapuis. "I'd rather it was bolted. So much convenience doesn't say anything good to me. When someone insists too hard that I go in somewhere, I scarper. But think what you like—perhaps I'm in a contradictory mood."

"You are," the engineer told him, smiling. "At any rate, you're wasting your time and effort if you hope to get me to abandon such an opportunity and not to attempt to free the prisoners."

"I'd never advise you that cowardice, M'sieur Jean. I'm only preaching prudence... because there's more than one way of doing things."

"Tell me what you prescribe... I'd be curious to hear it, because I can't see very many. For a quarter on an hour we've been waltzing around the sphere without attempting anything. Is that reasonable? That mobile cell without warders and defenders is here, within reach, with an opening permitting us to reach those we're searching for. Can I hesitate any longer?"

"I didn't say that." Laridon felt defeated. What, in fact, could he advise his young master to do? Circling the mysterious apparatus indefinitely was not a solution; from outside, it was impossible to see more than they had already observed. As for what awaited them inside, had the two young women not affirmed that the sphere as empty? There were also the machines they had mentioned, but in any case, and whatever the mastery of the unknown woman possessed in utilizing waves, she could hardly have recourse to that means to attack and vanquish three resolute men in possession themselves of various means of defense, and being on their guard.

There was, of course, the aluminum trawl; that had proved redoubtable and caused the mechanic to reflect. In fact, why that their enemy not employed it against them while they were passing under the sphere? It had been a fine opportunity for fishing for the Halcyon-Car like a mere whale.

She had not done that. Was it because she felt impotent? Or did it signify, as Jean Chapuis thought, that she had lost control of her aerial dredger, and that it was drifting, abandoned in space?

"Necessary, all the same, to reassure the girls," Laridon suggested, taking one hand off the controls in order to scratch the back of his neck. He had a prescience that they were about to suffer some extraordinary thrust, but did not have the pretention of being able to hold Jean Chapuis's impetuosity in check any longer.

In any case, as he had no practical plan to propose in order to correct the imprudent attempt that the young engineer was contemplating, he had to give in.

Nevertheless, the worthy fellow took account of an idea suggested to him by his devotion.

"Go with God!" he said aloud, replacing his hand on the lever. "It's necessary to risk everything to get the captives back. For that, it's necessary for one of us to get inside, if possible. Only, M'sieur Jean, it won't be you. Without commanding you, it'll be me. That way, since I've got the wind up, I'll be more tranquil."

"I'll be much less so," replied Oronius' pupil. "You have a heart of gold, my dear Victor, and believe that I appreciate the sentiment that pushes you to want to take my place in an exploration you judge to be dangerous, but I wouldn't think much of myself if I hid behind that suggestion of your devotion.. What do you imagine that my Cyprienne would think of me? You don't want me to dishonor myself, I hope? Stay at your pilot's station, my friend. You're my reserve and my hope. If anything happened, I know that you wouldn't abandon me...or Cyprienne. So let me go and content yourself with facilitating my gymnastics by bringing me as a dead weight into proximity with that opening."

"That's no trouble, M'sieur Jean; I can deposit you in the hole without a jolt. But truly, it breaks my heart to see you go, especially to let you go alone. If Julep was capable of holding the broomstick for ten minutes, the two of us could go. At least, take that Indian cashmere with you."

"No," replied the engineer, firmly. "At one time, a certain Foch demonstrated that its necessary never to deplete one's reserve, except in case of urgency. Well, you and he constitute all my reserves; I don't want to weaken them, in the interest of those we want to save and I'll have to count on you if I fail."

"That's sworn, M'sieur Jean," the mechanic consented, emotionally. Then, affecting to joke, he added: "All the same, Boss, don't lead with the back of the spoon; better to succeed right away so we don't have to replace you. Linings, you see, never make good cloth."

He did not say any more, and contented himself with giving his superior one of the energetic handshakes that is worth as much as all protestations of devotion and affection.

Smiling, Jean Chapuis took the black and white hand that Julep dared to hold out to him, and shook it similarly.

"I have full confidence in you, my friends," he said, cordially.

The effusions stopped there. It was not a moment for Laridon to let himself go to emotion. He had too much need of his sang-froid to succeed in the delicate maneuver that would permit Cyprienne's fiancé to pass into the interior of the sphere. Fortunately, the mechanic was an ace and toyed with difficulties; in his hands, the Halcyon-Car was as docile as a well-schooled horse. Taking to the field he returned to the traveling ball, which he brushed in passing exactly at the height of the opening, as he had announced.

Having emerged from the cabin, Jean Chapuis had advanced to the tip of one of the wings, and was waiting for the favorable moment. When he aircraft brushed the sphere, he only had to push the panel and slide into the opening, which the panel returned automatically to close behind him, silently.

"Good luck, M'sieur Jean!" cried Laridon's vibrant voice.

"Good luck, master," continued Julep's echo.

Oronius' pupil was in place.

Chapter Fourteen
CONFRONTING A MYSTERY

As he set foot inside the strange machine, the young man's first concern was naturally to look around. He did not perceive anything suspect. As Cyprienne and Turlurette had declared, the sphere, completely hollow with the exception of a metallic floor, the upper side of which sealed the glass cap in which the young women must be, seemed absolutely empty of any human presence. It was only filled, as if by the flutter of wings, by the evolutions of silent machinery. Flaps, connecting-rods, transmissions and wheels were purring, beating, running and turning along the walls and above the bewildered engineer's head.

In fact, the mechanism was surprising; it did not resemble in any fashion the propulsive apparatus of dirigibles, or the engines of maritime or terrestrial transports.

Jean Chapuis suppressed his surprise and overcame his professional curiosity; he had not come to study a problem in mechanics, and he did not linger in that examination. He was in feverish haste to join Cyprienne and Turlurette and bring them back to the automatically-sealed opening. There would commence the most difficult part of his task: to get the young women and the lap-dogs, if possible, aboard the Halcyon, which it ought to be possible, by means of appropriate veering and looping, to maintain in continuous contact with it.

With the collaboration of his two devoted companions, he thought he could succeed in that audacious transshipment.

A kind of cage fitted between the machines remained free in the center of the sphere; it occupied its entire height. Jean divined an elevator and went to place himself on the metallic platform at its base. He only needed to press a malachite button forming a projection on one of the four columns framing the cage; immediately, without any shock, the platform rose up, caring him toward the interior ceiling of the sphere.

When he reached it he saw a trapdoor open automatically above his head, through which he emerged without having a gesture to make or a question to pose himself.

His desires were realized. He was in the glazed cabin, and Cyprienne and Turlurette were standing before him.

He had, of course, neither the inclination nor the time to examine that retreat, which, adapted to the summit of the sphere over its active works, affected a semi-lenticular form.

A little dog raced toward him, yapping with joy. It was Pipigg; Kukuss had disappeared.

Jean Chapuis scarcely noticed that, just as he only responded with a simple gesture to the cries of joy and the enthusiastic signals with which Laridon and Julep, aboard the Halcyon—which had returned above the sphere—saluted his appearance.

For the two brave fellows, the minutes that had elapsed since the entry of their master into the aerolith-prison must have been fecund in anguish, so the sight of Jean emerging safe and sound at the goal he had fixed had liberated them from that anguish. They thought it was proof that their fears had been exaggerated; no danger threatened Oronius' pupil.

For his part, however, Cyprienne's fiancé, who ought to have been at the peak of gladness, scarcely seemed disposed to associate himself with the demonstrations of the Halcyon's crew. A new and cruel anxiety was assailing him.

He remained icy and as if nonplussed in confrontation with Cyprienne, who no longer appeared to recognize him. In fact, he was looking at her with an expression of stupor and disquiet. That was because the uncustomary welcome of the young woman appeared to him to be extraordinary and, to say the least, disconcerting.

What was the matter with the two of them? Why was Cyprienne not throwing herself into her fiancé's arms? Why was the chambermaid, at the appearance of their liberator, not manifesting a noisy and delirious joy, as Pipigg was doing?

For it was a fact; only the minuscule lap-dog was welcoming Jean as usual, like an old acquaintance. In the eyes of the two young women, by contrast, one could have sworn that he seemed to be a stranger.

Yes, their attitude certainly have that impression, since they had not made a movement or a gesture at the entrance of the liberator; limiting themselves to turning toward him gazes that were empty of expression, but filled with a bleak sadness.

Jean Chapuis could not stand it; all the anxiety of the previous hours took hold of him again with a new vigor. He ran to Cyprienne and seized her hands.

"Cyprienne! My dear Cyprienne! What's wrong? Don't you recognize me?" he implored, in a tremulous voice.

In order to respond to him, that of Oronius' daughter remained perfectly calm and colorless. "Yes," she said. "You're Jean Chapuis, my fiancé."

"You're Monsieur the Engineer," said Turlurette, in her turn, with the same absence of emotion.

Disconcerted, the young man gazed at them alternately. Why that incomprehensible attitude? Oh, how he missed Oronius at that moment.

"Weren't you expecting me?" he asked,

"Certainly we were expecting you," Cyprienne affirmed, serenely.

There was only one possible explanation for such insensibility. The excess of the terror they had experienced, acting as a narcotic, must have anesthetized the two young women, momentarily taking away from them any means of expressing what they felt.

That's certainly it! Jean thought, to reassure himself. *They'll recover their spirits when they find themselves in safety, surrounded by calm.*

He resumed speaking to them gently, as if he were addressing invalids—let us say the word, madwomen.

"I've come to fetch you. You'd like to come with me, wouldn't you?"

They acquiesced with a nod of the head, without appearing to be in the least surprised or emotional. If their gazes did not express any opposition, nor did they mark the joy that ought to have animated them. They seemed to have become automata, uniquely capable of gestures and simple statements; they were passive and docile, as far from joy as from dolor.

It was as if something inside them had died.

Did that idea cross Jean's mind? His heart lurched frightfully. Immediately, he no longer had any desire but one: to get them out of that enigmatic sphere, the atmosphere of which put both thought and feeling to sleep, and to bring them back to pure air.

Was not that inertia, that indifference, so cruel for a fiancé to contemplate, the result of some pernicious influence of which the aerolith, created by a demonic hand, was the magnetic field?

As soon as that thought had crossed the young man's mind, he seized the hands of the captives.

"Come!"

Then he tried to draw them away, while Pipigg, as if he understood his intention, bonded around him, barking in fanfare. But his action was not completed, because it was in vain that he searched with his eyes for the trapdoor by which he had entered, in order to get out of the deceptive chamber. Moved by the infernal automatism that directed everything in the Spherus, the trapdoor had closed.

In his turn, Jean Chapuis was a prisoner, like Cyprienne and Turlurette, who had become so strangely cold and insensible.

The perspicacious engineer had glimpsed the terrible truth.

And yet, he still refused to believe it, and did not yield to it; he wanted to think that it was a simple accident. With the aid of his knowledge, it ought to be possible for him to remedy it. If the trapdoor had closed by accident, he thought, he ought to be able to open it again. Who could believe that an invisible and active will, watching at a distance what was happening inside the mechanically-animated ball, was able to intervene at its discretion and provoke the incidents? To accept that was to believe in the supernatural, in a sort of sorcery.

On reflection, however were the mysterious apparitions and all the evidence given thus far of an extraordinary power any different?

Jean Chapuis struggled in vain in that dilemma, To conserve the illusion that the unknown woman had nothing to do with the closure of the trap-door, as well as the incidents that had brought him into the sphere, it was necessary to deny that she disposed of a mysterious power. In all frankness, could he do that? Certainly not; the anterior facts were conclusive, alas.

Her fell to his knees and searched for the location of the trap-door. The grooves were invisible, there was no breach in the continuity. After a few minutes of futile searching, he had to concede that, whether it had been provoked by his persecutrix or not, the closure of the trap-door left him helpless.

Victor was right to mistrust, he thought. *In my precipitation, I've acted less sagely than a child. Henceforth, Oronius being no more, who will be capable of getting us out of this magical snare?*

Having risen to his feet, he mimed distress signals to Laridon and Julep, who were observing him through the unbreakable glass, with an increasing anxiety.

"I'm locked in!" he shouted to them at the top of his voice, through one of the air inlets. "The trap-door separating the interior has fallen shut and I can't find the mechanism to activate it."

"We can see that, M'sieur Jean!" replied Laridon and his companion, in a strange specimen of human phonography, almost simultaneously.

The Halcyon plunged, disappeared under the sphere, and reappeared on the other side.

Jean Chapuis was waiting anxiously. The evident consternation painted on the faces of his devoted companions informed him immediately of the negative results of their inspection. In any case, Laridon vociferated angrily: "Stuffed!

The orange is closed too. No chance of joining you. Oh, M'sieur Jean, why weren't you mistrustful? I knew you were going to fall into a trap."

The young man made a dejected gesture, which signified: *What's the point of recriminations? What's done is done. Better to think of what to do next.*

Laridon understood it thus, and at the same time he felt a slight remorse at having yielded to the initial impulse of chagrin instead of consoling his dear boss.

To redeem himself, he shouted: "You're not done for, M'sieur Jean. You'll get out of that mouse-trap. Think about your situation; Julep and I will do the same. I'll be damned if we can't figure out a way of getting you out of there. In the meantime, we won't leave you. Since the Sphere is carrying you off without it being possible for you to steer it, the Halcyon-Car will keep that prodigy company."

"Thank you, my worthy Victor!"

As you will have suspected, that conversation between the two aircraft was not without difficulty. On either side, many phrases had to be repeated or accompanied by explanatory gestures.

Claude Chappe,[10] dead for two hundred years, would surely have experienced a proud surprise if he had been able to see his semaphore telegraph reappearing in the year 2000.

---

[10] Claude Chappe (1763-1805) was a French inventor who in 1792 demonstrated a practical semaphore system that eventually spanned all of France. His system consisted of a series of towers, each within line of sight of others, each supporting a wooden mast with two crossarms on pivots that could be placed in various positions. The operator in a tower moved the arms to a sequence of positions, spelling out text messages in semaphore code. The operator in the next tower read the message through a telescope, then passed it on to the next tower. This was the first practical telecommunications system of the industrial age, and was used until the 1850s when electric telegraph systems replaced it.

Although very touched by the devotion of his mechanic, the engineer could not see the present or the future in a rosy light. Oh, if he had only found Cyprienne quivering with joy and tenderness! If, on seeing him, she had thrown herself into his arms in order to affirm her happiness and her confidence, he would have envisaged things from a very different angle. Knowing that he was in a trap would not have frightened him, since he would have found himself in the company of his fiancée, speaking, acting and loving, ready to encourage or to be protected. How happy he would have been then to be able to devote himself to fighting for her.

That was what he had wanted. Initially he had seen himself within reach of the goal, all his desires fulfilled, in penetrating the young women's prison. Unfortunately, the strange attitude of Cyprienne, her coldness and inertia, spoiled the joy of the reunion and posed a disquieting problem. Whence came that dolorous change, which Turlurette also presented? To what influence were the unfortunate captive obedient? What perfidious philter had been employed on them to cause their brains to atrophy to such a degree?

Facing them, gripped by a terrible doubt, Jean Chapuis felt that he would not recover his mental tranquility until that point had been clarified.

So, going to his fiancée again, he took hr hand a murmured a prayer: "Cyprienne, my gentle, my beloved Cyprienne, don't hold me in such rigor. What veil has been extended over your mind? One might think that you no longer experienced the tenderness for me that as my joy. We're together again after terrible and dolorous events I have a thousand questions to ask you. You must be impatient yourself to know how we were able to pick up your trail. You must also be anxious not to see your father among us."

At the memory of the recent catastrophe a contained sob troubled his voice.

By contrast, the young woman remained impassive. She was listening to him indifferently, as if the words he was pro-

nouncing were merely a tiresome noise devoid of any significance.

"Cyprienne," Jean Chapuis went on, anguish putting
droplets of sweat on his brow, "since the moment when mysterious enemies snatched you away from my affection, an abominable crime has been committed... but in contemplating you,
in searching to penetrate the enigmas of your visage, I'm
wondering if other crimes, even more frightful have not unfolded in this sphere between your abduction and my arrival
here? Here you are, looking at me like a stranger. You remain
ice-cold. You're manifesting neither joy, nor hope, nor
dread—no emotion of any sort. Why? I beg you, tell me what'
happening within you?"

"Nothing, absolutely nothing," said the young woman,
giving her beautiful eyes an expression of surprise.

And her pure gaze, in spite of a hint of atonality, did not
evoke any deception, any impression of duplicity or hypocri-
sy.

Before that face, now bleak, in which once had been reflected, as if through crystal, all the charming thoughts of
Oronius' daughter, her fiancé felt an atrocious despair.

He could not understand it. Doubt insinuated itself within
him. After all, was this really Cyprienne? He seemed to be in
the presence of a stranger. His own heart remained strangely
icy, and he had to make an effort not to abandon himself to an
impression of discouragement and indifference.

Indubitably, that originated from a maleficent influence.
Was he about to yield to the spell in his turn?

He repeated to himself: *It's Cyprienne, though! It's
Cyprienne. She's here, I'm holding her hand but I'm not feeling any relief... any joy... What's the matter with us? Are we
bewitched?*

Suddenly, just as he asked himself that question in the
secrecy of his consciousness and his heart, as if it were an
ironic response, the image of the unknown woman appeared to
him again.

He saw her again, in a halo of mist, mocking, triumphant and menacing.

He saw her again, and he had the sensation that she was really present, by virtue of her omnipotent will, invisible, impalpable and implacable.

He shuddered, and squeezed Cyprienne's hand.

Ought he not to be trembling for his dear fiancée, certainly a victim of the hatred of the unknown woman?

The enigma was there, behind that mocking face, which refused to give him the key.

The Spherus was keeping its mystery… the time had not yet come for Jean Chapuis to know it.

The image faded away...

Devastated, blaspheming his science, the pained young man took Cyprienne's hands again, plunged his anxious gaze into the empty stare that did not even attempt to escape his own.

"For pity's sake," he implored, "enlighten me! Recall your memories, my beloved Cyprienne. Tell me exactly what has happened since the moment when you were introduced by force into this accursed ball."

Motionless and immutable, without even the shadow of a shadow altering the serenity of her features, the young woman let fall: "I don't remember anything."

And Turlurette, as calm, and as distant, equally estranged from everything that had happened, confirmed in the fashion of Master Julep: "Don't remember… anything."

Chapter Fifteen
THE PRISONERS OF SPACE

Both of them! Abomination! Neither of them remembered any longer... they had lost their memory.

Was that possible?

However, they were still conscious when the sphere carried them away, surrounded by its cloud, and, pale and tremulous, they had responded to Jean Chapuis' questions.

Yes, they had been in full possession of their minds during the first phase of the pursuit.

It is finally necessary for us to report what had happened to them between the moment of their brutal abduction and the arrival of Jean Chapuis in the sphere.

Issued from the flanks of the mysterious bolide and provoked by the distant will that was directing its course, noxious vapors had then isolated them from their defenders. The Spherus had carried them away through space.

They had found themselves alone in the great sky, the two of them, with the two little dogs, anxious and agitated.

Where were they going? What strange voyage had they effectuated and into what region of the earth or the sky had the airborne cell taken them?

That, truly, they could not have said, because, vanquished by fatigue and emotion, or ceding to the influence of soporific vapors, they had fallen asleep.

When they awoke, they realized that they must have been removed or transported during their slumber. In fact, not figuratively, but veritably, they were no longer in the sphere, the fantastic apparatus with the silent machinery. No movement, no matter how light, was causing their bodies to oscillate, like that produced very recently in the course of a maneuver or change of direction of the trawling apparatus.

They were lying on rich cushions in the middle of a domed room worthy of a palace, the style of which immediately enlightened Cyprienne.

"We're in India!" she murmured. "Is it possible that our abductor is a rajah?"

Involuntarily, she admired the splendor of the décor that surrounded her and the marvelous light spread by the open bay windows.

Impregnated with memories of voyages accomplished in the company of her father, the young woman imagined the panorama that ought to be perceptible.

Doubtless, at the bottom of the stairways of terraces, on to which the bays must pen, the Ganges or some other river was flowing, bathing the foundations of the palace with its sacred waters.

Quitting the cushions that had served as her couch, Cyprienne got up in order to go and lean on the interior balustrade, for the bay was sealed by a double plate of glass enclosing an intermediate air.

Turlurette followed her mistress.

Together, the two young women uttered an exclamation:

"Where are we, then?"

It was certainly not a terrestrial landscape; the mirage of India vanished at the first glance darted outside.

No river, merely an ocean of cloud extending as far as the eye could see, down below, like an immense fleecy carpet.

Disconcerted, Cyprienne abandoned the bay.

Was she in some aerial palace then, around which complaisant clouds extended their veil to hide the sight of the earth?

Footsteps glided over the carpet.

Cyprienne and Turlurette turned round and found themselves in the presence of a young Chinese woman.

She considered the prisoners with a fearful and melancholy curiosity that was not exempt from sympathy.

Cyprienne sensed it with so much certainty that she did not hesitate to smile at the young woman as she asked: "Who are you?"

"Ypu may call me Mandarinette, Madame," replied the Chinese woman in a timid voice.

"Is this palace yours?"

Mandarinette made a fearful gesture. "Nothing is mine, here or elsewhere," she protested. "It's me who belongs to..."

She hesitated.

"To whom?" questioned Cyprienne, increasing her mildness and benevolence. "You can respond to me without fear, my girl. I'm not wicked and won't betray you. Alas if you're subject to some kind of slavery, the position that awaits me can scarcely be any better. My companion and I arrived here as prisoners... and I don't even know into whose power we've fallen or in what part of the world we are."

"The world?" repeated Mandarnette, with a astonished expression, which showed that she did not grasp the significance of the word.

"The Earth, if you refer," Cyprienne explained.

"The Earth?"

That expression seemed as strange as the other to the young Chinese woman. But in fact, in spite of her appearance, to what race did she belong?

"Have we not descended among human beings, then?" asked the daughter of Oronius, anxiously.

"Human beings?" repeated the little slave, in the same manner as before. Then, sketching a gesture of ignorance, she finished by saying: "Here, we're outside everything."

"You can't tell us where we are, then?" exclaimed Cyprienne.

"That won't be convenient to give our news," sighed Turlurette, evidently thinking about Laridon.

"How does one arrive where we are, then? Doubtless you weren't born here. You must at least be able to tell us what kind of voyage you accomplished in order to reach this place," Jean Chapuis' fiancée insisted.

The young Chinese woman's features contracted. She put one of her frail hands to her forehead and her face reflected a dolorous expression. In a melancholy tone, she affirmed: "Here, one no longer has memories."

The two young women considered her fearfully. The fantastic, which had not ceased to surround them since the beginning of their adventure, was not relaxing its grip. On the contrary, it was tightening. How could they resist the invasion of fear?

"Oh, I beg you," said Cyprienne, putting her hands together, "tell us who commands in his palace? What names to they have? You must now the names of your masters."

"The masters?" replied Mandarinette, meekly. "They're..." A great frisson than shook her from head to toe interrupted her thought. "Oh!" she exclaimed. "There she is! She's calling me. I must go..."

She fell silent; her head inclined over her breast; her eyes closed and she remained as motionless as a marble statue.

"Mandarinette!" cried Cyprienne, frightened. "What's the matter?"

But no matter how she shook the little woman, she did not obtain any sign of sensibility from her. Her body, which thought seemed to have deserted, had suddenly acquired a frightful rigidity. Oscillating between the hands of the terrified Cyprienne, it suddenly collapsed and remained inert on the carpet.

Going pale, the young woman and her maid stepped back, holding one another by the hand. They did not understand anything of what had happened, but nevertheless had the intuition of witnessing the manifestation of a power unknown to them, of a tenebrous character.

"She's calling me; I must go," the young girl had said. And her body was lying there, inert, while the thought that had animated it a moment before seemed to have departed. Could the mind escape matter, then, at the summons of a strange will?

121

Cyprienne and Turlurette would not take long to experience themselves the response that it was appropriate to make to that question.

Trembling and silent, they were huddled in a corner of the room, half-lying on the cushions. Suddenly, Oronius' daughter felt a singular impression within her. An electric current appeared to traverse her body, which immediately became so light that she had the illusion of rising up and floating in the air.

She had got up without having to make the slightest effort, like a sylphide snatched from the ground by an imperceptible gust of wind. Oh, veritably, she must be disengaged from her heavy envelope, since the movements whose necessity she conceived were executed by her as soon as she had formulated the intention mentally.

She headed toward the door—or, more exactly, she thought was heading, for she felt imperiously drawn in that direction. At the same moment as she imagined herself drawing away from the cushions, however—an unexpected demonstration of her own ubiquity—she had the amazement of perceiving herself, still lying down.

She drew away... at least, she had the sensation of doing so... but she left her body behind, in the place that she had quit.... her body, apparently asleep or derived of sentiment, as Mandarinette's had been a moment before.

However, Cyprienne still had a body. She could no longer sense it, but she could still see it. She was walking; she was acting; it, on the contrary, remained immobile and visible, if not palpable.

Was she then duplicated, in two forms, one of which—the one that was active and conserved the faculty of thought—was only an appearance?

For the moment, Cyprienne was far from being able to ask herself questions, for in a space of time that was absolutely inappreciable and certainly inferior to a tenth of a second, she found that she had gone through the doorway of the room, traversed various galleries that she glimpsed in a flash, and

122

penetrated into another room whose dimensions remained imprecise because of the mysterious light that reigned there.

There, sitting on a divan, a man and a woman were waiting, watching Cyprienne arrive.

The man was short and round, with a powerful head on the hideous face of which the worst instincts were inscribed: immeasurable pride, ferocity, domination and violence.

Of a mysterious beauty, which did not seem to belong to this world, the woman was entirely clad in a transient veil, which allowed her pale face and sparkling eyes to be divined rather than seen. Under that gaze, of an almost unsustainable intensity, Cyprienne had the impression of being consumed by the radiance of an ardent flame.

The man was also staring at her, but the only impression that his gaze caused was repulsion. Instinctively, Cyprienne detested him and was scornful of him, while the unknown woman inspired an inexplicable terror in her, at the same time as a fascination, against which she tried in vain to struggle.

The man sniggered.

"Here she is, then! You're admirable, Yogha. You keep all your promises. Yes, on my faith, it's the pretty daughter of that imbecile Oronius. She's fallen well to hear the news, the slut. Eh! Stop here, beauty, and open your ears."

It was not that coarsely uttered order that Jean Chapuis' fiancée obeyed, but an imperceptible suggestion of the unknown woman, who immediately interrupted the impression of movement with her.

The fat man certainly had a brow whose dimensions indicated a rare intellectual power; despite his ugliness and the deplorable penchants in the service of which he put his faculties, his brain certainly placed him above the common run of mortals. In appearance, he remained abominably material, and formed a shocking contrast with his ethereal companion. A glance from the latter was sufficient to make the most recalcitrant individual understand and obey; her companion, by contrast, took pleasure in speaking loudly and accompanying his words with brutal gestures. By those mans, he did not always obtain such a rapid response. Like almost all his overly obese gestures, he possessed one of those voices whose shrill intonations always astonish, coming from such a mastodon.

Turning toward the tapestry, he launched in a fluty roar: "Come in, Wiwar!"

It was as if Cyprienne's ear had been flayed.

At that order, Oronius' laboratory assistant, the servant with the suspect manner in whom the clairvoyant Laridon had divined a traitor, advanced in the same sly manner. Bowing in a servile fashion, he pronounced: "Hail to the omnipotent Master! Hail to the genius Hantzen!"

Hantzen!

We know that name. It had made Paris tremble when the challenge brought by the mysterious waves had been announced to the world by the "voice of the Tower."

So Hantzen was this repulsive man? The proud rival of Oronius, after an eclipse of many years, was avid to hear his name pronounced and to avenge the humiliation that his old defeat had inflicted on him.

What was he doing next to this woman? What role was she playing in his regard?

He was a hippopotamus and she, a gazelle! A strange couple! A disparate association if ever there was one. Which of the two was empowering the other?

With an imperious gesture, Hantzen had Wiwar come forward.

"Well? What happened? Speak! Is Paris annihilated?"

"No, Master."

In making that response, which he divined to be disappointing, Wiwar's fugitive gaze avoided the furious pupils of Otto Hantzen, but could not hide from the luminous and penetrating radiance of the unknown woman's eyes.

However, she was visibly disdainful of him. Addressing Hantzen, she murmured: "I told you, Otto; your nebulous accumulators simulated, in verity, clouds very similar to real ones, but you didn't have an adequate electrical pressure and your hurricane ran into a superior power. Your rival has thwarted it."

Convulsed with rage, the monster hissed: "I don't doubt your marvelous power, Yogha. You've furnished me with many proofs of your faculty of vision at a distance. Don't find it bad, however, that I desired confirmation by an eye witness of that incomprehensible check."

"That confirmation Wiwar has just given you," riposted the implacable woman. "Your envoy couldn't belie me with what he has seen with his mortal eyes. Oronius defeated you by capturing the lightning that you claimed to have unleashed."

Hantzen was acting in a demented fashion, making adipose waves roll over his pectorals and his Buddhaesque abdomen.

"Is that true?" he howled, withering Wiwar with his gaze, whom he held to be responsible for the failure.

The laboratory assistant bowed his head. "That's right, Master," he confessed. "The lightning bolts came of their own accord to lodge in a reservoir in the laboratory; one might have thought that the scientist was collecting them one by one from the sky, in order to put them in storage. The lightning only fell once."

At the peak of exasperation, Otto Hantzen was looking for something to crush. "You're lying!"

For want of any other object, his fury fell upon the envoy, as in ancient times, when Emperors did not hesitate to put bearers of bad news to death.

Wiwar dreaded that fate and hastened to add, in order to appease Hantzen's wrath: "Omnipotent Master, your rival is dead!"

At that incredible declaration, Hantzen was dazzled, and thought he might choke.

"Oronius? Dead?" he cried, finally, straightening up, ready to be delirious with joy. His eyes devoured Wiwar, and did not see the ironic smile that was born on Yogha's lips.

"Yes! The old man is dead! Everything blew up!" proclaimed Wiwar, energetically, delighted by the effect he had produced. "The famous magical Villa sank into the ground with a good part of Belleville."

Impassively, Yogha confirmed with a nod of the head the triumphant glance that Hantzen directed at her. "That's true. Oronius' Villa sank into the fire of the ground."

"Into the fire? You saw that too?" said Hantzen, trying to make his tone ironic. "Why didn't you tell me that?"

The mysterious Yogha made no reply; she contented herself with shrugging her shoulders, attaching a gaze of scornful pity to her companion.

Exultant, Hantzen disdained that gaze. He stamped his feet, and might have danced had he not been afraid of a probable fall.

"Oronius and his shack have blown up! I'm victorious, then!"

The smile still lingered on Yogha's lips. She remained silent, but an imperceptible sigh raised her breast, which seemed delectable.

"And the volcano—for it was a volcano—spat out the skeleton of Oronius, to which Paris gave an imposing funeral," Wiwar concluded. "Everything supports the belief, of course, that Jarrousse left his hide in that crater."

"No matter," replied Hantzen, jovially. "Jarrousse's hide against Oronius' isn't too dear an exchange. I'd have given yours as well, my dear Wiwar, and many others into the bargain."

The laboratory assistant made a grimace. He found the pleasantry indecent. Laridon would have said "salty." But there was no point in protesting against the gibe. Furthermore, Hantzen was now in an excellent mood.

"Tell me, Yogha, did you also see the burial of Oronius?" he joked. "Oh, you're lucky to be able to displace yourself at will through time and space while your body remains in the house! I'd have liked to be at that little celebration! Did you hear the speeches?"

"Paris gave the skeleton an imposing funeral," pronounced the enigmatic Yogha, attaching an indefinable gaze to her companion.

"Good riddance!" growled Hantzen. "Let's share his heritage. To me, his glory; to me, the empire of the world! And to you his daughter... with, a little later, the man who was to be his son-in-law." He sniggered facetiously, and then became serious again. "I must ask you for one more service, my dear... if it's possible for you to render it to me. For it's truly... it's a little service..."

"Keep talking. Don't I have the habit of satisfying you?"

With a gesture, Hantzen dismissed Wiwar.

Cyprienne—or, at least, the thinking image of Cyprienne—remained alone with the couple; but the couple did not seem to attach any importance to her presence.

"Here it is" said Hantzen. "Perhaps you're going to find me very indiscreet. I'd like to know Oronius' secrets... if he hasn't taken them to the tomb. You, who see everything, do you know a means of informing me?"

Yogha inclined her head. "I can have him interrogated."

"Who?" said Hantzen, alarmed.

"Oronius."

"But he's dead."

The strange creature pursed her lips. "What does it matter? Perhaps he'll reply anyway. Besides which, I wouldn't be sorry myself to know what is going on in that skull."

"Oh, nothing at all can be happening there any longer," sniggered Hantzen.

"Who knows?" murmured Yogha. But those words were pronounced too quietly; Hantzen could not hear them.

"How will you proceed?" he asked.

The smile of the unknown woman suddenly took on a cruelty compared to which that of her companion was honeyed. She started at Cyprienne and her eyes emitted a flame.

"Through her," she announced. "It has to be through her."

Then, addressing the young woman and extending one of her hands toward her brow, she pronounced, imperiously: "Follow my thought! Go where I wish... enter and see!"

After a moment's silence, during which she appeared to concentrate and exteriorize all her strength, she added: "Say what you see! I order you to do it!"

Something strange happened within Cyprienne. Revolted by the unknown woman's words, she wanted to stiffen herself, to rest the order; but she felt herself impelled, curbed like a frail reed. She glided through space with a vertiginous speed.

Where was she going?

Abruptly, she had the sensation of an impact, and it seemed to her that she retraced her steps. She found herself back in the room, before Hantzen and Yogha. She advanced, pushed by the same mysterious force, of which she was the prey.

She advanced toward Hantzen. She stared at him. And suddenly, she spoke. Oh, it was terrible!

"*He* is Otto Hantzen," she said, in a mechanical voice, a voice that was not obedient to her own personality and seemed to be emerging from a strange throat. "*She* is Yogha, the daughter of Yoghis and the heiress of their power. Otto was wandering through the world, humiliated and vanquished. He encountered her. She, Yogha, saw an instrument in that tramp. She offered him an alliance..."

"Stop! I wish it!"

Convulsed, stiffened, braced as if to resist a formidable, invisible assault, Yogha had just stood up in order to hurl those words, brushing Cyprienne with her two extended hands.

An intense amazement was painted on Hantzen's face.

"What is she saying?" he stammered. "But that's my history...! It's *our* history! Why is she saying that?"

Yogha did not reply; breathless, she was visibly making desperate efforts to impose her will on Cyprienne, undisciplined and rebellious.

"Get away!" she cried, wildly. "Wake up! Wake up! I command it."

And she fell back exhausted, on to her cushions.

But for Cyprienne, that long nightmare vision was abruptly effaced, at the same time as the room, the divans and Hantzen disappeared.

Exhausted, as if after a night of nightmares, the young woman found herself lying in her original place, next to Turlurette and Mandarinette.

Both of them were looking at her fearfully...

Chapter Sixteen
YOGHA'S HATRED

Yogha's exhaustion only lasted a few minutes. Then she remained curled up, plunged in a grim mental contention. In that state, her strange eyes threw forth magnetic flashes, which interrupted gleams of anguish.

Evidently, Yogha had just suffered a defeat, and was devouring her rage silently.

But how had the will of the frail Cyprienne been able to oppose victoriously one that had just revealed itself to be possessed of the inexplicable power of the yoghis, adepts of a mysterious sect of India, venerated and terrible magi whose superhuman faculties seemed to accomplish miracles.

That fact, Hantzen could not think of denying. He had just witnessed it.

He was astonished by it, but he welcomed it with a sort of mocking satisfaction; it was like a revenge of his science—too often inferior in its results—against the secret practices of Yogha, of which he was jealous, while pretending to treat them disdainfully as conjuring tricks.

"Aha!" he jeered. "You've encountered your mistress, it seems to me. That sly little girl, without having the air of touching it, had just shown herself to be as indocile as she is rebellious to your influence."

Yogha shrugged her pale shoulders, semi-visible under the veil. "In fact," she admitted, calmly, "I wasn't able to impose my will on her. For the first time, I collided with a will equal to mine."

"Equal? Superior, you mean my dear," Hantzen insisted, with an ungallant stubbornness. "In the end, admit it, it was you who had to capitulate and interrupt the experiment."

Yogha must have been far above the mockery of such a boor. She did not allow herself to be moved. "You're right," she acquiesced simply. Then, with a slight smile, she added: "I consider myself so completely beaten that, in order to reduce that stubborn young woman and achieve my objectives, I'll be obliged to have recourse to your enlightenment."

That was, for Hantzen, an opportunity to feign modesty and to declare that he did not see very clearly how scientific knowledge could prevail where the occult forces at his partner's disposal had failed. His soul, kneaded by pride, refrained from making any appeal to that restraint; he was rendered extremely credulous as soon as anyone flattered his vanity. He therefore welcomed Yogha's declaration as a merited homage.

"Aha! You're come round," he chuckled, with a coarse, satisfied laugh. "You admit that, after all, Old Hantzen's knowledge has some good, and that in its genre, it too can realize prodigies!"

"I'm convinced of it," Yogha replied, gravely. "And I'll immediately offer you the opportunity to furnish the proof. Do you know what you're going to do with that child? An experiment... one of your dear experiments..."

Leaning toward Oronius' rival, she whispered a few words in his ear, which made his cruel eyes gleam.

"Certainly, my dear Yogha, I'm perfectly temped by that little game," he assured her, warmly. Then, arrogantly, he added: "And I think that I won't fail!"

"That's my hope."

After clapping her hands, Yogha extended them toward the wall. Wiwar reappeared.

"Take the young women to Lord Hantzen's laboratory," she commanded.

"Good!" laughed Hantzen. "You talk like everyone now. Decidedly, that little check has done you good. Here you are, a convert to common sense. Congratulations! And believe me, my dear, you won't repent of abandoning forever these mystical fashions. Between us, they can only delude the ignorant. Does that species still exist? I've never believed it, I who am speaking. There's only science... only *my* science."

The conceit with which the fat man emphasized that phrase was so insupportable that it ought to have summoned a revolt and riposte on the part of the Yogh,

But no! Yogha did not give the impression of having been touched by that stupid provocation; she contented herself with smiling.

A few moments later, Otto Hantzen, utterly penetrated by his importance, made his entrance into a strangely furnished room that he called, pompously, his laboratory, and whose aspect and installation were strongly reminiscent of the torture chambers of the Middle Ages.

Cyprienne and Turlurette were already there, in the flesh and bone this time. They were pale and trembling. Next to them, no less terrified, was poor Mandarinette.

Hantzen's wide eyes strayed complaisantly over the group formed by the three young women.

"Aha!" he sniggered, amorously massaging his enormous belly, which affected the form and dimensions of the egg of an Atlantosaurus. "Here, then, are my subjects!"

Perhaps he should have said, with more verity: *Here are my victims.*

But pride blinded him, and it was with an absolute unconsciousness that he pronounced: "Don't tremble, my darlings. You belong, for the time being, to the greatest scientist of the century! Well, yes, Mademoiselle Oronius, not to displease you, to the greatest scientist of the century... a title that ornamented very unduly your charlatan of a father. Once again, don't worry—I operate painlessly!"

His rictus was frightful, sufficient to cause gooseflesh...

Behind him, standing voluntarily in the shadows, there was Yogha, whose gaze, and the slight movement of her mouth, were more frightful still, who was covering them intently with the ardent embers of her terrible eyes.

An hour later, Cyprienne and Turlurette, not accompanied this time by Mandarinette, reappeared in the doorway of the bizarre laboratory.

Cyprienne and Turlurette, not transformed at all in appearance, and yet, how greatly changed!

They were no longer trembling; they were no longer pale; they were walking with an astonishingly calm stride.

Alas, it was precisely that immutable calm, the kind of unfailing serenity—or rather, an absolute, abnormal insensibility—that would have inspired a profound pity in anyone that hazard had enabled to study the condition of the young women.

That calm, one could not fail to have the impression, could only be the result of some abominable sorcery.

Yogha and Hantzen no longer had any need to appear in order to direct their prisoners. With the assurance of automata, all of whose gestures are imperiously regulated by a mechanism, they advanced without the shadow of a hesitation through the galleries. They emerged thus into an immense room with a high ceiling. A bizarre procedure ensured its illumination. The compartmentalized ceiling seemed to be lost in space, supported by twelve enormous pillars of radiant metal rubbed with jellyfish oil.

At the median extremity of the room there was a framed opening resembling the opening of a fireplace. The young women placed themselves at the entrance to that covert and Cyprienne called: "Pipigg! Kukuss!"

Almost immediately, the two little lapdogs precipitated into the room and bounded toward their mistress, yapping joyfully. They seemed to be ready to devour her with caresses.

Then a singular reversion occurred; two paces away from them, both dogs stopped abruptly. Pricking up their ears anxiously they began to howl mortally.

"Pipigg! Kukuss!" Cyprienne repeated.

The appeal of the familiar voice only decided Pipigg. He came to sniff his young mistress, with a certain reluctance, and allowed himself to be caressed, with a piteous expression.

Kukess acted differently. Evading the attempt of Turlurette, who bent down in order to take him in her arms, he seemed frightened. Uttering a dull growl and, turning around, his tail between his legs, he fled with more rapidity than he had arrived.

Placidly, without astonishment or giving evidence of the slightest displeasure, the chambermaid stood up again.

Holding Pipigg, who was licking her hands and lamenting, Cyprienne had just gone into the covert; Turlurette joined her there. Behind them, sliding soundlessly in its grooves, the door closed behind them.

Immediately, in that closed tube, it was as if they were sucked up, lifted and carried away by an irresistible air pressure. Like two dead leaves, colliding with one another and seeming to pursue one another, they rose into that wind tunnel, at the exit of which the airflow, suddenly easing, let them fall on to a metallic floor.

A click was heard, than the impact of a steel plate rejoining its emplacements, and finally the purr of a motor.

The two young women had just been reincarcerated inside the Spherus, which resumed its course through space again, taking them back toward the Halcyon-Car, Laridon, Julep and Jean Chapuis, for the greater emotion of the latter.

In appearance, nothing had changed. Only the absence of the flighty and capricious Kukuss could have offered evidence of that secret port of call...

Chapter Seventeen
THE EXCHANGED SOULS

Why that new machination, for the success of which the hateful Yogha had called upon the science of the vainglorious Otto Hantzen?

One thing was certain: it had succeeded. The prisoners of the sphere, sent back by her through space, but still and more than ever subject to her imperious power—had drawn Jean Chapuis into the trap intentionally left open, which had closed upon the overconfident engineer.

In fact, was it not as if, by the same coup. Hantzen's strange ally had capture the Halcyon-Car and its passengers, since, in order not to abandon Cyprienne's fiancé, the aircraft was condemned to follow the course of the sphere?

Imprisoned with Cyprienne and Turlurette, Jean Chapuis was reduced to complete impotence.

Freer in their movements, but without being able to do anything in favor of their young master, Laridon and Julep, drawn into the adventure, had to be considered, practically, as prisoners, like him.

This time, the habitual ingenuity of the mechanic appeared to be found wanting; Laridon racked his brain, and abused poor Julep, who thought nothing of it, but he could not find a solution to the problem.

"A thousand million Ottomans, as the late Claude Farrère[11] would have sworn at his Turks," he repeated, exasperated. "What have we got in this thing to make that sphere stop? Yes what is there to do, M'sieur Jean? It was certain in advance that it only opened its belly to capture him! All the same, it's annoying to be here, two cables away, while he's

---

[11] Claude Farrère, pseudonym of Frédéric-Charles Bargone (1876-1957). French author of novels, many of which are based in exotic locations as Istanbul, Saigon, or Nagasaki.

banged up with Mamzelle Cyprienne and that scatterbrain Turlurette—who, said without reproach, doesn't give the impression of paying much attention to my sympathetic photography! Yes, it's a little enraging to see them there and not to be able either to stop their vehicle or help them get out of it. Not to mention that they've got faces straight enough to stop a clock. The situation doesn't seem to lead them to expansion—what a look! Oh la la! Call those expressions amorous! One would think they were in a fridge. Pass for the kid Turlurette; I can admit that she isn't smiling, since she's separated from her flirt, which is I, but the other two! What are they offering? Let's see, M'sieur Jean! Reflect, Mamzelle Cyprienne! Not necessary to break like bottles. After all, you're together. You can have a party."

But those amiable encouragements—which, in any case, could not reach the ears of the fiancés—had no effect consternation continued to darken the features of the engineer confronted by the strangely closed expressions of the two young women. Only witnessing that scene from a distance, also embarrassed by the refraction of the armored glass that separated them from the prisoners, Laridon and Julep could not understand it. They had an intuition, however, that some new contrariety must be opposing the engineer's projects and that all was not well inside the airborne sphere.

So, regulating his speed to that of the flying prison and maneuvering in such a way as to maintain the Halcyon in permanent contact with it, Victor had the idea of using the wireless telephone—the Spherus, an ultrascientific apparatus, was bound to be equipped with one—in order to attempt to have a less awkward conversation with Jean Chapuis.

"Ahoy! M'sieur Jean, can you hear me?" he asked, after an initial appeal. He knew that his voice ought to reach the ears of the three prisoners automatically.

Let us explain: the usage of particular receivers had been abandoned a long time ago; aboard navigational apparatus especially, marine or aerial, installations now comported amplifiers permitting appeals to resonate throughout the space occupied by the passengers, without any regard to partitions or compartments, and, in consequence, to impose on their attention at any time without obliging them to change place.

In the same way, once the equipment was activated automatically by the initiative of the transmitter, those summon, in order to make themselves heard, had no need of the intermediary of any special instrument. They responded from wherever they were, and the vibrations of their voice, registered by an arrangement of plates and microphones, were launched toward the transmitting posy.

Laridon therefore saw Jean Chapuis turn his head mechanically at his appeal, and respond to it.

"Of course."

They could talk. Everything was working. The dialogue was engaged.

"Well, M'sieur Jean, it seems that you've been swallowed, as we thought you might be. What if we were to try to break the legs of the damned pirate that's carrying you away?"

"How would you do that, my poor Victor?"

"I don't know, but good God of wood, it's up to you to find a way. You're on the spot. Don't be afraid—clever fellow that you are, and an expert engineer, it seems to me that you'll quickly figure out where the heart of the mechanism is and take control of the direction of the flying puffball."

Jean Chapuis shook his head. "You're forgetting, my lad, that I'm locked in this glass cabin and that it's quite impossible for make to carry out the study in question.

"Break down the door."

"How? With what? It's invisible, and we're lying on a sheet of chrome steel."

"Damn! If I could pass you a petard to blow open the locker..."

"Along with the cabin we're in, and us. Thank you very much. Good idea, my friend. It's as if you were going to free us by firing a shell that would disembowel the sphere. Evidently, the door would be open, but we'd fall into the void without having had time to go through it. On reflection, your idea doesn't seem very practical, for you'd only have the recourse of picking us up in pieces."

"Don't say such things, M'sieur Jean. You're sending shivers down my spine... and making Julep change color... which makes one more. Let's leave the petards alone. Nothing to be done, then?"

"Alas."

"Don't say that, boss. It's too disheartening."

"It's the case, unfortunately, my dear Victor." The mechanic heard the engineer add, in a dispirited murmur: "If only I didn't have another worry!"

"What's upsetting you, M'sieur Jean?"

The other shuddered. "Nothing," he muttered, darting an involuntary glance at the impossible Cyprienne. "You couldn't understand. For the moment, we can only allow ourselves to be guided by events."

"Which is to say, be carried away by that damned flying flea. That's simple enough—but how far is it taking us?"

"As far as it wishes."

"And if it wanders through the sky like this perpetually? Will it be necessary to follow on its heels?"

"As long as your devotion doesn't weary, my friend."

"Then I'm in it for life, Boss, believe me. Victor Laridon isn't a quitter. Let's say no more about that. It's decided; we'll follow. Damnation! I was told in my youth that I'd end up as a star in the sky, going round and round... and as good as the Moon."

"That won't be our fate," Jean Chapuis assured him. "Without being able to specify the goal for which we're bound, I don't believe I'm mistaken in affirming that this sphere isn't gravitating in the fashion of the planets; it has a destination. No," he continued, becoming excited, "it isn't flying at random; it's carrying us toward the key to the enigma...all the enigmas presented to my mind. May I soon, at the risk of all perils, find myself face to face with our persecutrix, in order to know... to comprehend..."

Again he turned toward the indifferent Cyprienne.

Then, fearing that he would be indiscreet if he continued listening, Laridon interrupted the communication.

The visage of the fiancé expressed an ardent interrogation. "You, to comprehend you," he repeated, considering the young woman as if he were certain that she could not hear him, and could not even see him.

To comprehend the mystery that I have before my eyes and which is tearing my heart. Alas, here, facing me is the face of my beloved Cyprienne, but I sense that she's very distant, more absent then if millions of leagues separated us. My hand can touch hers, and yet, she isn't here. Where is she? I can see her features, her silhouette, but it seems to me that it isn't her. It's her body, to be sure—but her soul is no longer inhabiting it. What to believe? How to explain?

He darted a glance at Turlurette.

"If this bizarre amnesia had only struck Cyprienne," he murmured, pensively, "I could conclude that it was a new game of the unknown woman, invented to torture me. But what need would she have to influence a petty servant in the same way? That's inexplicable. She might want to raise the barrier of a kind of mental separation between my fiancée and me, but there's no reason to apply the same treatment to Turlurette. How can I find out what's happened? How?"

He put his head in his hands.

Neither Oronius' daughter nor the young chambermaid seemed to pay any heed to Jean Chapuis' anguish. The extraordinary insensibility that seemed to have paralyzed them was prolonged without any amelioration... inexorably.

In truth, if that was only a cruel game, a refinement of malevolence invented by Yogha; if, by indulging in it, she only wanted to inflict an unexpected torment on the unfortunate fiancé, it is necessary to admit that she had attained her objective. Invaded by an inexpressible despair, the unfortunate sensed his reason vacillating.

Cyprienne... his beloved and tender Cyprienne, was enduring his presence as she would have endured the presence of a stranger; for him, she had suddenly become the most indifferent of women. And, sensing that he was the victim of un-known forces, against which he could not react, he dreaded having lost his happiness forever.

A wall of ice separated him from his fiancée; to his most ardent supplications, to the passionate evocations he made of their past, she only responded with mechanical phrases, se-lected from the ready-made formulae that one pronounces idly and which signify nothing.

No cry attained that mysteriously sterilized thought. Cyprienne's mind was asleep, in a slumber so profound that on careful examination the suspicion arose that no heart was any longer beating in her breast.

Had someone stolen it?

Had she been robbed of her soul?

An atrocious suspicion, a torturing thought. In that ago-nizing expectation, Jean Chapuis tore his own breast with his fingernails.

Who could return his Cyprienne to him? Who could ex-plain the accursed mental malaise by which she seemed to be afflicted?

Suddenly, the same impression of trouble and malaise by which he had already been seized aboard the Halcyon-Car, when two adverse wills seemed to be disputing within him, made itself felt.

Like radiations, thoughts and desires traversed him, im-mediately countered and paralyzed by contrary thoughts and desires.

To begin with, a phrase—surely absurd—crossed his mind with an incomprehensible persistence: *It isn't Cyprienne.* Then, immediately, another, more logia: *Don't allow yourself to be abused; it's her.*

And like two alternating voices, the two thoughts were repeated, harassing him without either one prevailing and above all, without permitting Jean Chapuis, their common receiver, to comprehend either where they were coming from or to suspect the perfidious or friendly influence that was emitting them by turns.

Who could be suggesting that doubt? Who was seeking to plunge him into a further horror?

Who was striving, with that implacable tenacity, to reduce him to despair?

Like the first time, when he had acted to resist or to yield to the diabolical will that summoned him toward the sphere, he thought of the unknown woman. Only that hostile being could manifest herself in that subtle fashion. But he sensed another influence within him, hostile to the first.

That one, of course, seemed more difficult to identify.

Can the Dead not see us and guide us? What if it were my master, Oronius?

A new problem: how to discern the voice from beyond the tomb from the equally immaterial one that was making itself heard simultaneously?

One of the voices whispered to Jean Chapuis: *You want to know? Hypnotize Cyprienne. She'll recover her memory. She'll tell you the secret.*

But the other voice immediately added: *Who will guarantee its verity? Perhaps the enemy will lie via that mouth.*

Skepticism and suspicion divided Jean Chapuis' mind increasingly. He was struggling in the bosom of a nightmare, and the two voices ended up appearing to him to be equally infernal and hostile.

Were not those doubts, born of their contradictory suggestions, uniquely destined to torture him more?

He tried to reject them both, no longer to listen to either of the voices, without taking account of the fact that, by virtue of that passivity, he would be giving victory to the one that was counseling him to abstain.

He thought momentarily that he had recovered calm; the conflict within his seemed to be appeased. The two voices fell silent.

Suddenly, an irresistible flux of will-power impelled him; he acted against his inclination. Heading impulsively toward Cyprienne, he stared at her and enveloped her with magnetic passes.

"Sleep! I want it!"

He felt strong; he felt resolute. He was in control.

However, the dormant Cyprienne, inert and almost torpid a moment ago, defended herself. Now she confronted him, rebellious to his influence, struggling to escape it, struggling and turning her gaze away. It was her, now, who seemed to have become the battleground of the contest of the invisible powers.

Jean Chapuis took account of that. He was in the presence of a prey that two forces were disputing, one that held her captive and did not want to let go, the other that was striving to remove her from the power of the first.

But all that was happening outside Jean; he was only a simple spectator of the horrific struggle—and also an instrument, for, stiffened by the force that possessed him, he was striving to impose his will on Cyprienne's revolt.

And again, abruptly, he sensed that one of the wills—the second—coming to the aid of his, was about to give him the means to triumph.

The revolt that was shaking Oronius' daughter calmed down; she ceased to struggle and the desired statement—heard, however, with what fright!—finally sprang from her lips.

"I'm not Cyprienne. I'm Turlurette, simultaneously deprived of my appearance and my thought."

Then, pointing at Turlurette, who did not seem to understand, or to be interested in, what was happening, the apparent form of Cyprienne concluded: "And that one, to whom my face has been given, is no more Turlurette than I'm Cyprienne. It's a Chinese woman by the name of Mandarinette."

"But Cyprienne! Cyprienne!" moaned the fiancé, chilled with terror by the revelation of the infernal transformation.

Then, by the will of the more powerful of the two mysterious forces, these final words fell from the lips of Turlurette to complete terrifying Jean Chapuis:

"Cyprienne still exists, but she is no more than a soul imprisoned in another body."

Chapter Eighteen
THE INFERNAL CARNOPLASTY

Now, with the physiognomy and voice of Cyprienne, Turlurette, entranced by magnetic sleep, spoke and revealed to Jean Chapuis, frozen by horror, what had happened in the diabolical laboratory.

His eyes flamboyant, Otto Hantzen had attached the three young women to the operating tables while the silent Yogha watched him.

Oronius' rival seemed to be at the peak of excitement, preparing his instruments of torture.

What frightful operation was he meditating carrying out on his unfortunate victims?

While proceeding with impressive preparations, he indicated that himself, in a frightful fit of gaiety.

"Hee hee," he sniggered. "Institutes of Beauty would pay dearly for my secret. I can realize all the promises, as deceptive as they are habitual, of their prospectuses. By my method of perfected carnoplasty, I can transform any face whatsoever. You'll see! I'm going to render you unrecognizable—but not undesirable."

Carnoplasty—the surgical method that, on a more modest level, was uniquely devoted to the task of correcting facial imperfections—had been taken by Hantzen to the ultimate degree of virtuosity. It is true that he had at his disposal, in order to replace the outmoded scalpel and the slowness of sutures, the omnipotent influence of alpha and gamma radiation. No tissue could resist radioactivity, and magnetic effluvia, cleverly employed, permitted modeling new features in living flesh, in conformity with s determined model.

For Hantzen, therefore, it was a mere game to realize the astonishing transformation that the prodigious Yogha had imagined. Under his surgical sleight of hand, Cyprienne's smile was transported to the lips of Turlurette, while she was masked by the yellow skin of the Chinese woman, and the frightful jugglery continued, causing the eyes of one to pass into the orbits of the other, substituting for the Asiatic nose the mischievously turned-up nose of the mechanic Laridon's friend.

Presto! By means of that implausible conjuring trick, the chambermaid now had the face of her young mistress, and as able to contemplate her own features on the shoulders of Mandarinette. As for the latter, she had been obliged to yield her physiognomy to Jean Chapuis' fiancée.

"It's all done!" announced the operator triumphantly, as he detached the patients.

"Not yet!" Yogha intervened.

Because, for having changed visage and appearance, for having become respectively the appearance of Mandarinette, that of Cyprienne, and that of Turlurette, Cyprienne, Turlurette and Mandarinette had nevertheless conserved their personalities. Under features that were no longer theirs, they continued to think; they remained themselves; and that did not satisfy the sorceress.

With a haughty gesture, she dismissed the triumphant Otto Hantzen.

"Let me finish your work," she declared, in the guise of thanks. "Without being badly done, the task needs to be completed. I'll take charge of that."

Mortified, but docile, Oronius' rival immediately quit the laboratory, growling: "Charlatan!"

Then Yogha directed the gleam of her magnetic eyes at the young women. They did not pause on Cyprienne. The enchantress was under no illusion. She had experienced the resistance of Oronius' daughter, and did not care to observe her impotence to dominate her a second time.

It was precisely because Cyprienne escaped her influence that Yogha had, so to speak, exiled her from herself by relegating her to the appearance to Mandarinette. Otherwise, she would have simplified the comedy that she was preparing by simply substituting Turlurette for Cyprienne and the latter for her chambermaid—an exchange piquant enough in itself. But for want of being able to act on the will of Oronius' heiress, Yogha had decided that she would remain a prisoner, with the appearance of her Chinese slave

Turlurette-Cyprienne and Mandarinette-Turlurette, whom she sensed to be less rebellious to her power, would suffice for the execution of the plan that she had made. She stared at them one after the other.

"You are Cyprienne of the magical Villa," she said to the chambermaid" And to Mandarinette, she said: "You are Turlurette."

Immediately, the features of the hypnotized women froze and their eyes lost all their gleam, taking on the dull aspect of congealed organic matter. From that moment on, in their gaze and in their person, there was something dead, and they only acted like automata, under the unique impulsion of an external force, the will of the rival of fakirs.

That was what Yogha wanted.

Her hand extended. "Go!"

And as we know, obedient to that order, the "doubles" of Oronius' daughter and her maidservant had departed toward the sphere, first passing through the room of the luminous columns of the unknown palace, as then through the aspiratory chimney.

After their departure, Yogha turned to Cyprienne, con-sternated and confused under her new appearance, and di-rected a challenging gaze at her. "You, who can read the thoughts of others, try, then, to read mine in order to know your destiny," she mocked.

Her victim, with the eyes and face of Mandarinette, still possessed the energy of Cyprienne; so, without being dis-tressed, she riposted tit-for-tat: "Hatred cannot dominate or vanquish love!"

With a shiver of revolt, divined for the second time, Yogha quit the laboratory.

"Whence comes that magic in her, which opposes mine victoriously?" she murmured. "What is that force, and where does it originate?"

She meditated for a few moments and pronounced, in a menacing tone: "I want to know what it is in order to combat it. And to defeat it, whatever it might be."

To the question that Hantzen's ally had posed, Cyprienne would not have been able to respond herself. Left alone, the unfortunate child had collapsed on a chair and was sobbing quietly, hiding with her hands the strange face that had become hers. All the energy of a little while ago had abandoned her.

Suddenly, without taking account of it, since Yogha's departure, she had become a poor little girl again, weak and terrified. Separated from all those she loved, she wept for her dead father and her lost fiancé—her fiancé who would no longer recognize her!

How could she ever get out of the living prison in which she felt confined? Only death offered her a chance of escape. In the meantime, how much suffering and how many tears were in prospect! Unsteadily, she got to her feet. The laboratory in which Hantzen's cruel science had inflicted the transformation that had driven her to despair maintained an insupportable terror within her.

She went out, leaning on the walls, and started wandering in the maze of corridors and rooms, without encountering anyone.

The mysterious palace seemed to be uninhabited.

Where, then, were the pitiless Yogha and the ferocious Hantzen? What had become of the false Cyprienne and Turlurette?

A terrifying silence reigned; perhaps the solitude and the silence constituted a further ordeal invented by the malevolence of Yogha in order to torture the woman she seemed to hate.

Why that implacable hatred? Was it the fiancée of Jean Chapuis that the frightening and beautiful unknown woman was determined to persecute? Cyprienne did not think of asking herself that question. She was still unaware of the mysterious apparitions and occult pursuit to which Jean Chapuis had been the dolorous victim. She only observed the effects of that hatred.

What fear and what chagrin were hers on sensing that she was alone, all alone, without the comfort of a present friend.

In fact, in her present distress, now that she had lost her form, would she be able to find another amity?

Sad, languid and desperate, she found herself back in the room from which she had emerged an hour before with Turlurette and Mandarinette in order to embark on the terrifying adventure.

Overwhelmed, she let herself fall on to the cushions.

Yapping extracted her from her torpor. With mad bounds, an affectionate message of joy, tenderness and anxiety, the faithful Kukuss ran to her and harassed her with cajoleries.

Brave little dog! That was his manner of showing that he was not a dupe who could be taken in by a ruse. Wilier than Pipigg, he had been able to divine and discover his young mistress under the new appearance that had been imposed on her. So, wagging his tail, twirling before leaping on to his mistress' knees and looking at her amorously, he seemed to be saying: "I recognize you! I'll stay with you! You have a friend!"

Cyprienne took him in her arms.

"Nice doggie! Good doggie!" she murmured. "If you knew what a consolation and what hope you're bringing me! So the heart doesn't rely on the testimony of the eyes? Oh, if my beloved Jean could appear to me and divine me as you've done!"

Feeling more valiant, she stood up. "Come, my faithful little companion! It's necessary not to abandon ourselves. It's necessary to find out where we are and discover, if possible, the secrets of this strange place. Do we still have a chance of receiving help or of recovering our liberty?"

"Woof, woof!" responded Kukuss, affirmatively.

That was reassuring. But in the hours that followed it was in vain that the prisoner tried to find a way out of the labyrinth of corridors that served as her prison. Her footsteps always brought her back to the room from which she had departed. She understood then why she had been left without guards. Yogha knew that she could not escape.

Discouraged, the young woman went back to lean on the balustrade of one of the bays open over the strange sea of cloud, which seemed to isolate that singular abode from the rest of the world.

She looked up at the sky—the supreme horizon of prisoners.

Then her heart began to beat faster.

Above her head, close by—very close by, as if preparing to land on some terrace that she could not see, Cyprienne saw, face to face, the two powerful enemy machines, the Spherus and the Halcyon-Car.

Chapter Nineteen
THE SPHERUS REOPENS

After obtaining from Turlurette, asleep in a hypnotic trance, the revelation of the astonishing transformation realized by Otto Hantzen, Jean Chapuis stood there, as if paralyzed.

So, in spite of appearances, it was not Cyprienne that he had before his eyes!

That cherished face, which he could not contemplate without emotion, was only animated by a strange soul. He could no longer recognize his fiancée's gaze therein.

What hellish imagination had invented the odious mockery of sending him the body while keeping the soul?

Whether he was duped or not, the effect was to inflict a veritable torture on him. As long as he had been able to believe that he was in the presence of the veritable Cyprienne, had he not suffered cruelly from the apparent indifference of his fiancée, and also from unconsciously sensing that she was so different from herself? And now that the key to the enigma had been delivered to him, was he not suffering even more from a worse anguish?

Yes, the body of Cyprienne was here—at least, her face, her appearance—but she had become a stranger because of the divorce of that body from its cerebral motor. And he wondered what had been done in the meantime with Cyprienne's soul. Was she not being tortured as he was being tortured himself, savantly and ferociously, by herself? Oh, truly, their persecutors had surpassed the bounds of cruelty.

"The unknown woman! Always the unknown woman!" he murmured, gnashing his teeth.

Anger took possession of him and made him want to find himself in the presence of that frightful tormenter, of whom he only knew the cloudy image. He felt capable of killing her; his hands were quivering with murderous desire.

What was the point? He was a prisoner in the sphere, at the mercy of the unassailable will; He had been borne away into limitless space, and he did not know where that course would stop.

He would have given half his life to be able to extract himself from that impotence.

Grimly, now avoiding looking at his companions, he concentrated his attention on the parallel course of the Halcyon, which had become a satellite of the Spherus. It was his only hope henceforth. If Laridon could do nothing for him, he would have to submit until the end to the destiny that the unknown woman reserved for him. On that destiny, alas, it was better not to reflect. Toward what mental tortures, if not physical ones, was the moving ball taking him?

A sudden shudder agitated his body. He was about to find out.

Without a shock, the spherical apparatus had just immobilized, and in the steel floor, the trap-door was opening slowly.

Jean Chapuis did not hesitate, not even thinking about the possibility of another trap. What was the point? Was he not in the hands of the unknown woman? And was that not better than imprisonment at the summit of a metallic globe? His impotence had ceased, since he was able to act.

Taking just enough time to summon the attention of Victor Laridon with a joyful hurrah, he precipitated himself into the trap-door and placed himself on the platform of the elevator. The latter immediately sank.

Only then did the engineer perceive that the two young women—the false Cyprienne and the no less false Turlurette—had followed him automatically and placed themselves beside him, probably summoned by an order from the invisible.

That observation did not cool his ardor. He was feverish and impatient.

The elevator reached the inferior part of the engine-room. There, all the pendulums, wheels, transmissions, sliding rods and actinometers were at rest. The pause definitely announced the arrival.

The other automatic door, the one to the exterior, joyfully agape, seemed to be inviting the young man to resume his liberty.

"Victor!" he shouted, drunk with joy, leaning over the opening. At the first glance that he darted outside, however, he uttered a cry of ecstasy and forgot everything except the marvelous landscape that was offered to his gaze.

Victor Laridon and Julep had not missed a single one of the young engineer's gestures. They had seen him agitate his arms in a sign of delight, and they had heard his cry of joy.

Then Jean Chapuis and his companions, for a reason as yet unexplained, had plunged into the interior of the sphere.

"That's good! It appears that the boss has found the key!" Laridon had exclaimed. "Get ready, Julep. We'll need to offer the demoiselles a hand to help them come aboard."

Swiftly, the mechanic made the Halcyon plunge and turn around the Spherus in order to bring his apparatus opposite the opening.

But that opening he could not discover. He frowned.

"Have the tricks recommenced?" he growled, ill-humoredly.

Neither Jean nor his companions appeared. The metal sphere seemed to be immobilized, stuck to the flank of a cloud. Drowned in the fog, the opening was invisible.

"Damned thing!" swore the Parisian, regaining height. M'sieur Jean will surely have bumped his nose on the closed door. He must be stumped."

Executing ellipses around the glazed cap, he waited to see the engineer come up again, in order to inform him of his disillusionment; but the minutes passed, and none of the inmates of the lenticular cabin reappeared.

Laridon felt the bite of anguish, increasingly sharp.

"Some dirty trick is happening," he muttered between his teeth. "Truly, our friends must still be hidden inside that infernal wagon."

In the end, he lost patience.

"That's it! I'll find out. It's necessary to go and see. The Boss might need help."

Hailing Julep, who came down from the post where he was stationed, he installed himself before the dashboard of the electrical controls.

"Get hold of the broomstick, son of Ham. And don't let go of the ladder, above all. I'm going to town."

Without being a first-class pilot, Julep had been trained sufficiently by Laridon to be able to substitute for him.

"Don't worry," he declared, laughing broadly, flattered by that mark of confidence. "I'll be watching the shop!"

Already the mechanic had emerged from the control room, having first attached himself by means of a rope and equipped himself with a singular instrument that he suspended from his belt."

"Make the sheep jump over the bulge and circle in place by pressing the gyroscopic lever," Laridon shouted to Julep.

Having consulted the altimeter and observed that the height at which the Halcyon was moving rendered that precaution necessary, the mechanic fitted a respiratory mask to his face, complete with an oxygen generator. Then he went out, passing through the isolation compartment that assured the interior of the Halcyon of a consistent temperature.

Once he had descended beneath the central cabin, by means of a special apparatus, he moored the end of his rope solidly to a tender and then, letting himself slide into the void, he remained suspended, lightly swayed by the course of the Halcyon, which descended toward the Spherus.

When Laridon felt the asbestos of the latter's upper surface beneath his feet, he cast off his sling and crouched on the cap, while the Halcyon, obedient to the gyroscopic commands, began to rotate slowly above him.

In his perilous position—for the curved carapace was very slippery—Laridon gave evidence of the greatest sang-froid.

He had an idea.

"I have Oronius' blow-torch!" he exclaimed. "The radiations will quickly reckon with that glass plate, no matter how thick it is."

And, as at ease as if he were operating in absolutely normal conditions, he set about cutting as circular opening in the glass dome that surmounted the sphere, with the blow-torch he had brought with him.

Attacked by radiations of an extraordinary power, the glass dissociated and melted; soon the plaque excised by Laridon's labor was detached, and fell noisily into the lenticular chamber.

"My turn!" said the mechanic.

And boldly, he leapt into the opening.

That chamber, as we know, had remained empty since the abrupt departure of Jean Chapuis and the two women, but the elevator had not come back up. The panel remained open over a gaping hole.

Laridon, who was ignorant of its existence, did not examine it closely, and after a few appeals launched in vain, in the hope of obtaining news of Jean Chapuis and his companions, he bravely took hold of one of the four columns and let himself slide down into the inferior part of the sphere, where the sphere's machinery was dormant.

Having only darted a distracted but marveling glance at that original and well-regulated mechanism, the Parisian searched for his friends.

Alas, the place was empty, and a large hole open to the void showed the path that the engineer and his companions must have taken.

The mechanic went very pale.

"They haven't done that!" he groaned. "No, it isn't possible that they were able to decamp through that hole. Where would they have gone, since we're in mid-air?"

However, the fact was there; doubt became impossible. Neither the young engineer nor his companions were in the Spherus any longer.

"Come on, come on, I'm going crazy," murmured Laridon, putting his hand to his forehead. "They can't have flown away on wings!"

With a final glance he searched the slightest coverts; he inspected the entire space that contained the machines. The steel floor shone brightly; no dust or human foot, it seemed, could ever have brushed it. As for the walls, where all the apparatus was slumbering... nothing!

Laridon really was alone.

Shivering, he knelt down next to the opening, leaning over, and looked out. In front of him, however, there was only mist, and empty space... the great vertiginous void, which continued all the way to the ground.

A jump of nine thousand meters! Was it permissible to imagine that without going pale?

Laridon got up again. He tottered...

"What's happened, then?" he lamented. "Nothing to say—one can't escape like that into the open sky!"

Mysteriously... very mysteriously... Jean Chapuis and the women that Yogha had sent to him by way of a summons, had disappeared into the bosom of the clouds.

Chapter Twenty
THE MYSTERIOUS MOUNTAIN

In his despair, the unhappy Laridon tore his hair. He imagined a catastrophe, an imprudence on Jean's part, a drama… in short, a horrible fall from high altitude.

"Oh, the poor dab!" he moaned, hiding his face in his hands in order to try to escape the frightful vision. Then a little calm returned to his mind and he began to reflect.

"Who knows? I'm too imaginative. I'm thinking the worst. Perhaps hope still remains. What if it's simply a matter of more devilry like the artificial cloud or the flying trawl? With individuals of that reach, it's necessary to mistrust. Don't throw in the towel before having taken a punch, my dear Victor. Rather go back up to the honest Halcyon and open your eyes… perhaps you'll discover something that will explain the trick."

In order to acquit his conscience, he carried out another inspection between the decks of the singular mechanism; but it was in vain that he studied the apparatus and touched the levers; he could not succeed in putting the Spherus in motion. Perhaps that was lucky for him.

Nevertheless, that inexplicable immobility in the open sky troubled him.

"Do they have a fixation cell like that of the late Monsieur Oronius?" he asked himself. "I don't see any indication of it, though."

In any case, it was easy for him to take account of the fact that no generators of force were in action around him; in consequence, the present immobility of the apparatus was not attributable to any dynamic intervention. The Spherus had simply stopped.

It was illogical not to admit that conclusion. But such an arrest of something heavier than air that appeared to be a suspension in the bosom of the atmosphere constituted a truly incredible phenomenon

For want of being able to fathom that mystery, the Parisian decided to return to the upper part of the sphere, climbing along a column; then he hoisted himself out of the glazed cabin and observed with satisfaction that Julep, faithful to his order, was pursuing in the Halcyon the movement of a squirrel in a treadmill.

In the fashion of a guide-rope, the cord was hanging down above the mechanic's head. He seized it, knotted it around his waist and, by means of the strength of his wrists, climbed back up to the Halcyon.

A few minutes later, rid of his apparatus and his respiratory mask, he replaced Julep in the direction cabin.

"Hup!" he said, imprinting an oblique direction on the Halcyon. "Get the lotus bulbs ready, my friend. Careful and extraordinary tricks are happening. M'sieur Jean, Mamzelle Cyprienne and Turlurette have disappeared."

"No more M'sieur Jean? No more Mamzelles?" inquired the worthy Julep, squinting.

"You understand me," Laridon went on, feverishly. "It's a little stronger than playing hunt the thimble. I've looked everywhere... under all the furniture... which was all the easier because there wasn't any. No boss, and no more Mamzelle Cyprienne or Turlurette than in my eye. Do you know what I said to myself, my clever lad?"

"You talk a lot to explain nothing, and Julep not know," replied the negro, with a capable expression.

"Well, I said to myself: 'These are stories to bite me in the bum.' For in the end, they're no longer inside, and that means they've debunked into the cabbage-patch. You understand? Where can they have gone? There's no floor! Explain that; it's a catastrophe. Not possible that M'sieur Jean took his fiancée and mine to take a tour of that part of the garden."

"That's not possible," Julep approved.

"Then only one thing remains," concluded Laridon, with a discouraged expression. "Perhaps they're hanging on to the outside of the sphere... Well, that's what I think. The law says that any aircraft abandoned in space is a fair prize, so we're therefore the owners at present. Shall we make a tour of it to see?"

First floating above the sphere, then descending by degrees while describing circles that permitted him to inspect the apparatus on all its faces, the mechanic, without any great hope, attempted to execute his decision.

His expression darkened gradually, and he shook his head, for at none of the points of the absolutely smooth surface, devoid of asperities, would there have been any possibility for human beings of hanging on.

Monotonous and desperate, the conclusion returned to the mechanic's lips:

"They've flown away... flown... flown!"

He could have made use of another word with more exactitude, but that one did not pass because of the tragic horror of what it evoked.

What was there below—far below, thousands of meters? What would Laridon find when he landed? What lugubrious vision of broken bodies? He shuddered in thinking about it.

The Halcyon continued its descent while circling. Now it reached the inferior part of the apparatus abandoned in mid-air.

Suddenly, a slight shock was felt, and the Halcyon-Car rebounded backwards, as if it had collided with an elastic surface.

Rubbing his eyes—for there was nothing in front of him but the gray tint of a foggy sky—Laridon tried to take his capricious apparatus forward again. A new shock threw him away from the route he was trying to impose on it.

He persisted, but all his further attempts remained as unfruitful.

It was necessary to yield to the evidence. There was an obstacle in front of him: an obstacle that he could not see, but which was blocking the Halcyon's path; and that object must

be directly underneath the place where the Spherus was immobilized, perpendicular to it.

"Oho!" said Laridon, emphasizing his exclamation with
a little whistle.

The disposition of the invisible object had just opened
his mind. He remembered the cloud that had once served the
sphere as a protective cloak. Could he not conclude, by analo-
gy, that he had something similar before him, with the same
purpose?

This remained immobile in one place instead of moving,
and it affected the form of a fixed funnel—a funnel having the
Spherus for a summit and for a base... perhaps the ground?
That was all the difference. It was therefore, fundamentally a
repetition of the same phenomenon.

"Something?" asked Julep.

"Let's see," riposted Laridon, slightly reassured; for, after envisaging the irreparable—which is to say, a catastrophe
that had cost the lives of Jean Chapuis and the young wom-
en—he considered almost as a favorable event the possibility
that they had simply been the victims of a further machination
of the invisible enemy.

And damn it, an enemy could be fought! Friends might
be liberated! To undertake a struggle, to attempt that deliverance could not be frightening—not when one's name was Victor Laridon!

Having brought the Halcyon-Car back into contact with
the obstacle, by means of a perilous maneuver, the mechanic
coolly attempted a frightful vertical descent.

"I'll see where it ends," he muttered between his teeth.

A cry from Julep suddenly rang out. "Beware crash,
Massa Laridon! Land! Land ho!"

The ground? Already!

Relying on his altimeter, the mechanic had thought that it
was still eight thousand meters away.

Was he landing on the peak of a mountain, then?

And what a mountain! The altitude indicated by his instruments was in excess of eight thousand meters. Weak in

geography as Laridon was, he knew that very few points on the terrestrial globe exist that can boast of extending as far.

A few seconds later, having had just enough time to stabilize the machine and deaden the fall by the employment of a device of which Oronius was the inventor, the mechanic touched down, and was able to observe that the Halcyon was perched on the slopes of a peak that extended far above the clouds.

The landscape presented a spectacle of perfect desolation. At such a height, life could not exist, even in the most rudimentary forms of the animal and vegetable kingdoms. It was on a block of ice that the Halcyon had landed.

"Brrr! That must be cold!" Laridon prognosticated, instinctively raising the collar of his jacket. Then he thought that the precaution would doubtless be inadequate to confront the external air, assuredly as piquant as it was rarefied.

It was therefore prudent to adapt his clothing before quitting the comfortable interior of the Halcyon, where the solarium maintained the temperature at an appreciable level, thanks to the impermeability of triple walls.

"Campaign gear," he ordered. "Put on a calorific pelisse, my old friend, or you'll catch a cold in the head."

The garment that he designated by that picturesque term was a kind of suit of armor in supple fabric, an atmospheric "diving-suit," which Oronius had devised personally, and which, by the judicious employment of certain radioactive substances and a oxygen generator, assured the person it contained, no matter what environment or attitude he was operating in, of the normal use of his respiratory and circulatory functions. The temperature remained constant and the body was protected against any variation of external pressure.

Julep did not need the invitation to be repeated. He proceeded with the change of costume at the same time as his companion.

Naturally, for the convenience of conversation, the ultimate diving-suits were equipped with the antennae of a wireless telephony apparatus, with the consequence that the two men could communicate, at close or long range.

"Do you have the pills against thirst and hunger?" Laridon inquired. "Good! We're going to make a tour of the fairground; there's nothing more to do than take our midnight-pass sticks, in case we have an unfortunate encounter."

Through the glass faceplate the negro's physiognomy expressed that this hypothesis appeared to him to be unlikely. Who, except for them, would risk themselves on those icy slopes? Nevertheless, he imitated Laridon and unhooked the electric weapon to which the mechanic had just made allusion. Infinitely more dangerous than an ancient revolver, the weapon assured its carrier of an undeniable superiority, for, apart from the fact that it permitted a spark to be unleashed at one's enemies as murderous as lightning, it could also electrocute any aggressor by means of a simple contact.

Similarly equipped, the crew of the Halcyon could believe themselves to be invulnerable.

"En route!" declared the mechanic. "I have an idea that, although the country doesn't seem overpopulated, it will nevertheless reserve surprises for us. Look up for a moment. What do you think of that sphere suspended like a Swiss apple on the head of William Tell's son, whose body can't be seen?"

"Not an apple," riposted the negro, shaking his head. "Julep has good teeth... but couldn't bite into that!"

With the usual precautions, they left the cabin of the Halcyon, which Laridon immobilized by a means known only to the disciples of Oronius, with utilized the fixation cell.

The silence was impressive; the two men could only hear the sound of ice cracking underfoot. No less impressive was the sight of the icy summit emerging from a sea of clouds like a monstrous iceberg. And yet, it belonged to the world. At its base, thousands of meters below the violators of that virgin soil, there were human beings.

"Perhaps we're the first to wander around up here," suggested Laridon, considering suspiciously the wall of mist that seemed to crown the summit. "Yes, the first, unless..."

160

Without finishing, he continued his ascent, followed by Julep, who was no more inclined to chat.

The worthy negro had enough to think about reflecting on all the singular incidents that had caught him up in their whirlwind since the previous day. If it had been necessary, however, to make known his intimate thought, he would have confessed that an excursion by dragonfly over the Avenue du Bois would have seemed infinitely more agreeable. As he did not have the choice, though, he continued marching behind Laridon's back, resignedly.

Suddenly, he bumped into that back, which had just stopped abruptly.

His hands extended, the mechanic appeared to be palpating something.

"It's just as I thought," he announced. "One can't get through. The barrier is still there. Oh, it's not worth the trouble of trying to see it. It's like a skin... not its own! And one can feel scarcely any more... nothing except something like a wind repelling you. It's odd. But that's the way it is. It's necessary to accept it. Come on; we'll look for a door."

And, still groping, he started to make his way along the invisible wall of air.

As he was a fellow not lacking in judgment, he was careful, at the moment when he made that decision, to mark the spot by piling up a few fragments of ice there, and tracing some signs on the ground with the point of his knife.

It was a wise move, because, after having conscientiously skirted the invisible obstacle, he found himself an hour later back in the place from which they had departed, and which he had marked.

"That's it! We've gone full circle," he said, philosophically. I suspected as much, and as you see, I've taken my precautions to make sure of it. You understand me, old friend? We've made a complete tour, and there isn't a door. How does one get in there, then? Tell me that. How does one get into this locker that can't be seen?"

It was evidently not poor Julep who could answer that indiscreet question. So, uttering a deep sigh, Laridon did not persist, and started down the slope again in the direction of the Halcyon-Car.

"It's necessary, though, that I find the trick," he muttered. "I've sworn to M'sieur Jean that I wouldn't abandon him, nor Mamzelle Cyprienne, without forgetting Turlurette, of course. Now, something tells me that if I could traverse that"—he indicated the misty summit with a gesture—"I'd find the boss. But it won't be easy, damn it. Do you have any idea, Master Julep...? No...? Oh, a jugful of prune juice! It's not a fellow of our stripe that will reinvent perlimpimpin powder,[12] the formula of which my four-times-great grandfather lost when he had the pip."

They had arrived at the Halcyon. They went back into the cabin and sat down.

"Let's go!" said the mechanic. "Next move! Fold up the wings; it's the auto we need to explore this satanic mountain."

As we have indicated, the protean aircraft could, in accordance with the necessities of the moment, be transformed into any kind of vehicle, terrestrial, marine or submarine.

In two minutes it was ready to roll over the flanks of the mountain. The Parisian set forth at low speed. Fundamentally, he was only drawing away regretfully, sensing that it was at the summit that the interesting location was to be found. But in the same way that the occult force had guided Jean Chapuis' actions, Laridon yielded at that moment to an exterior suggestion—perhaps the same one.

He did not take account of it, however, and he continued to grumble while obliging the Halcyon to execute prodigies of acrobatics.

"I'm crazy! What if we fall down below?"

Suddenly—was it his hand that had braked involuntarily, or something else that had immobilized the vehicle?—the Halcyon stopped.

_____

[12] Fairy dust.

"A breakdown! That's too much!" the mechanic swore, hastily donning his atmospheric diving suit again.

Julep hastened to do the same, and they both went out to examine the apparatus and the terrain.

A kind of monument, manifestly erected by human hands, attracted Laridon's attention.

It was a pile of blocks of stone, which supported another, shaped in the form of a column.

Laridon and Julep drew nearer.

"An inscription! There's an inscription!" exclaimed the stupefied mechanic.

And, leaning over the stone he read: *OTTO HANTZEN.*

"Hantzen! The rascal who challenged M'sieur Oronius and sent that swine Jarrousse to him!" he gasped, rubbing his eyebrows. "Well, you can believe me if you want, my old Julep, but finding the visiting-card of that rogue isn't calculated to delight me. Damn it! I almost expected it. That clarifies things, pal! Yes, that clarifies things."

The black man tugged his sleeve. "Read again," he intimated.

"There's more? You don't have your finger in your eye. Oh, nice! That's a fine spoonful of angelic jam!"

Under Hantzen's name there was this:

Go no further, audacious mortal, if you do not want to incur the wrath of the god who, like Jupiter on Olympus, has fixed his abode on the summit of Mount Everest.

"He puts it nicely," joked Laridon, mockingly. But he would have been cleverer just to engrave, simply: *Beware of wolf-traps!* That would have more effective. Ah! Here's another little advice…"

To mortal eyes, the gods are able to remain invisible. Renounce attempting to discover the Etheric Palace.

"Etheric Palace? Damn! Is it a new Bar of Dreams?" wondered the mechanic. Then, more seriously: "Have you finished? Me, renounce my task? That citizen must be obtuse. He doesn't know Victor Laridon. If Hantzen and his clique are in the palace it mentions, it's because they went into it, so I can get into it too. That's obvious."

In spite of those proud words, he felt somewhat perplexed, and his gaze, wandering in all directions, sought inspiration.

It was then that, between the stones that were beginning to strew the ground, he saw something running, which plunged into the flank of the mountain.

Chapter Twenty-One
THE MUD-EATERS

"Did you see that?" cried Laridon

"Julep saw!" declared the negro, laughing loudly. "That's a rabbit. I run, catch it and have it roasted, as we do in my country."

"Flesh-eater!" protested Laridon, with a sincere indignation. "No, don't show me those sickening mores. It doesn't disgust you, then, to imitate the savagery of the men of the last century?"

"Good roast better than Massa Oronius' drugs," riposted Julep with a conviction that proved the limits of civilization when attempting to transform certain natural traits.

"Shut up, wretch. You're unworthy of our enlightened era. But let's get back to your 'rabbit.' I got a better glimpse of it than you. It was running on two feet, and one might have thought it was a little dwarf. Yes, shrug your shoulders, pal! I know that it seems improbable to imagine human beings at the summit of this mountain. We can only walk around here thanks to our masks, and if we didn't have the drugs you scorn, it would be impossible to ensure our subsistence. And yet, I got a good look at that thing. In any case, the presence of a large four-footed creature would be just as extraordinary as that of a biped."

"But that rabbit… It's gone back to its burrow," insisted Julep.

"Well, let's go see the warren, my lad. I'll have a clear heart."

Having made sure that the Halcyon, hidden behind an outcrop and perfectly immobilized by means of the currents of the fixation cell, was not running any risk, Laridon headed for the place where the animate creature had disappeared.

The so-called burrow was, in reality, an opening large enough to allow a representative of the human species to pass through.

Laridon and Julep engaged in it, one behind the other, and they soon found themselves in a kind of tunnel plunging into the mountain.

"Julep not see anything, Massa Victor. Too dark!" murmured the negro, in an uneasy voice.

"Joker! It isn't you who ought to be afraid of the dark," protested the mechanic, in a mocking tone. "Little as M'sieur Oronius has left on your hide, there's enough to rival the night that surrounds us. You understand that I'd light up, but I don't want to frighten the tenants of this Métro, who might be interesting to visit. Let me keep the incognito."

"Oy," moaned Julep, for all response, twitching as if a legion of demons were assailing him. "But I can hear, I can feel... beasts running... all over my skin... tickling...p inching... biting."

"Don't exaggerate. They'd break their teeth."

However, the mechanic could hear strange noises too: there was a mixture of little running footsteps and stifled sniggers; rapid living forms brushed him, surrounded him and palpated him, perhaps preparing to attack him.

"Damnation! What can that be? It's small... swarming... can Julep be right? Have we come into a warren of little monkeys?"

Intrigued, and slightly disturbed by the disquieting movements, he decided to switch on the electric lamp that was integrated into the metallic hood of his suit. The tunnel was illuminated.

Then Laridon and Julep perceived a crowd of singular little beings around them, who fled in panic, blinded by the light. They disappeared into the darkness of the corridor, with the single exception of one that the Parisian was able to seize.

"Whassat?" he exclaimed, bewildered. "Here's an escapee from a bottle! This monster would make the fortune of a fairground showman!"

In fact, the minuscule creature that was wriggling in the mechanic's hands and uttering plaintive cries was a fine specimen of the whims that nature sometimes permits herself. A vague humanity characterized the form; it had a head, legs and arms terminated by hands; but the face had a grimacing simian expression; the eyes were phosphorescent; the body scarcely comprised a sort of bladder of distended skin; the limbs were cartilaginous.

The bizarre pygmy, which resembled the goblins of folktales, was evidently constituted to live in a rarefied atmosphere; specially adapted and simplified organs facilitated a diminished life. It only measured twenty-five centimeters in height. On what was it nourished?

Putting it down on the ground, having attached it to him by mean of a leather thong, Laridon saw it pick up a handful of moist dirt and bear it to its mouth avidly.

"Eh! Well, obviously, it isn't easily disgusted, the knee-high!" the mechanic exclaimed. "It's guzzling mud!"

That was exact, and it was doubtless the secret of the life of that geophage; a scientist could have explained to Laridon that the singular specimen must possess a special digestive apparatus that permitted it to isolate from the damp earth the oxygen it contained.

Laridon did not care about that. He had not captured the mud-eater with the design of studying its anatomy; he was simply meditating employing it as a guide.

"It will lead us to its comrades," he explained to Julep. "I'm curious to know their abode. It must lack a certain comfort."

In fact, the captive, after having addressed furious grimaces to its conductor, was now tugging at the leash and manifesting the intention to plunge into the tunnel.

"Let's follow it," said Laridon.

With long strides, the two friends accompanied the rapid course of the pygmy, who drew them into the heart of a veritable labyrinth.

Incessant bifurcations, glimpsed in passing, demonstrated that tunnels hollowed out the mountain in all directions. Was that the work of nature or that of the geophages? Laridon judged the second hypothesis to be infinitely more probable.

Prudently, he had refrained from extinguishing the electric bulb that illuminated their progress. At each new corridor left behind he frowned, in an anxious fashion.

"We're going, we're going!" he muttered. "It's a curiosity that might cost us dear, for we don't have a map of his concentration station. If the midget escapes, or becomes indocile, we'll never get out of here, for I'd be quite incapable of finding my way on my own. What got into me, then, to go into it?"

He did not realize that he had yielded to the same force that had drawn him over the mountainside toward the stone erected by Hantzen's vanity. An invincible attraction was exercised upon him. Toward what was it drawing him?

As he went further forward into the interior of the mountain, a muted sound reached him; the sound grew louder incessantly, to the point that the mechanic was puzzled by its nature.

"Louder and louder!" he exclaimed. "One would think that we were approaching a factory in full activity. Have you ever visited the ruins brought to light on the site of old Le Creusot, Julep? No? It's much similar."

He suddenly thought: *Hantzen!* And instinctively, he began to advance more rapidly.

At the extremity of a tunnel, a bright light appeared to them. One might have thought it the entrance to a furnace; the din became formidable.

Prudently, Laridon switched off his lamp. He did not intend his approach to be detected.

"In order to get a good look, it's better to do it by surprise," he murmured. "Like that, people let their nature show, and one knows what one's dealing with."

By way of extra precaution, he tugged on the lead, bent down and picked up the pygmy.

"You, my chick, I'll hold tight. Otherwise you might take advantage of the dark to scarper. And then, one doesn't know whether you might be able to communicate with your mates and give us away. You have a tongue, I suppose?"

Those sage reflections incited him to tie up and gag the little creature before stuffing him into the vast pocket of the diving-suit.

"There! You'll be nice and warm, and when I need you, I'll know where to find you. Now, my old Julep, it's no longer a matter of a stroll in the park. Let's advance on tiptoe, and no noise. There's the devil of a racket in that cavern; it isn't possible that it's the mud-eaters. I rather think..."

He interrupted himself and stifled an exclamation of surprise. A veritable factory in a feverish activity of labor was revealed to his gaze; and it was the most curious spectacle that he had ever contemplated.

In a vast hall artificially hollowed out in the bosom of the mountain, and ruddy light emerging from the mouths of formidable furnaces, a population of imps was scurrying. Hundreds of geophages were there, stoking fires, hanging on to wheels whose course carried them away, pushing little wagons which they unloaded into the bellies of monstrous machines.

As far as the wonderstruck, but forcibly rapid, contemplation could reveal to him, the mechanic estimated that before his eyes there as a gigantic compressed air factory.

Masses of air drawn from the base of the mountain through giant conduits, opening into the hall, were concentrated in a central reservoir and directed from there toward extraordinary bellows that projected them, with an incalculable violence, into a dozen openings disposed in a circle

Laridon could not divine what the purpose was of the work of a machinery surpassing in power anything he had previously seen. He was living in a century of marvels, but what as happening in the cavern was prodigious; the pygmies were accomplishing a titanic labor.

But why? What function did it serve, the mechanic wondered, bewildered.

He was able at that moment to remember the mysterious breath of air that surrounded the summit of the mountain like a circular wall. How was that wall, which repelled the indiscreet and rendered invisible whatever there was behind it, produced? The strange labor of the subterranean factory might have something to do with it...

Another indication was about to attract the attention of Julep and Laridon, When they raised their heads they perceived, in the center of the hall, suspended from the vault, a flamboyant cartouche bearing a name in letters of fire: *Otto Hantzen.*

Him again! Always him!

Did he reign over this strange tribe?

On reflection, what he saw in that cavern, and what it allowed him to suspect, represented the disciplined work of formidable forces. How many arms had it required to pierce a mountain more than eight thousand meters high—which, if Hantzen's inscription could be believed, was none other than Everest, the Asian summit regarded as the highest on the globe. And how many machines too! Even while employing all the resources that human mechanics, multiplied a hundredfold by what the science of an Otto Hantzen—for want of an Oronius—could put in the service of a creator, it must have required an army of workers, and that for many years.

That race of geophages, which alone could live normally in these conditions of altitude and subterranean life, must be able to render great services to the mysterious man who had been able to discover and exploit it. It was, properly speaking, the ideal manual labor. By what means had Hantzen succeeded in discovering it, mastering it and employing it in the execution of his designs? That was an enigma.

In appearance, the pygmies were free; neither Laridon nor Julep perceived supervisor among them belonging to the human race; it was, therefore, benevolently that the minuscule creatures were bending to a discipline and giving themselves with so much zeal to the rude labor of the subterranean factory—but in appearance only.

In fact, the ears of the two intruders were suddenly assaulted by piercing cries, and they saw three of the extraordinary dwarfs emerge from a hiding-place where they had undoubtedly huddled in order to avoid labor.

Deployed through the air—an extravagant vision!—was a mechanical arm that terminated in a net, multiple elongations of which permitted the arm to extend its radius of action as much as was necessary, and its speed was vertiginous. In the blink of an eye, it had caught up with the mud-eaters that were fleeing before it; the net caught them and lifted them in the air, wriggling like fish in a keep-net.

Immediately, other arms departed from the same machine, some terminated by pincers and others by various instruments of correction, were extended. Plunging into the pocket of the net, the pincers, very delicately, plucked out the delinquents one by one, which mechanical whips fustigated conscientiously and pitilessly. After that, the correction having terminated, the moaning homunculi were replaced on the ground. Made wiser by that severe lesson, they hastened to go, piteously, to rejoin their comrades, whose zeal had been reheated by the scene.

"Well, that's not ordinary," murmured Laridon, rubbing his eyes. "Here's a place where the amusements are refined."

Directing his gaze toward the machine with the multiple arms, which had just given striking proofs of its vigilance, he discovered above it a glass cage enclosing a human silhouette.

"A typist!" exclaimed the mechanic, increasingly amazed. If he had been more informed of memories of ancient times, he might well have thought that the supervisor evoked a telephone or linotype operator. Coiffed in a helmet of which powerful lenses formed the eyepieces, with two microphones instead of ears, she was sitting before a kind of keyboard, each key of which activated one of the agile arms of the machine.

In her isolation, hearing and seeing everything that was happening in the hall, it was sufficient for her to press one of the keys to have the indocile or the negligent pursued, seized

171

and punished. Laridon could now explain the urgency of the labor of the geophages.

"Marvelous!" he said, admiringly. "Yes, marvelous, that machine, for stimulating labor. With the rich encouragement of the 'turbinophile,' there's no means of letting the grass grow underfoot. What would one get for one's promotion if that employment were vulgarized! They certainly wouldn't be demanding a three-hour week! What a brute that Hantzen is!"

Less enthusiastic, Julep pulled him backwards.

"This not good, Massa Laridon," he whispered. "If they discover us, we can't save ourselves. The Machine run after us and grab us."

"Let it come!" riposted the bellicose engineer.

After having launched that bold defiance, however, he reflected that Julep was seeking the language of wisdom in identifying a very real danger.

"On due reflection," he decided, "you're right, old boy. Let's take a walk. While admitting that the entry to Hantzen's domain must be in that direction, it's not by that door that we can hope to pass into it. It would be too stupid to get ourselves pinched without being able to defend ourselves. Against that machine, the 'turbinophile,' we wouldn't have any strength."

Wisely, he sketched a movement of retreat, which his companion hastened to imitate.

A retreat that was perhaps a trifle belated! Had the presence of the two friends been detected by the pygmies and signaled to the surveillance? Or was the tumult that suddenly rose up a coincidence, by which Laridon would have been wrong to be worried? A roar, which appeared to be an alarm signal, suddenly ripped his ears, and the multitude of little beings, uttering shrill cries, precipitated toward the gallery in which the imprudent explorers were lurking.

"Damn! They're after us! We're done for!" swore the mechanic, dragging Julep away.

Imagining that they could already hear the rattle of mechanical arms behind them and feel the wind of the net, they fled along the tunnel, turning into the first bifurcation, taking a third, and then yet another.

Behind them, the noise had died away; they must now be a long way from the factory, and certainly out of reach of the machine commanded by the "turbinograph."

Slowing down, in order to save their breath, which was running out, they continued nevertheless to plunge into the maze of subterranean galleries, searching for a way out.

Sometimes they seemed to hear murmurs and frictions, a while a series of confused and slight noises than gave them the impression if being pursued.

"Of course! The supervisor has launched her little beasts on our track," muttered Laridon, "That's awkward!"

He lit his lamp again and turned round. Thin shadows recoiled in disorder and disappeared from the illuminated part of the corridor.

"What did I tell you?" said the mechanic. "We're being followed. If I could only find the door again. It's doubtless the exit that they have a mission to stop us reaching. A thousand million curses! If I find them between it and me, I'll make a ratatouille of them."

"That much too stupid," observed Julep gravely, shaking his head. "If you have fleas, Massa Victor, you scratch yourself and crush the jumpers, but if you have many, many stingers, you can't scratch or crush, you get tired... and then they scoff you."

As one can see, the dappled negro had learned enough argot at the school of the Parisian worker.

"Thanks for the prediction," said the latter, amused. "You haven't anything more cheerful to serve me? Good! You're a funny mate, my old friend. At least, you understand enough to give you heart in your belly. Let's trot! We'll make the midgets run. We'll see whether we can get rid of that vermin."

As soon as they started to run, the muffled rumor resumed behind them.

A crossroads where a number of galleries intersected stopped the two fugitives.

Which to choose? Laridon wondered, scratching his head. *Is it this way or that way that one can climb up to Hantzen's lair? Fundamentally, that's all that interests me. We're underground. It's necessary to find the stairway that leads to the ground floor. Come on, boy, an inspiration! Which route do we take?*

The third.

Laridon started; he did not recognize Julep's voice.

"What did you say?" he asked, turning toward his companion.

"I not say anything," Julep protested.

"Then who just spoke?"

"Don't understand, Massa. No one spoke."

Laridon looked round, pulled a face, and muttered: "Now I'm hearing things! I would have sworn, though, that someone whispered in my ear to take the third opening. After all, why not? I asked for an inspiration; I got one. Whether my lugs rang or not, whether I only thought I heard or a mysterious voice really whispered to me, I accept it. We'll see whether it's serious, One, two, three... let's go this way."

They took a few steps. As they went into the tunnel, a loud rumor rose up in the depths of the corridor they had just quit. Then, immediately, all sound ceased.

"That silence! Nobody's following us any longer. Is that a good or a bad sign?"

Julep uttered a deep sigh. "Julep not confident," he declared.

But Laridon sketched an entrechat. "Sheath your palpitations. We're on the right path. There's daylight! Daylight!"

A pale light, which became bluer as they advanced, shone at the end of the corridor.

It was not daylight, in fact. It was a rather faint light falling through large glass portholes in a rocky room carpeted with moss, algae and seashells, which resembled an aquarium—except that instead of water, one could only see a kind of mist, colored with a blue tint by the light coming through the portholes.

Columns of rock, similarly encrusted with shells, sustained the vault and gave the place a mysterious profundity.

The explorers had stopped at the entrance, on the edge of a few steps that gave access to it. They both hesitated to penetrate into the bizarre grotto.

It opens like a trap, and that's quite clear, thought the mechanic. *Why haven't the microbes followed us?*

Some distance away, between the columns, it seemed to him that he could see an opening and a section of a stairway that rose up in a spiral. His heart was beating forcefully.

"Thunder of Oronius! What if that's the entrance to Hantzen's lair over there?"

It appeared to him that something within him was pushing him, encouraging him and murmuring: *Go on, poltroon.*

Windy, me? In fact, we won't get eaten. You're not chicken, Victor.

His decision was made. He pushed Julep.

"Go on! We'll take a steam-bath. You'll see how things are at the Hammam."

They touched he ground covered in plants. The soil was spongy and damp. As if water had covered it a few moments before. Under the feet of the two men the carpet went *Floc! Floc!*

Julep did not seem at all reassured.

"Go on, old boy!" said Laridon. "You're not afraid that the water will come back? Nonsense! If they try to drown us they'll be wasting their liquid. We're wearing diving-suits!

More resolutely, he started walking... but suddenly, he stopped, shivering.

Living straps, which terminated in suckers, had just fallen upon them, paralyzing them. And in the shadow of the columns, hideous and gigantic shadows agitated; they resembled giant spiders and they emerged from every corner of the room.

"Squid! They're squid!" cried Laridon, gripped by the terrible tentacles.

175

Chapter Twenty-Two
MAGIC!

As soon as Jean Chapuis had found himself outside the sphere, surprised and wonderstruck by the enchanting spectacle that was unfurled before his eyes, he had abruptly forgotten his agonizing preoccupations.

Was this the land of enchantments?

Without being irrational, he could believe it. Drawn outside as if by an irresistible magnet, he had jumped and had fallen back on ground covered with a carpet of grass speckled with flowers.

Above his head was a radiant firmament of gold and azure, and in that paradisal sky there was no somber or menacing patch; the rascally sphere was no longer visible.

Nut Jean as scarcely thinking about wondering by what miracle that incomprehensible monster had vanished into thin air; nor was he worrying about what might have become of his two companions, who had previously been the incessant object of all his thoughts.

He was alone, in the midst of a magical world, suddenly surged forth in the sky as if under the thrust of a magic wand.

As far as the eye could see, there was nothing but a perspective of Edenic gardens, palm groves, florid hills and enchanting horizons, invaded by the luxuriant vegetation of the tropical regions.

It was a feast of colors and perfumes. Marvelous birds were traversing the sky or singing in the trees. Graceful animals were bounding on all sides; wild beasts were frolicking and crawling at the feet of the young engineer, offering their large purring heads to his caresses.

Was that due to the intoxicating atmosphere? Mildness and joy seemed to reign as mistresses in this privileged abode. For a few moments, Jean Chapuis no longer thought about anything but breathing the odor of the flowers and rejoicing his eyes. His light body and mind floating, he advanced through the splendid country. He was so much under its charm that it did not occur to him to reflect on his surprising adventure. He walked nonchalantly, looking around, as if he had no other interest henceforth than admiring it. It seemed to him that he had entered Paradise, where the first condition of happiness was doubtless the necessity of forgetting all the past, our affections as well as our cares.

The young engineer was no longer conscious of time or the extent of space. He was certainly advancing at a extraordinary speed, traveling considerable distances without the slightest effort, as if borne by a breeze that he could not feel, but he did not take account of any of that.

Around him the landscape changed incessantly, unfurling its successive perspectives like the canvases of an interminable diorama.

He passed lakes and rivers; he traversed woods, climbed mountains, followed valleys, always in the midst if the marvelous vegetation, amid the most beautiful flowers and the most extraordinary plants.

Abruptly, he found himself on a lawn where a tent stood, before a background of palm trees. Under that tent, nonchalantly extended on cushions and surrounded by an entire court, to which Jean paid no attention, he perceived a woman.

Under the splendid and almost indiscreet costume of rajput princesses, the marvelous creature seemed to be the flower-queen of the delectable Eden.

Rising from the sparkling robe as far as the face, Jean's gaze encountered two female eyes, and he experienced the sensation of being transported by a burning double radiance. It produced the effect of fire on ice.

The armor of forgetfulness by which he had been surrounded since his spontaneous introduction into the strange world shattered as rapidly as it had formed.

He shivered as he identified the mysterious gaze and the visage that he had before him.

It was the unknown woman, It was Yogha.

177

Next to her, sarcastic and scornful, pontificating in order to mark how superior he was to the puerile comedy to which he was condescending, there was Otto Hantzen.

Jean Chapuis, of course, did not know that it was Hantzen. He had never met him, so, for him, he appeared to be just a man, of elephantine and unpleasant appearance, but, apart from those flaws, quite insignificant.

How mortified the proud scientist would have been if he had been able to read the impression in the mind of Cyprienne Oronius' fiancé. Fortunately for his vanity, Otto Hantzen did not possess the same faculties of second sight as the strange Yogha. He was therefore able to conserve the illusion of producing his effect.

In reality, Jean Chapuis only had eyes for Yogha. Oh, not by virtue of sympathy, but because the magnetic gaze of the magicienne captured his own. It was encountering their irises that provoked the reawakening of his memory.

Suddenly, he recalled is adventures, his anxieties on the subject of Cyprienne, the Spherus and how he had escaped from it.

Then he became anxious at being here; he turned round mechanically in order to see what had become of his companions—or, rather, he tried to turn round. But, frightfully, the victim of a further enchantment, his body no longer obeyed is mind.

A kind of duplication had just taken place in him, at the very moment when he had rediscovered the faculty of thinking and remembering. Only his thought had escaped its torpor and become accessible again to all human emotions: dread, suffering, despair. By contrast, none of those impressions could be translated, either by a gesture or even by a simple facial expression.

Jean Chapuis could see, feel and understand, but he could not express anything.

Facing the beautiful and abominable Yogha, and under the fascination of the great brilliant eyes, his body remained enslaved; he felt passive, incapable of obeying his own will.

With an increasing anguish and fear, he sensed that if it pleased the witch who was staring at him, he would pronounce words and perform actions that would fill him with horror.

He no longer belonged to himself, but he conserved the sad privilege of being the sickened spectator of that infernal disgrace.

What cruel game was in preparation? In what perfidious design had that woman drawn him to this place and reduced him to this frightful state of conscious impotence.

A smile wandered over Yogha's lips. She murmured, with an unspeakable expression of triumph: "Bonjour, Jean Chapuis. So you've finally responded to my summons, my handsome friend."

Horror: he heard himself speak, but it was his lips that emitted the reply; his thought played no part in to.

"I salute you, O Yogha, suzeraine of occult power and most beautiful of women."

"Well said, my friend," Yogha approved. She added, designating Hantzen: "And for him, my equal and my ally, can you not also turn an agreeable compliment?"

Involuntarily, the unfortunate bowed before the enemy of Oronius and pronounced: "Master, accept the tribute of my admiration. Savant Hantzen, I recognize in you the omnipotent god of science."

That blasphemy escaped his lips while he suffered atrociously from pronouncing it. Against such words his thought revolted; he detested his blasphemous tongue. Alas, it was no longer his will to which his lips were obedient, and the ironic smile of Yogha thanked him for it.

For his part, the vain Hantzen blossomed; as if he were unaware of the artificial and deceptive character of it, he respired with delight the gross incense that his partner offered him.

"Young man," he declared, arrogantly, "I am glad to see you in these sentiments... glad above all that you have escaped the grotesque influence of that beaten donkey, Oronius."

"What was Oronius compared to Hantzen?" proclaimed poor Jean, against his will.

"You're deserting his banner to range yourself under mine? Young man, you won't lose by the exchange. You'll replace the unlucky Jarrousse, who died, I can say, in the service of science... of *my* science."

"I shall be proud of that honor," the servile lips of the young engineer assured him.

But his thought protested: *Horror! Lie! Abominable blasphemy! Can't I succeed in breaking this bewitchment? I feel that all this is only a trick. I'm a prisoner of an association of charlatans and impostors. They're marvelous illusionists... but they're only illusionists. Their victory is only an appearance. The means they employed to subjugate me must similarly be no more than that... I'm dreaming... I'm living a horrible nightmare.*

Yogha's eternal smile enveloped him. Could she read his thought? Was she enjoying his suffering?

"Jean Chapuis," she said, all of a sudden, "am I not the one who occupies your thought uniquely?"

"You alone! You alone occupy it," Cyprienne's fiancé affirmed, fervently.

"I have always occupied it? I will occupy it forever?"

"Forever!"

Imposture! How it abominated him to launch that apostasy in a loud voice.

Yogha clapped her hands. It was a summons. A slave ran to prostrate herself before her and kissed her knees.

At the sight of that slave, Jean felt his heart lurch. Horror! It was Cyprienne... at least, it was the appearance of Cyprienne.

Poor Jean was too upset to remember immediately the transformation due to the carnoplastic methods of the virtuoso Hantzen. He did not think right way that he only had Turlurette before his eyes. He thought he was going to die.

A bizarre suffering, which could not manifest itself externally, since his visage remained as indifferent as if he had been in the presence of a stranger.

In any case, the scene was so rapid that images and thoughts collided within him. Cyprienne stood up—Cyprienne-Turlurette—but the fiancée only saw the beloved physiognomy, overwhelmed for the moment by an intense fear.

"Pille!" shouted Yogha, bursting into laughter.

Jan then saw one of the wild beasts that had been crawling at his feet a little while before and licking his hands bound forward in response to the appeal of the enchantress, knock down with a swipe of its claw the woman who had the features of Cyprienne, seize her and carry her away in its maw. It disappeared with her.

Impassive in appearance, the young fiancé was agonized.

"Imbecile!" cried Yogha, joyfully. "You know very well that that isn't Cyprienne!"

That's true! thought the young man, recovering slightly from his emotion. *It isn't Cyprienne.*

He was relieved by that, almost joyful. Only then did he think that it was Turlurette that the lion had just carried away in order to devour her.

He saw the wild beast reappear, voluptuously licking its bloody chops.

But that horrible spectacle could not succeed in moving him; he only repeated, with a sort of satisfaction: *It wasn't Cyprienne!*

"Would you recognize her?" questioned his persecutrix, at that moment.

He could not shudder, but all of his thought was stirred. He foresaw a new proof, perhaps more terrible than the one he had just undergone.

The revelations of the hypnotized Turlurette returned to his memory.

Cyprienne still exists; but she is no longer anything but a soul imprisoned in another body.

What body contained the soul of Cyprienne? What appearance had been inflicted on her? Such were the questions that obsessed the mind of the disciple of Oronius at that moment.

Again, Yogha clapped her hands. A second slave was detached from the group and came to stand before Jean Chapuis. He could not recognize Mandarinette—the *appearance* of Mandarinette. He only saw a young Chinese woman, who was considering him with a melancholy gaze. That was enough for him to be moved and to know further anguish.

For Yogha insinuated, with intention: "Perhaps this is her." Then, imperiously, she added: "Recognize her! I wish it!"

A little lap-dog surged forth, yapping at the Chinese woman. It started covering her with caresses. This time, Jean Chapuis recognized Kukuss. That was a revelation.

Advancing toward the Chinese woman he looked into her eyes. Then, with a frightful contraction of the heart, caused by an excessively violent mixture of joy and terror, in that olive-tinted visage, beneath those hooded eyelids, he recognized Cyprienne's gaze.

How sadly, how eloquently, that gaze met his own!

Recognize me, it implored.

And his mind clamored tumultuously: *It's Cyprienne! It's Cyprienne! Here she is, my beloved, under the new form that has been imposed on her.*

Yogha's impudent smile became ferocious. Oh, how she was about to make him suffer! The feline cruelty of a cat playing with an agonizing mouse was nothing compared to what that tenebrous soul contained.

"It's Cyprienne?" she repeated aloud, ironically. "You're quite certain that you recognize her? At present it seems, doesn't it, that you could rediscover her in a thousand? Well, we shall see."

She clapped her hands joyfully.

Young Chinese women, who were all wearing the same costume as Mandarinette, ran from all directions, surrounded the one who perhaps contained the soul of Cyprienne, seized her hands and drew her into a round dance. When they stopped in front of the bewildered Jean, there were thirty... fifty... a hundred similar faces, impossible to distinguish from one another.

There were a hundred Mandarinettes.

"Which is she?" demanded Yogha, mockingly. "Come on, make your choice." And as he kept silent, she added, redoubling her irony: "It's necessary, however, to decide to speak. I want to leave you the care of saving her or dooming her, for among these Chinese women, you are going to designate one who is going to die before your eyes, by your order. Perhaps that one will be Cyprienne!"

Her hand extended toward the group of young women. Her gesture commanded, irresistibly.

"Choose... and condemn!"

A stronger will dominated Jean Chapuis. He had to carry it out. He was about to choose... he sensed it. No revolt was possible, since his body no longer obeyed him.

In spite of himself, his hands made a gesture, redemptive for all, except one.

Horror! What if he were about to pronounce Cyprienne's death sentence without knowing it!

Anxiously—alas, that anxiety only existed in his thought; in the eyes of everyone, in the eyes of the woman who, in the midst of the group, was doubtless seeking his gaze, he remained impassive—anxiously, he studied the faces, interrogated the eyes.

All the faces resembled one another, all the eyes had an identical expression. Everywhere, everywhere, he saw no one but Cyprienne.

Multiplied by the magic power of Yogha, the unfortunate fiancé had before him a hundred exemplars of the face of Mandarinette.

"Well, go on then!" ordered the voice.

And his gesture, which he feared, his gesture, which he would have wished to retain, because it might be condemning

Cyprienne, Jean Chapuis made. Or, to put it better, his arm made it.

Moved by strings of which he did not have the direction, his hand extended, at random, and designated one of the young women.

"That one," said his lips, coldly.

Instantaneously, there was no longer more than one Chinese Mandarinette before him; for at the moment when he pronounced that phrase, all the others had disappeared, seeming to vanish into thin air.

Now, the only one that remained—the condemned one—Jean sensed with a frightful acuity, was Mandarinette—was Cyprienne.

Holding in her hand a sort of slender yataghan, Yogha stood up and approached the young man.

Shrugging his shoulders, Hantzen turned away, with a weary expression. "In truth, my dear, such affectations, in our epoch! You're stupid!" he growled.

Perhaps that was pity. Even monsters might be capable of it.

Yogha paid no heed to it.

She raised one of her hands.

A rope, uncoiling, appeared to fall from the sky and remain in the air.

The enchantress made another gesture. Mandarinette seized the extremity of the rope and began to climb.

Jean Chapuis, a prisoner of his inert body, followed her with his eyes, prey to horror and anguish.

He would have liked to hurl himself at Yogha; he could not. He remained there, nailed to the ground by her magic power. It was necessary for him to be an impassive witness of the scene.

Mandarinette climbed.

When she reached a certain height, there was a flash: the blade of the yataghan.

With a rapid semicircle traced in the air with the aid of the weapon, Yogha had just cut the rope.

Mandarinette collapsed on the ground.

What torture not to be able to utter the cry that remained in the breast of the young fiancé, stifling him. Oh, what torture!

On the grass, Mandarinette, her limbs broken, was still agitating, trying to get up and groaning, but Yogha, pouncing on her, assailed her with blows of the yataghan, making her arms and legs fly into the air, and then the head—which became invisible as soon as it was severed. Then the torso, launched by her, vanished in its turn... And of the victim, nothing remained but a little blood reddening the green grass.[13]

That was too much horror—more that Jean Chapuis could support.

Finally uttering he cry of horror that was rumbling within him, he fell full length, and fainted.

Immediately, the décor changed.

There was no longer any lawn, any palm grove, or any marvelous horizon.

Nothing remained but Hantzen and Yogha, lying on their divans in the same bizarre room where we saw them attempt to subjugate Cyprienne.

On a carpet lay the unconscious Jean Chapuis.

Hantzen pronounced disdainfully: "Have you finished with your phantasmagorias, my dear Yogha? I can amuse myself a little, then! It's the turn of science, if you please."

---

[13] Author's note: "These scenes, which are only phenomena of suggestion, are produced at will in India by certain fakirs, and notably by yoghis.

Chapter Twenty-Three
THE TRANSFORMATRIX

When he recovered his senses, Jean Chapuis no longer found the marvelous world, the mirage of which had vanished.

Before him, Otto Hantzen, surviving the recent illusions, was shaking him and looking at him with a feigned commiseration.

"Come one, young man, nerve!" he said. "Ought one to allow oneself to be taken in by such nonsense?"

"Cyprienne?" stammered the fiancé.

"Eh? She's quite well, of course… apart from the little modification that she owes to my genius, and which is only an insignificant pleasantry. Oh, you've been taken for a ride, young man."

"I saw!"

"Mirage! Trickery! It doesn't exist. Nothing of what that satanic Yogha inspires exists. She suggested everything to you, understand? It's not sorcery, in spite of appearances. I can show you much better things… yes, more solid. The veritable marvelous is about to commence… the real marvelous."

He helped the engineer to his feet.

Jean Chapuis stared at him fearfully. Who was this man?

"Come on, follow me," said Hantzen, paternally. "You're going to learn to know Otto Hantzen."

Majestically, he took the lead. Jean Chapuis followed him mechanically. The best proof that he was not yet liberated from the strange influence under which his intelligence was pliant and his will extinct is that he had not even shivered at the execrated name.

Whatever Hantzen said, the illusions persisted.

They both went into a room fitted out as a laboratory. It was there that the famous carnoplastic operation had taken place.

Jean was unaware of that detail. He only gazed with indifference, therefore, at the multiple items of apparatus that Hantzen's proud gestures indicated to him.

The eyes of Oronius' rival were flamboyant; a tumultuous passion agitated his adipose face.

"Young man," he said, majestically, "you are penetrating here into a sanctuary. This tabernacle contains more secrets than the cracked brain of the decrepit Oronius knew. Here beats the heart of Otto Hantzen; here dwells his soul. The profane do not have access to this room; to cross the threshold is to be condemned to death..."

He interrupted himself and marked a pause in order to enjoy the effect produced on his new subject.

Alas, it is necessary to admit that the effect was null, Far from being moved or marveling—above all, far from being sensible to the honor that was being granted to him, the young engineer listened to the words of his introducer with a perfect indifference.

Again, and more than ever, his thought appeared to be absent. He had fallen back into the apparent insensibility to which the magnetic influence of Yogha condemned him; but the vain scientist was nevertheless content; he could interpret everything to the taste of his pride. Hantzen wanted to take that attitude as a mark of deferential attention.

Taking care to emphasize by his tone the importance of the honor that he was doing his guest, he announced: "For you, young man, it won't be the same. You are, it appears, destined to finish your days among us and become one of ours. Yogha assures me that she will render you worthy of that favor. I have no reason to doubt her word; that excellent friend has already furnished me with numerous proofs of her possibilities. I only regret that she indulges in certain nonsense and that she employs empirical procedures... but let's pass on. Being one of ours, I no longer want to have any secrets from you. From this moment on, you'll become my confidant, my pupil, my disciple. Well, prepare to know the grandeur of my work and the audacity of my projects."

A further solemn gesture having commanded an increase of attention, he proclaimed: "This room stores a quarter of a century of formidable labor. Between these four walls, my genius has finally been able to blossom, thanks to the liberalities of the gracious Yogha and the unlimited means of which she disposes. Here I have been able to dream freely, to realize my dream and to accomplish the task for which I was born. It is not, believe me, young man, a paltry spirit of jealousy that led me to oppose Oronius. If I wanted to eclipse him it is because I know that my forehead is marked with the glorious sign of predestination. I am the awaited Reformer; I will remake the world!"

Jean Chapuis greeted that formidable pretention without blinking. Unleashed like a torrent, the improbable vanity of Otto Hantzen only succeeded, via his impressive declamations, in giving him an impression of fatigue, as if it were only the emptiest and most tedious of verbiage.

The person swollen by pride that he had before him was not impotent, he knew; his science, although it did not equal that of Oronius, could nevertheless do a great deal of harm. He ought, therefore, have paid more attention to the affirmation: "*I will remake the world*."

Perhaps he was announcing formidable upheavals, an entire era of frightful scourges.

In fact, in order to reconstruct, was it not necessary first to destroy. Was the existing order of the world truly menaced by Otto Hantzen? In that case, Humankind entire could expect to suffer. Perhaps horrific cataclysms were about to descend upon it.

In a corner of the laboratory, a sort of diabolical kitchen was installed; gigantic vessels were simmering gently over electric heaters; alembics were distilling multicolored liquids that passed into glass serpentines; veritable armies of bottles, flasks and test-tubes were arranged in the shelves.

Hantzen indicated all of that with a broad gesture.

"Here are my troops," he declared. "They're awaiting the hour of the great clearance. There is the wherewithal in here to rid the planet of everything that encumbers and spoils it, everything that opposes progress and the final perfection. Young man, until now, every time there has been mention of ameliorating humanity and commencing the reign of the age of the ideal, impressive stupidities have been pronounced. No one has imagined beginning at the beginning. Before talking about edifying the future world, it's necessary to make room—which is to say, to make everything that exists disappear. The present world reposes on error; it was spoiled in its origin; thus, it must disappear. I condemn it!"

The gesture accompanying those words would certainly have made Jean Chapuis shudder if the young scientist had enjoyed the plenitude of his faculties.

Hantzen, having mounted his favorite hobby-horse, was developing theories that were dear to him; he was exposing a project caressed for a long time.

"It's quite simple. The human race is utterly worthless; I shall suppress it. Don't protest, young man. Thanks to my colonies of microbes, my bacilli, my bottled epidemics, it will be an affair of a few weeks. A straw! A wind of death will pass over the five continents of the world and the Earth will be covered in cadavers. The scientific deluge will have given its proofs!"

"But the beasts?" stammered the engineer, whose eye reflected the horror involuntarily.

"A bagatelle, my dear. The beasts will perish too, that goes without saying, It's necessary to start from scratch. When there's no longer, on the surface of the continents, any living creature except for those I shall conserve as evidence of the past, I shall sanitize the world by means of a regenerative fire. I shall light the conflagration that will purify the Earth of all its flaws, all the memories accumulated by centuries of obscurantism. Can you glimpse the marvelous youth of what will grow, what will be edified, in that field of ashes? This time, it will be necessary to make anew! There will be no imitation, because all the models will have disappeared."

"But who will undertake that work of creation, since you will have annihilated the human race at the same time as the various species of animals and vegetables?" Jean objected.

"Have I not told you, petty inconsequent?" riposted Hantzen, serenely. "I shall conserve a few select subjects here and on a chosen island. But everything will be modeled in accordance with my will and the general lines of the new plan that I intend to follow. Don't be astonished. I've foreseen everything, and I'm ready. Do you see this machine?"

He opened the door to a hall and took the young engineer to a sort of metallic monster composed of pipes, boilers, towers and wheels; it could be recognized as a amalgam of a hundred machines, from a mechanical mortar to a pile-driver. It must have been able to crush, mold, laminate, saw, peel, polish, model and connect; it resembled simultaneously a perpetual motion machine and a digestive apparatus formed by complicated tubing.

At each of the two extremities of the monstrous organism, always in operation, from which a deafening noise escaped, there was a metallic door. Hantzen approached one of them.

"This is my machine for transforming people," he announced, while his face expanded, illuminated by a arrogant smile. "Would you like to see it function? One puts in a man and one takes out a dog, a seal or a dromedary. Thanks to my method, any organism is no more than an assemblage of interchangeable pieces, the disposition of which one can modify at will. If I lack one category of individuals, I can take individuals from another that is superabundant and pass the subjects through my transformatrix. For example..."

He whistled. A paltry and deformed little man presented himself, with no great enthusiasm. Hantzen looked at him scornfully.

"That's the work of nature," he sighed. "One can't claim that it's beautiful. For myself, this is what I make of it..."

He opened the steel door and shoved the runt brutally inside the machine. When the door was lodged in its grooves he

190

approached an indicative control panel, turned its handles, and punched five buttons.

The machine rumbled, roared, shook and shuddered; the tumult became infernal.

Then the fat man opened the other door and brought out a chubby and bestial colossus, who exhibited the muscles of an athlete.

"Perhaps the other was a thinker," said Hantzen, laughing loudly, "but from his filtered and softened substance I've taken a boxer, who is infinitely more useful. Darwin and his transformism are sunk; he explained, I realize. It's admirable, I tell you. Never any spoilage, never any malformations. One obtains exactly what one desires. And the functioning is so simple! A child could work the apparatus."

Successively, for the edification of Jean Chapuis, who was absolutely petrified, he delivered himself to a few surprising or ludicrous transformations. Thus, he metamorphosed a few subjects into a selection of various animals.

Then, taking on a malign expression to which his listener paid no heed, he proposed to him in a semi-amiable tone: "It's your turn, to conclude the session. Into what skin do you have the whim of introducing our last subject?"

Before Jean had time to think or wish, words sprang from his unconscious lips: "Into that of a white cat."

Sardonic laughter made him turn round.

Yogha came in, conducting Cyprienne under the features of Mandarinette. "As you wish!" she said.

Hantzen had seized the young woman and lunched her into the apparatus.

Astounded, Jean Chapuis did not have time to utter a cry.

Already, the diabolical transformatrix had functioned, and the second metallic door opened to let a white cat escape.

The nightmare gripped the young fiancé again, crushing his brain. With a groan, he leapt forward to seize the victim of that new malefic operation; but the cat lashed out at him with a clawed paw and fled through the door, which was ajar.

Bewildered, Jean Chapuis exited from the infernal study, leaning on the walls. He sensed his reason vacillating.

Behind him, Yogha and Hantzen were holding their sides; both of them were writhing with spasmodic laughter.

Chapter Twenty-Four
THE BODY AND THE SOUL

The young engineer's persecutors had not opposed his exit. They did not follow him.

Perhaps they estimated that he needed a little respite. By toying further with his brain they would have risked rendering him mad.

Cyprienne's fiancé had thus been able to draw away freely from the room in which he had just lived that new nightmare. Holding his forehead, he advanced, staggering.

"Have I lost my mind?" he murmured, with anguish. "Have I really seen what it seemed to me that I saw? Once already, under the suggestion of that terrible woman I've been able to believe that Cyprienne was dead, butchered before my eyes. Perhaps that metamorphosis machine that Hantzen claims to have invented is no more real.

His eyes revulsed. An immense despair invaded him. He was suffering the agony of a drowning man whose desperate efforts cannot hang on to anything.

"Where am I? What's happening to me? Do I still belong to myself?" he moaned, wildly. "Where does the power of that wretched female end? Is she going to torture me for much longer? I'm afraid... I'm afraid... for it isn't only my body that's in her hands, it's also mu mind that she can stop, en-slave and delude at the whim of her abominable caprice. That slavery surpasses everything imaginable."

He arrived at the end of the corridor in which he was en-gaged. Mechanically lifting the door-curtain by which it was terminated, he took three or four steps into a room in the Ori-ental style, uniquely furnished by a carpet and cushions. Jean Chapuis let himself fall on to the latter.

"What can I do? Does Cyprienne still exist?" he won-dered, desperately, hiding his face in his hands. "I've never experienced anything like it. Where does the phantasmagoria commence? Where does the real end? When am I a dupe? I no longer know. I no longer know!"

It was truly as if he were going insane and that Yogha's diabolical skill was triumphant. The unfortunate young man began to doubt everything that surrounded him; abused several times, having lost control of his will, he was not certain of having found it again. Overwhelmed by a sensation of utter impotence, he could no longer see anything to do. Everything seemed futile.

Death would have seemed less cruel to him.

Prostrate, he remained extended on the carpet, refusing to contemplate a world whose reality he doubted. He suspected that, since exiting the Spherus, he had not ceased to be the victim of successive mirages. Of two things only he could have no doubt—two equally terrible things.

On the one hand, he was in the hands of Yogha and Hantzen—the mysterious woman who persecuted him, and the rival of his master Oronius, now deceased; for in his terrible agony he had finally been able to understand the name pompously repeated by his latest torturer.

On the other hand, Cyprienne had been abducted by the Spherus. That he could not doubt. But was it her that he had seen from the Halcyon? Perhaps. In any case, it was only her appearance that he had found since. So where was his dear fiancée, if she still existed? Would he ever find her again?

"Jean! My poor Jean!" appealed a voice that he believed he recognized: his fiancée's voice.

Although his heart leapt, he dared not raise is head; he was so afraid of being the dupe of a mirage. Was this not a new invention of Yogha in order to take hold of her victim again, to torment him further?

The appeals continued, insistently.

"Jean! Answer me! Is it really you? What have they done to you?"

The temptation became too strong. The young man sat up, and perceived three feminine silhouettes a few paces away,

In appearance, they were Cyprienne, Turlurette and Mandarinette. Deceptive forms? Undoubtedly. Interchangeable physiognomies? Probably. He had been fooled too often not to be on his guard.

It was Mandarinette who was speaking. The other two conserved their unintelligent appearance, and the exterior they had presented when the young engineer had joined them inside the flying ball.

"Jean!" repeated the one who had Mandarinette's features, in a suppliant voice. "Come round. Talk to me. Be strong. They can be resisted; I can affirm that. Sustained by a force that inspired me, I stood up to Yogha and Hantzen. They've been able to steal my appearance, but, stronger than the two wretches, I haven't abandoned my soul to them."

"Is that true? Is that sure?" stammered Oronius' pupil, half radiant and half fearful. "I've seen prodigies... so frightful... that I no longer know what I can believe."

He stood up and tried to approach her. The false Mandarinette had sketched a similar movement—but at the moment when they came together they both bumped into an invisible obstacle: a wall of air that encaged the young man, while permitting him to see and to be seen.

Laridon, if he were still alive, might have been able to give them the key to the mystery; at least, he could have put Jean Chapuis on the track of the explanation.

In fact, would that have been very useful to the two disillusioned individuals? Jean and Cyprienne observed the new phenomenon without seeking its cause. They could only take account of the fact that the mysterious force that kept them apart originated from the floor.

Desolate, the fiancé murmured: "You see... it's continuing."

Cyprienne remained calm. "What does one prodigy more matter?" she said. "We're in a land of illusion. That's what you need to understand."

Jean Chapuis looked alternately at Mandarinette, who was speaking with his fiancée's voice, and Turlurette, who offered her living mage.

To see them and hear them thus, in duplicate—an insensible form and a mind imprisoned in a strange envelope—to hear her speaking with another voice, to sense her gaze in eyes that were not hers and did not even have the same color, was a very strange and very cruel impression.

Under two distinct forms he had the body and soul of Cyprienne before him. Separated, neither of those two parts of herself could succeeded in rendering Jean the impression of her dear presence.

He remained anxious and disconcerted.

Cyprienne, in her new body, was also suffering from her fiancé's anguish.

"Ah!" moaned the young man, pressing his forehead. "Who can get us out of this damnable nightmare? It would require the genius of Oronius... and your poor father is no more."

"The spirit is immortal," Cyprienne retorted, with an impressive confidence. "I can feel the spirit of Oronius within me. It makes use of my flesh, it guides my soul. It will save us."

The engineer shivered. Suddenly he remembered the strange struggle that he had sensed within himself twice. It was the struggle of two wills external to his.

He too, at that moment, had had the same idea. Like Cyprienne, he had thought of the Master's spirit, the spirit surviving and making itself manifest. Oronius dead against Yogha alive! Oronius struggling from the beyond against Otto Hantzen's ally! Was it necessary to share Cyprienne's faith? To believe that extravagant collision possible and realizable?

She's deluded, he thought. *It's her own will that is struggling, unknown to her, against our enemy. And it's only by virtue of a pious error of her filial amour that she imagines that she recognizes her father's intervention... for myself, I've been the dupe of an analogous sentimen*t.

Translating his discouragement, he murmured: "All hope is chimerical, all struggle vain. If, like me, my beloved Cyprienne, you had experienced the infernal power of the woman who reigns here, you'd be convinced that it only remains for us to wish for death. It's the only deliverance on which we can count. But even that hope is forbidden to us. Other illusions are reserved for us. Why are we in this place? What do they want to do with us? What destiny awaits us?"

To that question, it was the voice of Yogha that replied: "You shall know!"

And the mysterious silhouette reappeared, hieratical, radiant and more ethereal than an idol.

Surrounded by servants, Yogha advanced toward her prisoners. Her gesture tried to move aside the three young women.

The false Cyprienne and the false Turlurette, still submissive to her magnetic influence, obeyed meekly. Only Mandarinette resisted. With her eyes, in which the gaze of Cyprienne lived, she stood up to Yogha.

"You know full well that you don't control and can't subjugate my will," she said.

Fiery radiance darted from the Hindu woman's eyes.

"We'll see about that before long," she replied. "The day won't pass without witnessing your defeat, proud girl. If your mind resists me, remember that I'm the mistress of your two bodies—the one that belongs to you and the one that I've imposed on you. You'll obey me, therefore." Turning to her servants, she said: "Take her away. But let her remain within earshot. I want her to be convinced of the inopportunity of her resistance to my power."

The women drew Cyprienne into one of the corners of the room.

The, attaching the gaze of her glittering pupils to Jean Chapuis, Yogha seized his hand.

The wall of air that had separated the two fiancés had vanished before her like a dying breath.

197

Jean had attempted to repel his persecutrix with horror, but as he sketched the gesture a sudden numbness had paralyzed his arm, and it had fallen back devoid of strength. He abandoned himself, since his body had ceased to obey him once more.

"When I wish it," said Yogha, emphasizing her enchanting and mortal smile, "it will be your spirit that will become my slave. It's necessary that you understand that. Before then, we have to talk."

"Why are you persecuting me?" asked the young man, bitterly. "Have I harmed you? Had my fiancé had the misfortune to displease you? Tell me why you are attacking us thus."

Yogha's gaze transpierced him like a blade.

"Have you not divined it?" she sighed, in a profound voice. "If I have pursued you, it's because I love you, Jean Chapuis."

The young engineer felt an icy frisson. In truth, that declaration of love bore a singular resemblance to a declaration of hatred. She had hurled it at him like a threat.

He saw the group of young women in the distance; he saw the indolent and passive pose of Cyprienne, and the sad gaze of Mandarinette. That was the work of the sorceress.

At that thought, anger seethed within him. He tried to revolt, to slap the magicienne with his scorn in order to return a little of the harm that she had done him.

"But I don't love you, and I never will. I despise you, and you horrify me." His intention was to shout those words in order to be heard by Cyprienne, but he only succeeded in murmuring them in an imperceptible voice.

There again, Yogha's mysterious power intervened and enchained him. And her bland smile remained fixed on her thin lips, perhaps more malevolent. Her ardent voice became mocking.

"Don't boast. You're not unaware that I can oblige you to love me and forget Cyprienne. That will be my vengeance. Through you, I can even torture her. Do you imagine that you are anything but a plaything in my hands? Know that I can attain, within your skull, the mysterious cells that command your sentiments as well as your actions. Know that the personality doesn't exist in the presence of a superior will. If it pleases me—and it will please me—I could efface the image of Cyprienne from your mind, as easily as one faces chalk from a blackboard, and I could transport to her the horror that I inspire in you. Child's play! In the domain of the sentiments and impressions everything is artifice; the imaginary effaces the real. What difference could you detect between the spontaneous sentiments that you imagine you experience and those that I can suggest and impose upon you? Within two minutes, Jean Chapuis, you would be a new man. You would be plunged in a dream from which you would never awake, a dream that would be our life henceforth. Because of you, the beautiful eyes of the woman you claim to cherish would shed bitter tears. You would be her torturer. You would not know her, and no fiber of your flesh could be moved by her. Tell yourself that. Think about that before I put your thought to sleep, in order to insufflate it with mine."

The young fiancé tried in vain to escape the radiation of that terrible gaze; his fascinated eyes could no longer detach themselves from it. He could not even make them turn toward the form that contained the mind of Cyprienne.

Into that gaze he would have put so much love; he would have liked to make it contain all the tenderness with which his heart was overflowing and render it so persuasive that Cyprienne would never be able to doubt him in future, if Yogha's abominable design were realized.

That was not permitted to him. The implacable fascination mastered him.

"Go to sleep, Jean Chapuis," pronounced Yogh, imperiously. "Lose the memory of your present life and only open your eyes to see the world where my eyes will be the only light and my love the only joy. Sleep!"

With her hand she brushed the young man's eyelids and then his forehead; and the fiancé, still semi-conscious, saw the image that he had believed to be forever alive in his heart begin to blur, becoming vague and misty...

It was not only the room and the silhouettes of the three young women that were gradually effaced an disappeared from his memory. It was also, and above all, the beloved image of Cyprienne whose features ceased to move him. With a despair that was also about to weaken, he felt it gradually beginning to become foreign to him.

Her arm extended and her gaze fixed. Yogha completed her work of suggestion.

Vanquished Jean Chapuis collapsed on the cushions, his eyes closed and his face calm.

Triumphant, the dispenser of the secrets of the Buddhist Nirvana leaned over him, and then straightened up.

"Hantzen! Hantzen! Hantzen!" she called, three times.

Oronius' rival appeared immediately.

She designated Mandarinette to him. "You can take her now," she said, in a hateful voice. "Body and soul, she belongs to you. Do with her what you will. I have no further need of her."

At a gesture from the scientist the slaves were already taking away the three young woman when, changing hr mind, Yogha ran toward her monstrous accomplice and grabbed him by the arm.

"I want her to suffer," she insisted, in a hissing voice. "You understand? Make her suffer!"

"Don't worry," replied the odious scientist, with a treble grimace. "Don't worry. Yogha. She will suffer as no human creature has ever suffered."

Chapter Twenty-Five
THE PRISONER OF ILLUSION

Asleep in the hypnotic trance into which Yogha had plunged him, Jean Chapuis believed that he awoke in a new décor, but without knowing how he had been transported there.

He had lost all memory of the scene that had just unfolded.

But an indescribable passion, which he believed to be inked in his heart, had taken possession of his entire being.

"Yogha!" he murmured, passionately.

Where had he awakened? Once again he was scarcely anxious about that, and seemed to find it quite natural to find himself installed in a splendid solitude before a majestic palace.

He was on the summit of a mountain, and the world—the entire world—extended at his feet, as if it were being offered to him.

For those plains and valleys, the villages and forests, Jean Chapuis did not spare a glance.

He saw Yogha emerge from the palace, smiling and tender. He held out his arms toward her.

"Yogha!"

With the fervor to a deep-rooted passion he had pronounced that sweet name. Like he expression on his face, his attitude and all his gestures pronounced tht the woman who was coming was his uncontested idol, reigning without division over his heart.

A prisoner of the terrible illusion, he saw nothing but her, and he saw her with enslaved eyes.

The prediction and the desire of the Hindu woman were accomplished. Cyprienne was forgotten. Infidel without knowing it, the blinded fiancé imagined the he loved Yogha.

In order to savor her triumph, she made herself sweet and seductive.

And yet, was it truly a victory? Was all that real or artificial? Artificial, alas. That marvelous world, that palace, those expanses only existed, in sum, in her imagination, which passed the abusive mirage to Jean by means of suggestion.

He was dreaming all that. As for her, she was following his dream and delighting in it; for such was the bizarre and imaginary satisfaction that the woman was pursuing. In order to understand that, it is necessary not to forget that she had attained the highest degree of initiation among the sages of India, whose science and practices are aimed at the liberation of the mind from its prison of flesh and rendering it capable of immaterial joys.

In fact, if the material world is limited, if one can only travel it slowly and with difficulty, on the contrary, the domain of thought is limitless, and the mind of a yoghi is able to move there with lightning speed.

To the unlimited domain, infinite power!

Yogha knew that, and she also knew that, pushed to a certain degree of acuity, dream is confounded with reality, procures the same sensations, and leaves the same profound traces in the memory. That is why, following in the mind of Jean Chapuis what was only a simple fiction, she succeeded, by means of the energy of her fluid, in associating herself with it and according it the same value as if it had been reality.

What did the sleeping body of the young engineer matter, after all? Matter is perishable. Was not his true self the personality disengaged from that envelope—his thought?

That thought, captive of Yogha, followed the latter meekly in the imaginary world and yielded to her caprice. Yogha could triumph, for Jean Chapuis' dream continued.

Approaching him, the enchantress leaned her charming head on the young man's shoulder and murmured in a languid voice: "My beloved, do you truly only love me?"

"Who would dare to claim the contrary," replied the fiancé of Oronius' daughter.

"That Cyprienne."

"What Cyprienne?" The young engineer's face expressed a sincere surprise. One might have thought that he was hearing the name for the first time. By the will of his dominatrix he denied his fiancée... but Yogha was insatiable and meditating an even crueler game.

"You don't know her, you say? Then why does she claim to know you? She sustains that you love her. She outrages me. She tortures my heart."

Jean's eyes shone with anger. "It's an abominable imposture!" he cried. "Have that audacious person come; I want to put an end to her impertinent lie."

"I love you," said Yogha, tenderly. "Oh, my beloved, protect me! Deliver me from the persecutions of that infamous woman. Don't permit her to humiliate me further."

"Have her come, and you'll see."

The arms of the enchantress extended in the direction of the palace. "Cyprienne! Cyprienne!" she called, in a harsh voice.

And Cyprienne appeared—Cyprienne with her true face, as touching and pretty as the persecutrix wanted, in order to savor her implacable vengeance.

Jean Chapuis remained insensible. "On your knees!" he ordered, in a convulsed voice. "On your knees before the princess, little liar. Beg her pardon."

And, taking the unfortunate woman by the shoulders, he threw her to the ground brutally and forced her to bow down before the infernal Hindu.

As was her habit, the latter smiled.

In vain the unfortunate Cyprienne, more beautiful and more touching than ever, tried to implore pity, sobbing. In vain she cried in a heart-rending voice: "Jean! My Jean! Save me! Don't crush me! Don't torture me!"

Deaf to that adored voice, which did not reach his petrified heart, the young man weighed even more heavily upon the frail shoulder; and the young woman, in despair, yielded, groaning. Her forehead struck the ground; her marvelous hair spread out in a golden flood.

Jean was unmoved. "Beg pardon!" he thundered, again. "Admit your imposture."

Then, suddenly tearing herself away from the grip that held her pinned to the ground, Cyprienne stood up. "Never! Never!" she cried, with sobs in her throat. And she ran away madly, running down the slope toward a lake that extended below.

"She won't escape me!" Jean roared. "Have no fear, my beloved Yogha. I'll bring her back, dead or tamed." And he launched himself in pursuit of his fiancée.

The most insensitive of Nimrods does not bring a more cruel determination to forcing a tremulous hind than Oronius' pupil put into tracking Cyprienne.

She had reached the foot of the slope, but the lake barred her path. She was about to be caught; she threw herself into the water.

Immediately, she uttered a cry of fright. "Help, Jean! Save me!"

Horrible forms had just surged forth from the depths of the water. There was nothing but gigantic mouths, jaws bristling with monstrous teeth, and clawed feet extended in order to rip. They whistled, roared and growled. There were representatives of marine and lacustrian monsters of all the ages: saurians, sharks, plesiosaurs, and others even more hideous, which belonged to legend.

Struggling in the middle of the circle of death, Cyprienne extended her arms toward Jean.

He saw a monster with the upper body of a woman, covered in scales, but whose face was surmounted by tresses of serpents, like the Gorgon, seize the young woman and plunge fingers terminated by sharp claws into her neck. The gaping mouths opened wider, grabbing the delicate limbs. They were about to close again...one second more and, torn apart before her fiancé's eyes, Cyprienne disappeared in water tinted by blood.

Impassive, Jean Chapuis smiled cruelly as he contemplated that frightful spectacle. He listened to a voice that murmured to him, perfidiously: "She's going to die... you're going to see her devoured... rejoice..."

Suddenly, like a veil tearing, the horrible vision disappeared; and Jean Chapuis, abruptly recalled to the memory and the consciousness of everything that had just happened, found himself facing his persecutrix, an uttered a cry of horror. Reawakened, he remembered!

He was in a cage of glass and under a kind of shower apparatus. Facing him, under her transparent mask, Yogha seemed amazed by that abrupt awakening.

Jean did not give her time to collect herself; he hurled himself upon her, roaring.

Chapter Twenty-Six
THE FOUR PROOFS

What had become of Laridon and Julep? Seized by the squid, they found themselves in a terrible situation. It was not difficult for them, now, to understand the significance of the ironic sniggers they had heard as they entered he dried-out aquarium. Those sniggers had certainly been uttered by the geophages, who saw their fugitives throwing themselves into a trap.

Vigilant guardians, the squid stopped the mortals audacious enough to attempt to cross the portals of Hantzen's refuge. Laridon and Julep were certainly on the right path, but, seized by the murderous tentacles, they stood no chance of profiting from their discovery.

The squid, to give them he vulgar name that is generally attributed to them, were in reality clawed cephalopods, or *onychoteuthis*. It was a veritable tour de force on Hantzen's part to have brought them and acclimated the huge mollusks, which usually live in warm waters, to that subterranean aquarium.

The ones that were attacking Laridon and Julep at that moment belonged to the species *Onychoteuthis robusta*, known for its ferocity and its gigantic size; they came from the seas of Oceania, where they were particularly feared by pearl fishers, whom they did not hesitate to attack. Their tentacles were equipped with hooks and suckers, forming a formidable apparatus of prehension.

From such a grip it is impossible to escape; it is fatally mortal. Having recovered from their initial stupor, however, neither Laridon nor Julep was discouraged. Undoubtedly, the ferocious squid were surrounding them and enlacing them with tentacles, the grip of the suckers rendering them incapable of the slightest gesture of defense, but neither of them had let go of his electric weapon. It only required a simple pressure, therefore, to launch the mortal current, calculated to kill all those that were touching them.

A frightful shock convulsed the squid; the suckers let go; the tentacles became flaccid and dead, and the huge bodies collapsed at the feet of the two men.

Around Laridon and Julep there was nothing but the cadavers of cephalopods, and those that rushed to the rescue suffered the same fate. In five minutes the terrible battle was concluded. The cavern-aquarium was purged of its monsters.

Laridon and Julep breathed easier. They perceived then that they had water up to their waists. The initial alarm, and then the ardor of the combat they had just sustained had prevented them thus far from paying any attention to it, but behind them—and soon everywhere—as soon as they had crossed the threshold of the aquarium, the water had begun to flow back in through invisible fissures. It was running over the walls, springing from the ground and falling from the vault.

In a few minutes, the squids' aquarium was full again. Thus, to facilitate the victory of the terrible guardians of the cavern, a double trap had been set: the audacious violators of Hantzen's domain had as much chance of being drowned as being devoured. But that second peril only made Laridon and Julep laugh.

"Good, right!" mocked the former. "They're refusing us nothing. Now it's a bath. Fortunately, we're costumed for diving. In preparing his nice surprise for us, Hantzen hadn't foreseen that we'd be clad in diving-suits. Forward, old chap!"

Cleaving through the water, which was now above their shoulders, they headed for the extremity of the grotto and engaged in the spiral staircase.

"*Sapristoche!*" swore Laridon, climbing the steps precipitately in order to do so more rapidly than the water. "I forgot my little fellow—the miniature who's stuck in my pocket! It's not waterproof and he must have had a big drink, poor little thing!"

As soon as he had passed the last flooded steps he stopped, shaking himself like a barbet, and plunged his right hand into the pocket that contained the captive. He pulled the geophage out.

To his great surprise, the little being did not appear to have been inconvenienced in the least by his prolonged bath. Was he provided with a respiratory system that permitted him to lead the life of fish, if necessary? Could he isolate and absorb oxygen from water as he did from mud? It seemed probable. In any case, the fact was that he was alive.

"I prefer that," declared Laridon. "When we get out of his and return to Paris with M'sieur Jean and Mamzelle Cyprienne, without forgetting Turlurette, it will be a souvenir of my voyage. I'll show it off to amuse the mates, and then I'll give it to the zoo. You can see from here the scientific placard that they'll stick on his cage: *Sewage clown; donated by Monsieur Laridon, Parisian.* You can bet that I'll pass to posterity, my old Julep. Good, good, the kid's promising."

As the fellow pronounced those optimistic words, he emerged from the top of the stairway, with the negro on his heels, and discovered a new room. There, a furious concert of irritated hissing greeted them.

This time, terror chilled them, while a double cry escaped from their throats.

At their feet, above their heads, everywhere, a frightful swarm of snakes surrounded them. All ophidian genres were represented, from the smallest, which did not surpass seven or eight centimeters, to the largest, measuring eight meters in length.

There were vipers and spectacled cobras, and there were also those vulgarly called rattlesnakes, as well as boa constrictors, in company with elapids and vine snakes.

Furious heads with terrible little eyes rose up, mouths agape, showing fangs with mortal venom, coils whose grip could break bones, relaxing and stretching the body with a view to swallowing, favored by lubricating floods of saliva.

Before that swarming of imbricated scales, ventral plaques, horned, elastic and shiny, that unleashing of fury and menace of so many reptiles ready to bite or devour, Laridon and Julep thought their last hour had come. The electric weapons were insufficient to the task. At the most they could kill a few dozen snakes, but how could they prevent all the fangs attaining them? It would be sufficient for a single one to reach its target, and the venom would d its work.

"Mother!" murmured Landon. "Those are some teeth. When I think that I've never be able to abide dentists! If I could unearth a fine pulling crew at present, I'd have them operate on these individuals. *Bonsoir*, world! Instead of a diving-suit, I should have brought a suit of armor."

"That sting! That not good!" moaned Julep.

"Very bad! You're not exaggerating, my old zebra. But it's necessary to be reasonable. We've come where we're not invited. It might be that it's among these forked tongues that we're going to be put in the spicy sauce: too bad! Now it's necessary to finish well. It was bound to happen someday. I only regret not having seen Turlurette again. Let's go! Take the adventure full on. Laugh and see what they say to us. To the first of these gentlemen!

And the intrepid mechanic, as motionless as a marble stature, watched stoically as the menacing circle of reptiles tightened around himself and his companion.

It was then that an unexpected incident occurred that might have made the Parisian say: "That's it, old man, we've got charmed lives!"

At the moment when a veritable living wall of fangs enclosed the two men and seemed ready to fall upon them, a bizarre modulation became audible. The fury of the reptiles was suddenly appeased. It was a shrill and monotonous song—and it was coming from Laridon's pocket.

The later observed the immediate effect that it had on the reptiles. The hissing had ceased; still extended—but in order to listen with delight; the flat triangular heads were no longer menacing.

Stupefied, the mechanic looked at his pocket.

From there, as if on a balcony, the geophage was staring at the serpents while his lips modulated that singular tune. The little being possessed the art of charming snakes. Perhaps without suspecting it, for his personal preservation, by utilizing his talent, he was saving the lives of Laridon and Julep.

"What luck!" exclaimed the mechanic, already recovered from his alarm. "Here's a resourceful midget! My fortune is made. I'll pick up hundreds of them to sell. Against snakebite, who doesn't have his lucky charm! What a fetish! What did I tell you, Julep?"

"Massa Laridon never said," the worthy negro protested. "But I'm content. Serpents tame. Julep take them and put them in his sack."

"Don't do that, old man! By way of a sack you have a pocket, but not big enough to stuff them in. Better to profit from their melomania to break them. Let's go. And you, the band, go through your best repertoire."

Followed by the black man, the audacious fellow took two steps toward the living wall. Miracle! It opened up. Before the geophage charmer the reptiles moved aside meekly and formed a double hedge of ecstasized heads, swaying rhythmically.

The chamber of serpents was thus traversed without hindrance and the two men found themselves confronted by anther staircase. It was closed by a glass door. Laridon only had to pull to open it. It closed by itself behind him and the negro, separating them from the snakes.

The geophage immediately fell silent and the furious hissing resumed, louder than before; but the perilous passage had been crossed.

"After that, we can expect anything," Laridon pronounced philosophically. "What are we going to find next?"

They knew as soon as they arrived at the top of the steps; they found themselves at the entrance to a wide brightly-lit corridor. Flames were visible at the extremity, departing from the floor and rising all the way to the ceiling, which they were licking. It was the mouth of a furnace or the entrance to a brazier. In any case, it could be called an uncrossable passage.

Merely on seeing it, the boldest adventurer would have had to turn back.

Laridon went forward.

Like salamanders, did he believe that he could live in fire?

"Great! That must be warm!" he murmured. "But it's necessary to pass, though. We haven't come this far to go back. Anyway, the people of the house pass through, so there must be a trick to it."

That trick, if it existed, did not seem to be easy to discover. The two explorers squinted their eyes but they could not see anything but the prolongation of the flaming gallery. The alarming brazier continued for at least thirty meters.

"Not comfy," sight Laridon, scratching the back of his neck. "One hasn't learned to live in a grill-room. That's a mistake."

In fact, although the diving-suit protected them against the risk of asphyxia, and its asbestos could defend them against the reach of the flames, they would be unable to support the heat that the brazier was emitting.

However, they continued drawing closer. They arrived so close that by reaching out a hand they could touch the flames. They were not uncomfortable; they did not feel any elevation of temperature.

Julep took note of that first. "I'm not hot," he said.

Cold flames; a fire that did not burn—the Parisian had never seen that. "So it's a kind of bluff for those who believe it?" he suggested. "Well, well! Not bad. But it won't hold with us."

And without flinching, he advanced bravely into the brazier. The fire roared and growled; the flames hissed—but he did not experience any other inconvenience. And Julep, who followed him, did not suffer any either. Without encumbrance, as cool as when they had entered it, they arrived at the extremity of the corridor of fire.

"It's getting easy," said the mechanic. "The geophages and the animated machines, the squid and the snakes were dangerous, no doubt about it. But the moment it's a matter of trickery, we arrive in an armchair... not so, old chap?"

He was not exaggerating. With fellows of his stripe, the phantasmagorias of Yogha and Hantzen were insufficient barriers. They had just penetrated into the zone of harmless illusions, to which Jean Chapuis had owed so much suffering and terror.

The corridor of fire was succeeded by a small square room of very modest dimensions. Apart from the door through which they had entered it, there did not seem to be any issue. However, the paving stones of the floor and the vault were pierced by two circular openings facing one another.

"We can get out that way or go no further," decided Laridon, pointing at the upper opening. "I'm neglecting the hole in the floor. I haven't come up here only to go back down."

The upper hole was black and vertical.

No stairway," he muttered. Not even a haulage chain. In any case, the ceiling is so high that it can't be reached without a ladder. You don't have one on you, old pal?"

No. Julep had not thought of equipping himself with that utensil.

Not at all discouraged, Laridon switched his attention to the floor. He observed then that the hole that opened there had the form of a funnel. One could plunge one's arm into the hole, but the body could not follow it.

"Another mouse-path," the mechanic lamented. "This is becoming annoying. If we haven't a ladder, what can we use?"

He raised and lowered his eyes alternately to examine the two openings, and told himself that there had to be a reason why they were disposed thus.

In fact, he thought, *perhaps my midget knows the way. Let's see about that.*

Pulling the geophage out of his pocket, he untied his arms and legs, but attached him by the belt. Then, keeping the extremity of the leash in his hands, he deposited the pygmy inside the funnel. He only just had time to withdraw his hand

and release the strap, which slipped between his fingers, violently snatched.

The geophage had barely touched the surface of the funnel when he was seized by a blast of air emerging from the central orifice, and was lifted up like a wisp of straw by a whirlwind. The little creature spun in the air for a moment and then, lifted up by an invisible force, was hurled toward the vault, which absorbed him, and into which he disappeared.

"Damn!" swore the mechanic. "That's some draught! It's stolen my phenomenon. Go run after it now! Oh, well," he added, slapping his forehead. "I'll catch up with it, and by the same route. The hole's big enough. Too bad if there's a bump. I'm hurling myself into the unknown. After that, old Julep, if you want to use the elevator, there it is."

Having said that, he leapt bravely into the funnel and allowed himself to be seized in his turn by the current of air.

A violent wind whipped his entire body; he felt himself seized and thrown into the air like a simple ball. A second later, he was rising vertically through a black hole at an improbably vertiginous speed, and then his respiration was cut off.

Chapter Twenty-Seven
ON THE ROOF OF THE WORLD

The vertical chimney that departed from the vault traversed a rocky mass of an interminable height. Rapid as the ascension was, it lasted more than ten minutes.

If he had been capable of an approximate calculation, Laridon could have deduced that the blast of air lifted him several hundred meters. Not having mathematical knowledge adequate to devote himself to such reflections, he limited himself to thinking: *Funny elevator! It's a hoot!*

Abruptly, he surged out of the shadow.

In open air, the column of air, conserving its velocity momentarily, projected the mechanic fifty meters above the orifice of the chimney—but at that height, its force was exhausted; like a jet of water at the end of its course, it spread out in a bouquet to fall back.

Turlurette's suitor, sliding along that cascade of air, fell back gently on to the ground a few meters away from the well from which he had emerged. Stunned and stifled, searching for breath, he remained supine on the ground for a few minutes. It was in that position that he was able to see a black mass emerge from the well and rise up before falling back, as he had done. That was the faithful Julep; not wanting to be separated from Laridon, he had not hesitated to take the same "elevator."

The two living bolides did not take long to get to their feet. They were both somewhat bruised, but nothing was broken; they shook themselves and looked around curiously.

"Terminus," Laridon announced. "The funicular has deposited us at the door."

A simple glance, in fact, sufficed for them to realize that they had reached their goal. The ground on to which the jet of air had just thrown them had to be the mysterious summit to which Otto Hantzen and Yogha intended to forbid access to mortals. It was the summit of Mount Everest, or Gaurishankar,[14] the culminating point of the globe, the height of which attained nearly nine thousand meters.

If he had read that name on the monument edified by Hantzen, Jean Chapuis could have told is two friends that Gaurishankar—"the roof of the world"—is situated in the central region of the Himalayan mountains, on the frontier of Nepal and Tibet. For want of those geographical precisions, the Parisian saw with his eyes what Cyprienne's fiancé did not know—to wit, the real aspect of Hantzen's domain, at the entrance to which he found himself, and by what method that domain was rendered invisible and inaccessible to the rest of humankind.

The summit of Everest presented the form of a circular plateau with a radius of fifty meters. Its flatness and its regular form were doubtless due to the labor of adaptation of which Yogha's ally had been the engineer. Nature is more whimsical.

At any rate, that plateau bore in its central part a tower of aluminum, or some metal presenting the appearance of aluminum. The summit of the tower appeared to be lost in clouds—clouds of artificial origin.

The entire exterior edge of the plateau was surrounded by a ditch, or, more exactly, a circular trench, from which sprang, launching into the sky to close as a dome above the tower, a kind of liquid or fluid wall, the molecules of which seemed to be vibrating. That was the product of the subterra-

---

[14] In reality, Gaurishankar is not Mount Everest, but another peak, the second highest in the Himalayas. It lies near the western edge of the Rolwaling Himal, about 100 kilometers (62 miles) northeast of Kathmandu. It is almost directly between Kathmandu and Mount Everest, and is visible from Kathmandu. Mount Everest is known as Sagarmatha in Nepali and Chomolungma in Tibetan. The first official ascent by Hillary and Norgay was made in 1953, although Mallory and Irvine had made a ultimately unsuccessful attempt in 1924. At the time of writing, no one knew what the summit looked like.

nean factory of which Laridon and Julep had surprised the functioning. A curtain of compressed air projected vertically and circularly enclosed the summit of the mountain in a kind of diving-bell. Inside that bell, within the breathable atmosphere artificially produced and maintained by the slaves, rose the Tower of Mirages, the residence of Otto Hantzen.

"Of course! My comprehension is opening," murmured the mechanic, considering the wall of air, the vibrations of which, agitating its mass, ensured the invisibility of the tower. "Yes, I can understand how M'sieur Jean disappeared, and the Halcyon-Car bumping into the immovable obstacle. It's that hidden wall of which I made the tour, and which repelled me. That's the trick... we're inside. Above the tower there must be the Spherus; that's why it seems to be fixed in a cloud. There's an entrance in the attic. I've got that in the noggin."

The tower was high and broad; but how small it would have appeared and how that smallness would have surprised him, if he had been able to contemplate, like Jean Chapuis, the imaginary worlds that it contained!

It was in that aluminum cylinder that the mysterious power of Yogha enclosed the enchanting landscapes with which she had initially delighted Jean's gaze! What a revelation that would have been for the young engineer if he had been in Laridon's place! Observing the restricted dimensions of the domain of Yogha and Hantzen, he would have understood the truth immediately: in all that he had seen, there was nothing real except that tower of six floors, isolated from the rest of the world.

For the rest, there was nothing but illusion imposed by a creature expert in the occult art of suggestion.

Slowly and suspiciously, the mechanic made a tour of the secret refuge. Julep followed him nervously. The worthy negro could not get over it. After so many adventures, he conserved a vague anxiety about what might yet happen to him. In sum, he was mistrustful... but anyone would have been in his place.

"Not a good place," he muttered, darting angry glances around him. "I not want to go in, not want to risk the pretty skin I owe to Massa Oronius!"

The two companions arrived in front of a door. No servant ensured its closure; in order to open it, it was only necessary to push. Judging sufficient the precautions he had taken in choosing the geophages, the squid and the serpents as concierges, Hantzen had neglected to bolt it. He did not think that anyone would attempt successfully to penetrate his lair. He had counted without Laridon's perseverance.

Without appearing to have heard Julep's complaint, the mechanic indicated the door.

"That's the way it's necessary to go to rejoin M'sieur Jean and his company. What do you say?"

"Julep say, damn it, let's go!" the worthy negro replied, sighing wholeheartedly. "Even if Massa Laridon wants to kill him."

"How idiotic you can be, my poor chap. I intend to preserve your hide as much as your skin can take, firstly in the cause of your esthetics—you're what they call a rare specimen."

Flattered, Julep swelled with pride

"If there were a false step in there, the joker continued, "it would be a irreparable misfortune. Be convinced of this, then: if I push you to penetrate behind me into that tower, it's because there isn't any danger."

"I not believe those fine words."

"Impertinent. For incredulity, you could give lessons to Thomas himself. Hold on, dear chap, and you'll be convinced."

Pushing the door boldly, the mechanic went into the tower, certain of being followed by his multicolored Friday. As he expected, his entry did not cause any guardian to surge forth; it had not been thought possible that an enemy might get this far.

"No petard!" he murmured. "Since the way is clear, we'll proceed with a little domiciliary visit. It's a matter of knowing what has become of M'sieur Jean. It's also necessary to strive to recover Mamzelle Cyprienne and Turlurette. Hantzen better beware if he finds himself under my paw!"

The ground floor of the tower was only a kind of machine room, encumbered by distributors of energy, counters and apparatus of all kinds. Cables and wires ended there bringing through pipes all the forces produced or captured by the subterranean factory; electromagnetic and radioactive forces, and various gases, then rose to the other floors through glass tubes or metal coils.

Accumulators stored everything that was not utilized.

In order to regulate all that work, however, no human presence was necessary. Electric commands assured the automatism. From time to time there was a click, a needle vacillated, a bulb lit up or a reference-mark was displaced.

"As an installation, it's a full bath!"

Having paid his invisible host that tribute of admiration, the Parisian decided to take the elevator that he had quickly discovered, ready to rise up, in a central cylinder.

"Let's visit the first floor."

Prudently, he did not stop there. Through the glass of the elevator he had glimpsed, in passing, a number of silhouettes idly extended on mats in a large round room.

Were they human beings or domesticated apes? Slaves or subjects consecrated to the scientist's experiments? That question, Laridon did not want to investigate for the moment; he preferred not to be noticed and to arrive entirely incognito in the presence of the lord of the place.

There was no one on the second floor: only silent and deserted corridors, doors without battens over which tapestries fell and glass panes through which the interior of rooms could be inspected.

"Let's take a look around," whispered Laridon, stopping the elevator.

Followed by Julep, he ventured into one of the corridors, risking a glance through the window of one of the rooms and putting a finger over his lips to indicate that he had just discovered an interesting spectacle. Effaced against the wall, he lent an ear, and peeped.

What he saw was the laboratory into which Hantzen had taken Cyprienne, Turlurette and Mandarinette, each under the false appearance that she owed to carnoplasty.

Relying solely on the evidence of his eyes, the indiscreet individual believed that he recognized Jean Chapuis' fiancée and her chambermaid—an error mitigated by the fact that both of them were, indeed, in the laboratory. He therefore opened his eyes and ears wider, and held himself in check in order not to leap on Hantzen immediately. Suspecting that the person in question had more than one trick up his sleeve, he judged it wiser to study the situation first.

One never loses by self-instruction! What he perceived, it must be said, was of a nature to cause him a legitimate emotion.

Before his eyes were the appearances, not only of Mandarinette—whom he did not know at all—but also Cyprienne and Turlurette, in whom he was more interested.

The three young women were in an extremely awkward situation. Tightly bound and rendered incapable of making the slightest movement, they were each installed n one of the special armchairs that physicians and surgeons use for torturing invalids at their ease. To what diabolical operation was Hantzen meditating subjecting them? Sniggering, he was prowling around them like a wild beast.

"I have you, my beauties! That dear Yogha is truly generous! Three pretty faces like yours, three beautiful youths granted to Science, to serve in my research! That's a famous affair! I shall do good work, for it isn't ideas that I lack. It would be unpardonable for me to have come to lock myself away in this bubble of air—yes, it's a bubble of air, girls, a giant bubble of air that I've hatched out at the summit of this mountain to enclose my life—unpardonable to have cloistered the genius of Hantzen if it had not been to make impassioning discoveries here.

"I ought to be classified among those who have loved and served humankind best... yes, served it best! Have I not judged that the greatest service one can render it is to suppress it... almost? In view of that great work, you're going to be particularly useful to me. I'm going to inoculate all three of you with a variety of perfected bacilli, from which I expect marvelous effects. I hope that they'll find in you a culture terrain propitious to their development. Ha ha ha! I'm going to turn you into nurses, satanic nurses of microbes! Infinitely twenty-first century, isn't it? I'm a savant of my epoch, me! I'm not content, like that dear Yogha, to work in the domain of the imagination.

"Would you like an example of the difference between my rational method and her charlatanism? Here goes. Suppose she wants to render you entirely docile—what would she do? She'd hypnotize you. Pfft! That's her hobby-horse. She'd persuade you of an entire series of unreal sensations in formal discord with verity. Me, I operate differently, and scientifically."

He unhooked from the wall a bizarre head-dress, which resembled an ancient fireman's helmet, equipped with a mask and completed by a gorgerin. With the complaisance of an inventor, he turned it around, polished it and admired it from all angles.

"I take this; it's simply an interrupter of thought. Yes, my lambs! Otto Hantzen, who isn't an imbecile, has discovered this: thought is only a fluid like any other, a radiation, a current traversing space and captured by the brain. That doesn't produce thought, it plays the role of a simple accumulator. Having posited that, what did I say to myself? That there probably existed, for thought as for electricity, insulating substances. I made my researches and I found the substances that arrest thought-waves, just as glass, silk and rubber arrest or deflect an electric current. It's of those substances that the Hantzen interrupter is composed. As soon as one is coiffed with it, one can no longer think. That's already a result but I've arrived at a better one. Hee hee hee! I'm inexhaustible!"

He was the only one amused by his discourse. Cyprienne, Turlurette and Mandarinette were not about to laugh. They waited, bleak and resigned, for their torturer to progress from words to actions.

Laridon and Julep were both listening, but while the negro did not understand anything of what the scientist was saying, the mechanic did not miss a syllable, and he was beginning to be prodigiously interested.

"The better," Hantzen continued, "consists of this: I'm completed my interpreter with a radioactive keyboard that acts directly on each of the motor cells of the brain, able to excite the subconscious and the unconscious, permitting me, in sum, to make the subject execute a whole series of actions without being aware of it. In brief, my method transforms any human being into an automaton—but an intelligent automaton. The patient accomplishes in a reasoned fashion the actions desired by the operator, accomplishing them mechanically and under the sole condition that the mechanism exists in the memory. Do you understand, my charmers?"

That was not certain, but with respect to Laridon, Hantzen had much more success. If the slightly abstract theory escaped the mechanic, the application appeared to him very clearly.

"A marvelous machine," he said. "I've got it. Sufficient to coiff a fellow with it for him to cease cogitating and politely do whatever one demands of him. *Sapristoche!* I'm a subscriber! I'll put my name down for an interrupter—or a corrupter, which rhymes."

He began by eyeing the thought-interrupters hanging on the wall. They were almost within arm's reach. To attain them, he only had to slide his arm between the doorway and the tapestry.

"So, my pretties," Yogha's ally went on, brandishing the helmet he was holding, "we're going to experiment with Papa Hantzen's apparatus. It's admirable and instantaneous. One exists… one is thinking… and suddenly…"

221

His discourse was cut off cleanly and he was obliged to furnish the proof himself of the exactitude of what he was announcing; for the ingenious Laridon, taking advantage of the fact that the scientist had his back turned to the entrance, introduced himself like a whirlwind into the laboratory. Swift-ly, he had seized one of the interrupters, and with a decisive gesture he had jammed it on the head of Otto Hantzen.

The effect was instantaneous. In conformity with what he had revealed, the scientist, devoid of his intelligence, was no longer anything but an automaton.

Chapter Twenty-Eight
THE SAVANT MANNEQUIN

Laridon's first concern was to liberate the three young women. Hantzen could wait. If he had not been boasting, his docility could henceforth be assured.

In any case, Julep entered in his turn and kept watch on him, rolling his terrifying eyes. To remain calm before those eyes was to furnish irrefutable proof of a complete anesthesia.

"Salut, Mamzelle Cyprienne! Your servant, Turlurette!" said Laridon, bowing. Imagining that he was observing a hierarchical order, he had begun with the person who presented Cyprienne's features. He was astonished by the indifferent expression with which she welcomed his intervention, and vexed because the peudo-Turlurette did not show herself any more expansive.

"Good! If that's all your effusions, the game wasn't worth the candle!" he confided to the soubrette. "All the same, you could thank me. I must have arrived just in time to prevent you from coiffing, not Sainte Catherine,[15] but the thought-interrupter."

The admonished Turlurette did not seem to understand; she remained just as indifferent.

"Laridon!" called the third captive.

Amazed by hearing himself addressed by a Chinese woman whom he was seeing for the first time, the mechanic was bewildered.

"Where do you know me from?"

"From the Magical Villa," said the false Mandarinette, smiling. "Unfortunately, you can't recognize me. I'm Cyprienne."

---

[15] "to coiff Sainte Catherine" is an old French expression used when a woman reaches the age of 25 and is still unmarried.

"You, Mamzelle? No... but..." Bewildered and very anxious, he designated Turlurette, in whom his eyes persisted in seeing the daughter of Oronius. "Here's Mamzelle Cyprienne. I'm not crazy!"

"No, Victor, that's Turlurette, your fiancée."

"Turlur...?"

The mechanic put his head in his hands. Yes, he was going out of his mind. Was it not due to some diabolical apparatus of Hantzen's invention? His suspicious gaze made a tour of the laboratory; then it returned to Turlurette's face.

"What about this one, then? Who's she?"

"Her name is Mandarinette. She's the young Chinese woman when appearance I have."

"What! Am I losing my mind... do you hear, Julep? It's strong coffee, anyway! What do you say, Mamzelle Cyprienne who isn't Mamzelle Cyprienne? And you, Turlurette, who must be Chinese? Oh, my head! Without wanting to offend you, my little girl.... Especially if, as you say, that's you, Mamzelle Cyprienne... I'd like to believe you, but it's hard."

The false Mandarinette sighed. "I understand your amazement, my friend, and I'd like to be able to explain what has happened, strange as it appears. It's a machination of that Yogha and this Hantzen. I don't know exactly by means of what surgical operation they've interchanged our faces..."

Laridon was beginning to see more clearly. "They've made you permutate your skin?"

"That's it, very nearly. According to what I've heard and understood, this individual has acquired an extreme skill in the art of modeling faces; he can remake the features of a given person and impose on her the appearance of another. That's what has happened to us..."

"Don't finish, Mamzelle. I'm on the same page, Oh, what a boutique! I've had to rack my brains rudely already, but you're giving me gooseflesh. If he's amused himself like that in blurring your faces to switch them around, what might he have done to M'sieur Jean? Have you seen him, Mamzelle?

Has that rascal had the whim of making a dwarf of him? Pipigg, for example... or Kukuss?"

"No," replied Cyprienne. "Pipgg and Kukuss are locked in a cage at the end of the corridor. Go and set them free, Julep. The poor little beasts will be glad to see me again... Kukuss especially, whose superior sense of smell enabled him to recognize me in my new form... Pipigg was duped too."

"It's necessary to excuse me, Mamzelle."

While the mechanic was sweating blood and water, dividing his embarrassed apologies between the true Cyprienne and the apparent Cyprienne, Julep had librated the two little dogs. Mad with joy, they threw themselves successively on all the people they recognized, beginning with Cyprienne—for this time, doubtless scolded by Kukuss, Pipigg was no longer mistaken.

Before that new evidence, Laridon's last doubts crumbled,

"Well, he's a fine one, the fellow in the helmet," he muttered, menacing the savant Hantzen, forcibly impassive, with his gaze. "This will finish badly for him, for we have more than one account to settle between us. First of all, there's that of your poor Papa. Has M'sieur Jean told you, Mamzelle?"

A tear rolled down Mandarinette's cheek; it was Cyprienne's pain that caused it to flow. "Alas," groaned the young woman, "I had the story of my father's tragic end from the mouth of this wretch. And—shall I admit it to you, Laridon?—I can't accept the idea that such a splendid intelligence is extinct forever! No! Something in me protests and revolts against it. I sense... I think I sense..."

She interrupted herself, and appeared to extract herself from a reverie that she judged to be unreasonable. "Let's leave it there," she said. "We can't change what is... my father is dead, But Jean is alive. I've seen him... unfortunate... tortured by that woman."

"What woman, Mamzelle Cyprienne?"

"What she is, I can't tell you. They call her Yogha, and her power seems to be infernal. The man you've just paralyzed only makes the body suffer. Yogha attacks the mind... which is more terrible. Jean is her prisoner. To what despair has she reduced him? Unfortunates that we are, can we ever rediscover happiness? Even if you succeed in triumphing over that woman and delivering your young master, will we be able to rejoice? Look at me... look at Turlurette. Our minds might reestablish the identity of each, but the eyes and the body protest. We're no longer ourselves. And in condemning us to such an existence, that Yogha has pushed back the bounds of cruelty."

"It's surely a mess!" approved Laridon, scratching his head. "What will come out of it all? Turlurette might only be Turlurette, but I daren't even say '*tu*' to her while she's borrowed your face. I'd be too afraid of annoying M'sieur Jean if I talked to her as before. On the other hand, if I address myself to her natural person... the one that has her peepers and her little nose, the count isn't there again... its Turlurette's mug, but you tell me that there's someone behind it named Lemonade, Orangeade, or I don't know what, for whom I haven't the slightest fondness. Go and make sweet talk, then—the heart wouldn't be in it. It's inextricable."

"Inextricable," repeated Cyprienne,

Victor suddenly clicked his fingers and planted himself in front of the impassive Hantzen.

"Up to you, my old ruffian! You made the muddle, you can sort it out. Go on—get to work! You claimed just now that with your satanic machine one can make you operate at will. Well, the time has come. Let's see your keyboard. I'm going to make you slog!"

It was simple, but it was necessary to think of it.

Hantzen, having done the harm under Yogha's order, could now repair it at Laridon's suggestion. It was sufficient for him to reverse his carnoplastic operation and to render to each of the young women her original physiognomy.

"Get on with it!" repeated Laridon, slapping the savant automaton on the shoulder. "And afterwards, old fleshbag, we'll have a chat. In order to help me find M'sieur Jean, you'll initiate me into the secrets of your locker. We'll see how your mechanism functions."

In default of technical instruction, the mechanic was endowed with an instinct, a particular flair that enabled him to discover the secret of all machinery; none resisted him. With the flick of a wrist he could take them apart and put them back in working order as if he had been their inventor.

The new problem posed to his intelligence by the Hantzen interrupter and its keyboard could not embarrass him for long. After twenty minutes of exploration and trials, our friend had mastered the trick. By pressing the keys he could make Hantzen act with the docility of a puppet—except that the puppet was a scientist and he remembered that when Laridon wanted it. He only had to formulate his desires in that mathematical and energetic form.

"Pay attention. Mamzelle Cyprienne number one, Turlurette number two, Citizen Grenadine number three. Understood? Transport the face on number one to number three, that of number two to number one, and that of number three to number two. Carnoplastic operation. Go—and no gaffes, or beware for your medallion. I'll put the boot in, you know, my old mannequin!"

But, only operating under the influence of his subconscious, unleashed by a opportune pressure of Laridon's finger on one of the buttons of the keyboard, the savant automaton could not make any mistakes. He had never shown so much dexterity or surety of hand. The transformation, including the instantaneous scarring by radioactive procedures, took no more than three-quarters of an hour, and everything was back in place.

Cyprienne had become Cyprienne again, Turlurette Turlurette, and Mandarinette the mildest and prettiest of Chinese women. The bodies had rejoined the souls.

For Cyprienne, at least, the miracle was complete, but to Laridon's great disappointment, it was not the same for the other two young women.

They remained hypnotized and no reawakening of their thought was produced. To all questions, Turtlurette still affirmed that she was Cyprienne, while Mandarinette, for her part, answered to the name of Turlurette.

That mental disturbance, with regard to the young Chinese woman, was rather indifferent to the mechanic; by contrast, he was less easily consoled for not being able to reawaken the dormant heart of his Turlurette.

"It's Yogha who has hypnotized them," Cyprienne explained. "Interrogate Hantzen. Perhaps he can furnish you with a means of extracting her from that woman's influence."

"In fact, I have great many things to ask him," Laridon consented, examining the keyboard. "I see things at a distance, me. I've got you back, and Turlurette too, but M'sieur Jean remains. After that, it's necessary to get out of here. As for this bandit, it wouldn't be bad to know dear Otto's underhanded practices. Go take a tour of the city, Mamzelle, while I make my mannequin talk. When that's done, I'll call you."

The result of the interrogation must have been satisfactory, because a short while later, the mechanic's voice resounded joyfully in the corridors.

"Reassemble!" he shouted, "We're going up to the lantern. And hold hard... you're going to see things green and not ripe."

Chapter Twenty-Nine
THE INTERRUPTED DREAM

While following the brave mechanic to the elevator, as he had invited her to do, Cyprienne was surprised to see Hantzen, still helmeted by the interrupter, dogging their paces. As Laridon pushed the savant automaton into the cabin of he elevator, however, she divined that he had his reasons for acting thus. Without a doubt, a role was reserved for the unconscious Otto in what was in preparation.

The cabin rose up, carrying Hantzen and the young women, Laridon, Julep and the two little dogs. Another person had slipped into it. That one took up so little room that no one, except for Pipigg and Kukuss, had paid any heed to his presence. That was the geophage that the mechanic had launched as a scout into the funnel of the elevator. Having arrived at the summit of Everest, he had been able to penetrate into the tower in the wake of the invaders, and was now accompanying them.

The two dogs growled dully and wanted to bite that bizarre specimen of a race they did not know, but, fortunately for the homunculus, Laridon perceived the imminent drama and hastened to put the geophage in shelter, crying: "Be good, friends! Don't damage my pygmy. He's been very useful to us, and he might be again on the way back."

The elevator having stopped on the third floor, when they emerged, Hantzen took the head of the troupe, with his mechanical stride.

"No noise," commanded the mechanic. "The only chance we have of my little plan succeeding is to arrive on tiptoe. Let's let the mannequin go; I've given him the orders. It's marvelous how facile it is to direct a scientist when he's remounted and his brain has been put under a globe."

Unconsciously guiding the visitors to the Tower, Hantzen was marching with felted steps. He pushed a door and penetrated into a room filled with bizarre apparatus. In frames fixed to the walls, porcelain buttons were aligned, surmounted by curt labels.

Laridon and Cyprienne approached and read:

Bell of dreams.

Ecstatic state.

Cloud generator.

Image projector.

Voice projector.

Apparitions.

Stop visions; Awaken.

"Look over there, Mamzelle," murmured Victor. "That's the cabinet of mirages. M'sieur Jean must have been locked in there and he must presently be inhaling more drug than he'd like. I'll stay here. When you give me the sign, I'll stop the supply."

Obediently, Cyprienne darted a glance into the next room.

It was a simple cell devoid of furniture, over the walls of which a great many pipes were running; thy ended n a cage of glass. In that cage Cyprienne, her heartbeat accelerating, recognized Jean Chapuis. Next to him stood a masked woman: Yogha, who had put on a respiratory mask to protect her from the gases under the influence of which she was holding the young man. Her ardent eyes were fixed on her victim.

Collapsed and inert, Jean Chapuis retained on his face an intense expression of overexcitement. He was living a succession of depressing dreams. His persecutrix was feasting on the torment she was inflicting and savoring a bitter joy in following the progression of woes.

Divining that, Cyprienne begged: "Wake him up, Victor!"

The latter nodded his head and pressed the button that would extract Jean Chapuis from the baleful influence.

It was then that the mirage vanished.

Cyprienne's fiancé found himself back in reality, but retained the memory of the sufferings endured, and leapt upon Yogha in order to strangle her.

The magicienne did not have time to evade that attack, which she had not foreseen. It seemed inadmissible to her that a stranger might have been introduced into the next room. Nor could she envisage a dangerous intervention, the manipulation of various taps, handles and interrupters being a secret known only to her and to Hantzen. She therefore had to believe that no intruder was capable of operating the commutators that regulated the arrival and action of the gases.

As she sought instinctively to repel Jean's attack, she perceived the face of Cyprienne stuck to the glass of the cage, and she immediately understood that a metamorphosis had taken place.

It was the body *and* the soul of Cyprienne!

Behind Cyprienne, her gaze discovered all the invaders, including Hantzen, coiffed with the interrupter.

Then, divining what had happened, glimpsing defeat, she uttered a terrible scream and tore herself away from Jean Chapuis' hands. Her eyes were flamboyant. She got ready to have recourse to their terrible power.

For want of the scientific weapons put at her disposal by Hantzen, but of which Laridon had just taken possession, hypnotism remained. Apart from Cyprienne, no one had ever resisted her. She therefore extended her will-power, looking at all of them... all... and tried to order:

"Sleep! All sleep! I wish it!"

A strange weakness suddenly overtook her. A cloud passed before her eyes. She felt her brain fill with fog and obscurity. Everything within her blurred and vanished.

With a cry of despair and rage, she collapsed, vanquished by a will stronger than her own: the same will of which Cyprienne, Jean Chapuis and Laridon had already felt the effects, and which seemed to come from the mystery of the beyond.

Jean Chapuis, pouncing on her again, had just snatched away her mask.

At the same moment, yielding to an inspiration that traversed him like a lightning-bolt Laridon pressed the button whose label bore the indication *Sleep*.

And sleep—an invincible sleep—took possession of Yogha and Jean Chapuis simultaneously. They fell to the floor, unconscious.

"Victory!" cried Laridon, leaping up. "Go in, go in! The lioness no longer has claws or teeth!"

He pulled a lever, which caused a window to open in the glass partition, through which the mechanic and Julep swiftly pulled the inert body of the engineer. That rescue having been carried out, they closed the cage again on the inanimate Yogha.

A few minutes later, Cyprienne's fiancé opened his eyes again and held out his arms to the young woman. "Dear Cyprienne! We're reunited!"

Laridon felt something akin to a caress on his cheek. It was Turlurette's little snub nose. The pretty maidservant had just straightened up, fully conscious, at the same time as the same phenomenon unfroze Mandarinette: a consequence of Yogha's slumber. Dormant, the Hindu's will could no longer maintain its domination over the young women; the suggestion was interrupted.

"There!" cried Laridon, joyfully, clasping the chambermaid in his arms. "This time, one has all one's limbs. A little more and we'll be in clover. We'll boast when we're out of this nest of bandits. Let's get out of here!"

Chapter Thirty
THE BURST BUBBLE

The mechanic's words were golden. Brought up to date with everything that had happened since their separation, Jean Chapuis could only approve.

Hantzen and Yogha were defeated and reduced to impotence; but that was only a provisional solution. Prudence commanded that their work be destroyed and that they be rendered harmless.

The redoubtable mysteries that the Tower of Everest contained and its armor of compressed air, what Laridon had discovered of the secret forces accommodated in the bosom of the mountain were of a nature to make the engineer reflect. A threat had been suspended over the world that it was necessary to annihilate.

How?

He did not hesitate for long. Already, an idea was sketched in his thought. In order to execute it, it was only necessary to reach the subterranean factory that the mechanic had just described.

In any case, it was also by that route that the path of retreat went. In order to get out of the artificial world created by Hantzen, to destroy the bubble of air that protected it, the interior of the mountain was the only way.

"Do you think that we can go back by the route you followed?" he asked.

"Of course," said the brave Victor. "But it's necessary to expect a few hitches. We have Citizen Hantzen, who is there to guide us, the squid are dead and I still have my geophage snake-charmer. There's no encumbrance, therefore. We can pass those... but in the subterrains, we'll find the pygmies. We can bash them, I don't say the opposite... we can crush a few dozen... but there's a whole ant-hive. And there are some superior to our fellow. Beware of the net-machines. Necessary to see that we aren't fished up."

"It's necessary to pass through, though. Yes, it's necessary to brave the dangers of which you speak."

"You won't have to... we'll pull out all the stops. Julep and I can give you our electric weapons for you and Mazmelle Cyprienne... and there's also our diving suits, for it isn't pleasant outside. There's a nip in the air..."

"Thanks, but I don't intend to sacrifice you. It's necessary that you can follow us, as well as Julep and this young Chinese woman. Cyprienne doesn't want to abandon her. Interrogate your automaton. There must be respiratory apparatus here."

"Come and see for yourself, M'sieur Jean. I know where the collection's hanging. In any case, if your heart tells you so, visit the tower from top to bottom. The lady is quite tranquil in her box and Monsieur Hantzen is also snoozing in his fashion. In the meantime, as Julep and I are armed, we'll make a tour of the first floor. If that's the guard-room, we'll proceed with a little cleaning. When you come down, the passage will be free."

"Act as you wish—but be prudent."

The domiciliary visit with which the young engineer proceeded was as fruitful as it was instructive. Cyprienne had insisted on going with him. During her captivity she had been able to familiarize herself with the bizarre dwelling, and her indications were useful to Jean Chapuis.

Turlurette and Mandarinette, the former joyful at the turn taken by her adventure and the latter quickly domesticated, remained in the chamber of mirages. The guard of Yogha and Hantzen had been confided to them.

When the two fiancés reappeared, they brought back four costumes with respiratory masks. Hantzen must have foreseen excursions on the icy flanks of Everest, in the environment of irrespirable air, and he had consequently provided for them.

"Let's rejoin Victor and Julep," said Jean Chapuis when he and the three young women were equipped. "The hour of chastisement won't be long in sounding for the two enemies we're leaving here. They'll perish with the world that they made their lair. In declaring war on humankind and delivering themselves to the aggression that cost your father his life they've rendered themselves unworthy of pity. To grant them mercy would be to betray the human cause. The scourges accumulated in this Tower will never emerge from it."

Darting a glance at the vanquished, he drew Cyprienne and her two companions away.

On the first floor they found their saviors and the pygmy. Victor announced: "The spring cleaning is finished. I've opened the soporific reservoirs. Hantzen foresaw everything; he was able to place you under protection from the where-withal to get rid of hindrances. At present, apart from us, everyone camped in the tower is sound asleep. Shall we take the elevator downwards? What bothers me is rhe maneuver. I've seen how it functions upwards, but for the descent, I have no suspicion. Not to mention that if it tosses you about as it does on the ascension, that might not be to Mamzelle Cyprienne's liking."

"Don't worry about anything. I have all the necessary information. We'll get out of this lair safe and sound."

"That's okay, then."

Before quitting the tower the young engineer stopped in the ground floor room that we have mentioned. There were assembled the organs commanding the formidable mechanism; it was the vital center of Hantzen's work.

Successively, Jean turned various commutators, placed the needles of dials at certain numbers, opened some taps and closed others, and rejoined his friends,

"En route!" he said. "It's necessary for us to be out of the mountain in an hour."

The opening of the well was a few paces away. Laridon observed with a satisfied surprise that it was illuminated and that a metallic staircase had emerged from the wall.

"That's good," said Victor. "We've hit the right command at the first attempt. And Julep, resuming his role as an echo, repeated: "That's good."

The descent was easily effectuated, without them encountering the tempestuous air-blast.

The corridor of fire no longer showed any trace of the horrifying brazier.

In the chamber of serpents, the reptiles, numbed by a wave of cold, were lying impotently.

Laridon was profoundly vexed by that; he could see a mocking smile on the lips of the malicious Turlurette. Had he not advised her thus far to allow herself to be guided by him and to close her eyes in traversing the various terrifying rooms?

"You'll always be a joker, Victor?" she murmured. "These are your serpents? And your conflagration? I no longer dare believe in your mud-eaters. We haven't seen a single one."

"You've divined it, Turlurette," the engineer interjected, smiling. "But don't accuse the unfortunate Laridon of boasting because of that. Everything he reported to you really exists, but it only serves to forbid passage to those who attempt to introduce themselves into Hantzen's abode. On the descent, there's less risk... especially if one has taken the precaution, like us, of announcing the passage of the master."

"You've done that, boss? What cheek!"

"Cheek or not, from up there, I issued a warning that Hantzen was going out. For him, I think, the scarecrows call a truce...and the geophages too. That's why we can reach the exit without encumbrance."

"On condition that we don't get lost in the tunnels. It's a real maze!"

"Certainly, a maze...and very well-designed, as it's easy to see if you want to cast an eye over this plan."

Oronius' pupil exhibited that document triumphantly, which he had found among Hantzen's papers. Thanks to it, the fugitives easily reached the breach by which Victor and Julep had introduced themselves into the mountain.

As they drew away from it, a mighty explosion made the ground tremble; it seemed to them that the roof of the word was bombarding the sky.

"The bubble has burst!" announced Jean Chapuis.

EPILOGUE

A few moments later, reunited aboard the Halcyon-Car, the heroes of the singular adventure launched into the air while listening to the young engineer explain the end of Yogha and Hantzen.

He had simply disabled the mechanism producing compressed air, with the result that the protective envelope constituting the air bubble had no longer been alimented by the provision in the reservoir. There was only an hour's supply. At the end of that lapse of time, the wall of air, too thin and ceasing to have sufficient force to rise, no longer offered a sufficient resistance to the interior pressure, superior to the rarefied atmosphere of the heights.

At that moment, therefore, the interior of the air bubble, the tower as well as the artificial atmosphere enveloping it, had to burst and dissipate in space. And that had happened.

At the same time, however, the gases accumulated in the subterranean factory, no longer finding an issue, had caused an explosion, and the upper part of Mount Everest had been volatilized.

Thus, nothing subsisted of the vile work of the vainglorious Hantzen and his cruel associate Yogha. Both of them ought to be nothing more than atoms scattered in the space that they had subjugated.

"The world is saved," said Jean Chapuis. "And for me, dear Cyprienne, the prize of victory will be happiness, in Paris, where we'll return, although the loss of the best of Masters will put us all in mourning.

"Damnation!" swore the mechanic, letting go of the controls. "That didn't enter my head. Alas, we can't conserve the slightest illusion. I've looked into the bottomless abyss in which, in the midst of flames, the unfortunate Oronius was swallowed."

"Father, oh, Father!" moaned Cyprienne.

And, unable to contain her chagrin, her tears emerged in floods.

Then something improbable happened; in the middle of its vertiginous course through the serene sky, the Halcyon-Car was abruptly seized by a temporary turbulence, which caused it to "loop the loop" completely and resume its route, while a voice, which everyone could hear, clamored:

"One only mourns the dead!"

Reassured, without knowing exactly why, the Halcyon's passengers continued their path toward happiness... at least, toward the relative happiness that is the only one within the reach of human beings...